ISLAND
LOVE SONGS

USA TODAY Bestselling Author
KAYLA PERRIN
CARMEN GREEN
FELICIA MASON

ISLAND
LOVE SONGS

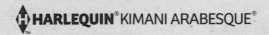
HARLEQUIN® KIMANI ARABESQUE®

ISLAND LOVE SONGS

ISBN-13: 978-0-373-09137-9

Copyright © 2013 by Harlequin Books S.A.

The publisher acknowledges the copyright holder of the individual works as follows:

SEVEN NIGHTS IN PARADISE
Copyright © 2013 by Kayla Perrin

THE WEDDING DANCE
Copyright © 2013 by Carmen Green

ORCHIDS AND BLISS
Copyright © 2013 by Felicia Mason

Recycling programs for this product may not exist in your area.

For questions and comments about the quality of this book, please contact us at CustomerService@Harlequin.com.

Printed in U.S.A.

www.Harlequin.com

CONTENTS

SEVEN NIGHTS IN PARADISE
Kayla Perrin

Dedication

This book is dedicated to my children: Jeremy Green, Danielle Green and Christina Green. I love you with all my heart. Mom

To the sparrow. I'll see you in the Rapture someday.

Acknowledgment

Thank you to Shannon for asking me to take part in this fun project.

Chapter 1

As the small seaplane soared over the turquoise-blue waters of the Fijian islands, Melanie Watts could hardly breathe much less look out the window. Her fingers were finally beginning to cramp after gripping the edges of her seat for the entire seven minutes that the small plane had been in the air. She felt tension in her back and neck as a result of not being able to relax.

To say that the seaplane with a seven-passenger capacity was not her preferred mode of transportation was an understatement. But it was the quickest way to get from Fiji's Nadi International Airport to Malolo Island, where she, her best friend, Richelle, Richelle's fiancé, Roy, and their wedding guests would be staying at the much-acclaimed Likuliku Lagoon Resort.

"Can't you just go to Jamaica?" Melanie had tried to reason with Richelle. "Four hours nonstop from JFK, same time zone as New York, nice and easy to get to."

"Roy and I want to do something different," Richelle had explained. "Something that not every couple does. We know Fiji's far, and expensive, which is why Roy's going to pay for everyone. And please don't tell me you can't make it. If you're not at my wedding, I'll be devastated."

In the end, even though Melanie wasn't thrilled with the idea of a superlong flight, she knew she couldn't deny her best friend of fourteen years. Of course she would go to Fiji and be Richelle's maid of honor. And with Roy, a recently retired multimillionaire NFL quarterback, footing the entire bill for seven nights in paradise? Melanie didn't have one good reason to say no.

"Oh, my goodness!" Richelle exclaimed, and Melanie flinched reflexively. "I see the resort! Look at all the bungalows over the water! Oh, Roy, we're really here!"

Melanie opened her eyes to peek through the window. She was sitting on the left side of the plane, and Richelle, who was to her right, was leaning against her as she tried to get a better view of the resort.

There had been room on the plane for everyone to have a window seat, but Melanie hadn't wanted to sit with one of Richelle's or Roy's relatives she didn't know. Richelle had wanted to sit with Roy, which was why they had crammed in the only row with three small seats.

"Oh, wow," Melanie said, taking in the sights below. It was extraordinary. Not to mention the stretch of pristine golden beach. Melanie inhaled her first relaxing breath.

But suddenly, the plane's engine, which had been loud for the entire trip, sounded like it had just conked out and the plane rapidly began to fall.

"Oh, God!" Melanie cried, fear seizing her body. "Did the engine just die?"

"We are beginning our descent, ma'am," the pilot, a man named Suli, explained.

"But—but the engine," Melanie protested.

"Relax," Richelle said. "We're in paradise."

"So it's okay if we die because we're in paradise?" Melanie countered.

Richelle giggled. "Mel, I swear, sometimes you let your fear stop you from enjoying life. Did you even see the view? All those small islands and the ocean's different shades of blue?"

"I...I saw some of it," Melanie admitted sheepishly.

"It was stunning. Priceless. Yet you had your eyes closed."

"At least I'm on this plane. Give me credit for that." Rationally, Melanie knew the plane would have to go down, but she was still beyond afraid. This was a new experience for her—one she'd never anticipated doing, or ever cared to do.

"The only reason you agreed to go on this plane was because you feared you might fly off the catamaran if it was going too fast," Richelle said. "Or that the helicopter would crash. You figured a seaplane was at least equipped to land on the water."

The seaplane swooped, and Melanie uttered a cry. Then it leveled off, and she was suddenly wishing she'd been sedated for this trip. "I'm starting to second-guess my decision. I'm feeling very Tom Hanks in *Cast Away*."

"You see the small island on the right?" Suli said, pointing. "That's where they filmed *Cast Away*."

"Wow," Richelle said, and Virginia who sat two rows in front of them echoed the sentiment. They had all heard that Monuriki was close to the resort.

Which didn't exactly impress Melanie right now. "We'll be landing momentarily," Suli announced, reading Melanie's thoughts exactly.

Richelle patted her hand. "I swear, Mel—sometimes it's not just about the destination. It's about enjoying the ride."

As the plane went lower and lower, Melanie closed her

eyes and braced herself. Then it crashed against the water, and she let out a small shriek.

Seconds passed. She was breathing frantically, but she *was* breathing. Water wasn't flooding the small plane. They were safe.

The other passengers on the plane began to cheer.

"Look at this place!" Richelle said excitedly. "I can't believe we're here! Open your eyes, Mel."

Melanie obeyed. And she finally drew in a calming breath and released her death-grip on the seat. The plane was slowing as it approached a dock near the over-the-water bungalows, and Melanie had to admit, the place looked magical. From the rooms that seemed to float on the water, to the mountains in the background, to the stretch of beach…it was postcard perfect.

"We're really here."

Melanie looked to her right to see Richelle slip her arms around her fiancé's neck and plant a kiss on his lips.

Massaging her fingers to get the cramp out, Melanie glanced at the relatives in the seats around her. They were mostly talking excitedly among themselves around how gorgeous the place was. But Edward, Roy's cousin, immediately met her gaze and smiled.

Melanie offered him a polite smile, and then turned back to look out the plane's window. Edward had been making awkward conversation with her for two days now, from the time they'd first gotten to JFK on Tuesday afternoon, but now that they were finally in Fiji, she hoped she could escape him.

As Melanie continued to look outside, she realized that the plane had come to a stop while they were still a ways from the dock.

"Um, excuse me?" Melanie called to the pilot, leaning in the plane's small aisle. "With all due respect, are we supposed to swim to the shore from here?"

"Miss, don't worry," Suli said. "Look."

She did. And she saw a boat heading toward them. Of course, the adventure wouldn't end with the seaplane landing on the shore. They had to get on a boat to get to the dock.

Melanie forced a laugh. What else could she do? At least the plane had landed safely and they were all in one piece.

Soon, they were loaded onto a boat too small for Melanie's comfort and taken to the safety of the dock. Only then did she truly start to relax. Members of the resort were on the wooden walkway with guitars, singing what she believed was the same welcome song they'd been serenaded with at the airport. It was lively and jovial, and in the native tongue, so Melanie couldn't understand a word of it.

But she did understand the warm, inviting smiles the staff members wore—which immediately helped to lift her spirits.

Melanie did a 360-degree turn once she was standing on the dock. She looked out at the dazzling view of the vast turquoise waters finally able to appreciate its beauty.

She spontaneously smiled. They were in Fiji. And it was truly an island of paradise. From the lush mountains to the stunning shoreline, it was clear that she had left the bustling world of New York City behind.

As the men continued to sing, a woman from the resort approached Melanie. "*Bula.* Welcome to Likuliku."

"*Bula,*" Melanie repeated. Once they'd landed at the airport, she had quickly learned that *bula* meant "hello."

The woman then placed a string necklace with a wooden trinket around Melanie's neck.

"Thank you," Melanie told her.

The woman moved past her to greet Richelle, and placed a necklace around her neck, as well. Once Richelle stepped past the cheerful woman, she came to stand beside Melanie and took hold of her arm. "Oh, my God, Melanie, look at this

place." Richelle squealed in delight. "It's even more beautiful than what we saw in the pictures!"

"I know," Melanie agreed. "It's incredible."

"I—I can't believe it." Richelle's voice caught. Melanie
met her friend's gaze. She saw the look of awe on her face
that matched the tone in her voice. "It's perfect, Richelle. The
absolute perfect place for your wedding. " *Even if it did take
a hundred years to get here.*

Richelle squealed again. She then giddily skipped over to
Roy. She threw her arms around his waist, and he pulled her
into a tight embrace. Then he brought his lips down on hers.

"Get a room," Roy's older brother, Lance, teased. But even
he was holding his wife's hand.

Melanie watched as Richelle snuggled close to Roy, then
as Lance slipped both arms around Lisa from behind. It was
as if just being here had quickly transfixed the two couples
with a spell of romance.

Melanie couldn't help but feel slightly wistful. Here she
was in Fiji for Richelle's wedding, a place that seemed to
ooze an aura of romance. It was hard to forget that just nine
months ago she herself had been scheduled to walk down the
aisle. Nine months ago, on a bright September morning, she
had gotten dressed up in her beautiful white gown, had gone
to the stylist to get her hair and makeup done, and Richelle
had been by her side, telling her that the day would go mar-
velously well.

But the wedding never happened. Melanie hadn't been
able to go through with it. En route to the church, she had
suddenly been seized with the fear that her marriage was
doomed to fail, and no matter how Richelle and her bridesmaids had tried to convince her that she simply had the pre-
wedding jitters, Melanie had ultimately instructed the limo
driver to turn around and drive her back home.

Richelle and the bridesmaids had gone on to the church,

where they'd told Melanie's parents her decision. And instead of seeing their only daughter married, her parents had had to break the news to the groom and wedding guests that she wouldn't be showing.

"Beautiful place, isn't it?"

Jarred from her trip down memory lane, Melanie spun around to see Edward standing behind her. "Um, yeah," she agreed. "Gorgeous."

"I love the still of the morning, don't you? No sounds of traffic. Just chirping birds and flowing waves."

"And the beautiful singing," Melanie added. She looked toward the trio of singers, where Edward's sister, Virginia, was shaking her heavy body to the beat.

"And the singing," Edward acknowledged. "We're definitely a long way from New York."

"Go get your necklace," Melanie told him.

"Oh, right."

When he walked away from her, Melanie went back over to Richelle and Roy. "We don't have to wait here for our luggage, right? The hotel staff is going to bring it to us when it arrives?"

"Right," Roy said. "All we have to do is check in."

"Then let's do that. It's barely after six in the morning, and I can't wait to take a long nap."

They all began to walk toward the hotel's main building, which Melanie could see was at the end of the path they were on. After a few seconds, Richelle came beside her and said, "Hey, why do you look so glum?"

Melanie faced her, forcing a smile. "How could I feel glum in a place like this? This is incredible. I'm just exhausted. We left New York Tuesday afternoon. And now it's Thursday morning."

"I know," Richelle said. "Quite the adventure getting here, but it's totally worth it."

"I just hope the beds are comfortable." As if to empha-size the point that she needed rest before doing anything else, Melanie yawned.

Until Richelle and Roy's wedding on Sunday, in just three more days, Melanie and Richelle would be sharing a room. Then Richelle and Roy would move into a honeymoon suite, which was a private bungalow on the beach.

They didn't have a schedule for today, other than to arrive, relax and recuperate from the jet lag. Tomorrow, for most of the afternoon, Melanie and Richelle were scheduled for time at the spa. After that, there would be a dinner for all the family and friends who had come for the wedding. And the next day, Roy and Richelle would become husband and wife.

"Have you ever seen a lobby like this in your life?" Mela-nie asked once they reached it. It was like a giant hut, with walls that doubled as the roof, angling on each side and com-ing together to form an upside down *V*. The walls didn't quite hit the ground, allowing a breeze to flow in from beneath them. There were no doors. The path from the dock simply led straight through to the lobby. It was a truly open concept type of building, blending with nature.

There were beams beneath the roof structure to give it support, and lighting fixtures that hung from the beams. The exterior of the roof was covered in straw, giving the place a true rustic island feel.

Had the resort in Aruba where she and Lawrence had planned to honeymoon been this beautiful? Melanie won-dered.

"Hey, something's wrong," Richelle insisted, moving to stand in front of Melanie before they reached the front desk. "Talk to me."

"I already told you, I'm tired."

Richelle shook her head. Then she led Melanie to a chaise with red cushions near the wall, while the rest of their travel party headed to reception. "You're thinking about Lawrence, aren't you?"

"Of course not," Melanie lied, forcing a smile.

"Mel, you don't have to lie to me."

Richelle knew her too well. "Look, this trip isn't about me. It's not about my failed relationship. This trip is about you. You and Roy. How you finally found the man you were meant to spend your life with. And how you're going to have the most amazing wedding ever, in this paradise."

Richelle beamed from ear to ear. "I am, aren't I?"

"Of course you are."

Richelle drew in a breath. "I just—I can't believe this is actually happening. That only six months after being devastated by Vern, I found my Mr. Right. Who knew that Vern cheating on me would be the best thing to ever happen to me?"

Four months before Melanie was to marry, Richelle herself had already had a date set to walk down the aisle. But a couple weeks before the wedding, she had discovered that her fiancé had been cheating on her. Not that he had cheated once, but that he'd carried on a long-term affair. The news had crushed her, naturally, and the engagement had been called off. But after allowing herself a few months to grieve, Richelle quickly got back in the saddle and started dating. Having created a profile on an online dating site, she was determined that fate was going to deal her a better hand.

And maybe it was that belief, that confidence, that faith, that had led to her finding Roy. Only as fate would have it, she didn't meet him online. She met him while trying to hail a cab outside a restaurant in Soho. And it was more like hate-at-first sight rather than love, considering they got into a little spat over who had hailed the cab first. Roy had acquiesced on one condition—that Richelle would take his number and call him.

Which Richelle had no plans to do until the colleague—

whose birthday she'd been attending at the restaurant—had encouraged her. What did she have to lose?

And from their first date, Richelle had known. So had Roy. The two became a couple after that night. Roy hadn't told her until their third date that he was a recently retired NFL player. The fact that Richelle had been clueless as to who he was had attracted Roy to her even more. It had been clear to him that she wasn't after his fame or fortune.

"Vern was a jerk," Melanie said. "But thank God he did what he did. Talk about a silver lining, you hit the jackpot, Richelle. The *love jackpot*. Roy's the real deal."

"How did I get so lucky?" Richelle asked. "I keep pinching myself. A part of me wonders if this is all a dream, but everything that man does shows me he adores me."

"He's the one," Melanie said.

"God, can you imagine if I'd married Vern?" Richelle shuddered.

"Sometimes something beautiful comes out of the ashes of disaster," Melanie advised.

A smiling woman approached them with a tray of frothy drinks, garnished with a slice of papaya. Melanie and Richelle took them, and after thanking the woman, sipped them at the same time.

"Oh, wow," Richelle said. "This is delicious."

"I don't think I want to leave," Melanie chimed.

Richelle took another sip, and then said, "There's only one thing that would make me happier than I already am." Richelle ran a hand over Melanie's shoulder. "Knowing that you've found the guy you're destined to be with."

Melanie waved a dismissive hand. "As I said, this trip isn't about me. Soon, you are going to be marrying the man you are meant to be with. One I feel confident will cherish you for a lifetime. I'm thrilled for you. And here he comes now."

Richelle turned, and her eyes lit up. "Room keys," he said, presenting them to Richelle. "For you and Melanie."

"Who are you rooming with?" Melanie asked.

"I'm with Edward until the big day. We're all staying in the bungalows on the water, or, as they say here, the *bures*."

Melanie looked toward their rooms in the distance and sighed. It was a far walk. And she was desperate to hit the bed.

"And don't worry. Hotel staff is coming with golf carts to take us there. All we have to do is head to the edge of the path outside the lobby."

Relief washing over her, Melanie looked at Richelle. "He's a keeper."

Richelle grinned. "No doubt."

A short while later, Melanie and Richelle were in their room, where the sense of awe continued. The room was elegantly decorated, and boasted a large bathroom with a spa tub that was situated so that you could see the ocean while you bathed. The words *Bula* and *Welcome* were written in colorful rose petals on the king bed they would be sharing. There was a living room area with a sofa and a coffee table. And outside, there was a large patio with lounge chairs and steps literally walking down into the ocean.

But the focal point of the room was the floor. Amid the wood, there were two giant panes of glass enabling people to see into the water below the room.

"Oh, my God, I could stay in this room forever," Richelle said, sighing happily as she sank into the sofa before one of the panes of glass. "Seriously—there are fish beneath our feet. Look!"

Melanie quickly hurried over to look, and sure enough, a school of fish was swimming among the coral beneath the room. "Breathtaking." Then she faced Richelle. "As I remember telling you, sure the Caribbean is lovely, but why not do something different for your wedding? You only do it once, after all."

Richelle grabbed a cushion off the sofa and hurled it at her. "You told me to do something different? Yeah, right! Remember your Jamaica solution? I'm lucky I even got you here!"

The two friends shared a laugh. "What I'm really saying," Melanie began, "is that you made the best choice. We came halfway across the world, and it took forever, and I'm totally a nervous traveler, but this is absolutely the best spot for your wedding."

"Mel, you're going to make me cry."

Melanie sat beside Richelle and wrapped an arm around her shoulder. "I'm happy for you, Richelle. I really am."

"Thanks, Mel. And thank you for being here. You know I couldn't get married without you."

"And you know there's nowhere else I would rather be right now. If I had to walk over hot coals to get here, I would."

"Now I'm crying," Richelle announced, and raised her hands to wipe her tears.

Melanie hugged her. "I love you, Richelle. You're the sister I never had."

"I love you, too. And I know you don't want me to say it, but I don't want you to give up on love. You're going to have your own happy ending. And I still think Lawren—"

"Eh, eh," Melanie chastised as she pulled apart from Richelle. "No talk about him, remember?" Melanie got to her feet. "Now as beautiful as this room is, I have got to get some sleep if I'm going to enjoy any part of this day. Don't wake me up for at least four hours."

Chapter 2

It was shortly after noon when Melanie woke up. She blinked as her eyes adjusted to the sunlight streaming into the room. Then, upon coming alert and remembering where she was, she turned to her right to see if Richelle was still asleep.

But Richelle wasn't there. Instead, there was a slip of paper beside her.

I'll be on the beach at the island bar.
Call for a shuttle. It's a long walk.
See you soon.
Love, Richelle

Melanie sat up, noticing that their luggage was now in the room.

She got out of bed, showered and dressed, and did as Richelle suggested. The shuttle arrived at her *bure* within five minutes.

As she rode on the back of the golf cart, she surveyed the resort. Fully awake now, she was even more dazzled by the impressive view of the lush foliage and beach. There were a number of rooms situated among the trees beyond the shore on the beach, which were lovely. But Melanie was glad that she was staying in an over-the-water *bure*. She could stay in a room on the beach anywhere. How often could she stay in a room that was actually on the water?

"How do you like the resort?" the driver asked.

"What's not to like?" she countered. It was lovely. She saw people walking along the golden sand or resting on lounge chairs. All couples. This resort catered to adults, and clearly was a choice for men and women in love.

The beach was extensive, and she didn't see Richelle or Roy on the portion that was visible. The driver continued on to the island bar, which was where they had originally arrived by boat.

She could hear the sounds of a live band before she saw the performers, and as the cart came to a stop, she looked around the small intimate bar with comfy cushioned seats and saw Richelle at the same time that she saw her.

"You're awake," Richelle said, rising to greet her.

"I'm awake." Melanie drew in a deep breath of the fresh island air. "When did you get up?"

"About eleven-thirty. Then I called Roy and woke him up." She smiled sweetly and rubbed his arm.

"What are you drinking?" Roy asked, looking up at Melanie.

"Is that a piña colada?" Melanie asked, indicating Richelle's drink.

"Yep."

"Then I'll have one of those."

"You'll want to see how they make it," Richelle said. "Fresh pineapple and fresh coconut. And the taste? To die for."

"I'm sold," Melanie said. When Roy began to stand, she placed a hand on his shoulder. "It's okay. I'll go get it."

"Just tell Manueli to add your drink to my tab," Roy told her.

"Why did you walk here with your purse?" Richelle asked her. "Just charge everything to the room."

"Oh. Right. I didn't think of that."

"Please don't tell me you have your phone in there," Richelle said, giving her a knowing look. "No one is going to call you for wardrobe work on a film set this week. And even if they do, you're taking a break, remember?"

"I can't even play Angry Birds?" Melanie countered.

"No," Richelle told her. "Good grief, there's so much more to do here than be tied to your phone."

"I was kidding," Melanie said, though she did have her phone in her purse. Force of habit. "I was only thinking about paying for food and stuff."

"Put all food and drinks on my tab," Roy said. "I'm taking care of everything. I will be offended if you don't."

"Thanks, Roy," Melanie said. "For everything. This place is amazing, and I already feel relaxed. Now how about putting off the wedding for a week or two? That way, we can stay in paradise longer."

"Already working on it," Richelle said as she took Roy's hand and smiled at him. "Meet us at the beach once you get your drink. We're headed down there."

Warmth filled Melanie's heart as she watched them stand and walk hand in hand out of the bar. As they strolled contentedly, Roy lifted Richelle's hand to his lips and kissed it.

Melanie made her way to the bar. *"Bula,"* she said to the bartender, whose name tag read Manueli.

"Bula. You must be Melanie."

Melanie's eyebrows shot up as she sat on a bar stool. "How did you know?"

"Because your friend told me you would be arriving soon. Said to make you an extraspecial drink."

"Richelle says you make an amazing piña colada."

"One Likuliku piña colada coming right up."

Melanie watched him cut slices from a fresh pineapple and put them in the blender, and then chop the top off a green coconut and pour the juice found inside into the blender, as well. He added some sort of cream, followed by a good dose of rum and ice, and then turned on the machine.

After about seven seconds of whirring, the blender came to a stop. Manueli poured the creamy concoction into a tall glass and presented it to Melanie. "Here you go."

She sipped it. And felt like she had just tasted heaven. "Oh, my goodness. This is delicious! Thank you, Manueli. I'll be back for more of these."

Turning on the bar stool, she took another drink of the delicious cocktail and surveyed the area.

And her eyes caught a glimpse of a seriously sexy body. Strong golden brown legs, washboard abs, perfectly sculpted pecs…

An odd sense of realization dawned a moment before her gaze went higher, to the man's face. Her heart slammed in her chest. And as she dared to look at his face, her eyes bulged in stupefied horror, and the liquid she'd just sipped went down the wrong way.

No! her mind screamed. *No. It can't be possible. There's no way that could be him!*

She coughed, almost violently, trying to clear her windpipe. With the commotion she was making, she knew she was drawing attention to herself.

Which was exactly what she didn't want, especially if the man she thought she'd just seen was actually not a figment of her imagination.

Perhaps the Fijian heat was getting to her. Obviously, that couldn't be *him*.

She turned back to the bar, where Manueli looked at her in alarm. "Are you okay?"

Melanie waved a hand to dismiss his concern. She slapped her chest, hoping to relieve the endless hacking. And as the coughing finally began to subside, she was certain now that the man she'd seen had simply been a look-alike. He had to be. Everyone had them, after all.

For God's sake, she was in Fiji, not strolling along Wall Street.

Surreptitiously, she glanced to her right once more. And there he was, still standing at the perimeter of the island bar as if frozen to the spot, staring in her direction.

And then she *knew*.

She saw, at the moment, that he knew, too. The question in his eyes morphed into complete surprise.

Clearly, he had just spent the last few seconds trying to determine if she was truly who she'd appeared to be, just as she had done where he was concerned. And now, there was no longer any doubt.

God help her, it was Lawrence.

The man she should have married nine months ago. The man she had left standing at the altar.

Lawrence looked in the direction of the coughing woman at the bar, and at first thought that he had to be hallucinating. He was halfway across the world, on one of Fiji's beautiful islands, a far cry from New York City. He had come here expressly to forget the very woman he feared his eyes now rested on.

She glimpsed in his direction once again, and then he was absolutely certain. The deer-in-the-headlights look on her face made it clear that he wasn't dreaming. That indeed,

Melanie Watts was here in the same bar at the same resort he was staying at.

Of all the islands that made up Fiji, Melanie was actually at the very same one where he was.

Melanie quickly jerked her gaze away from his and shot to her feet, and the purse that was on her lap went flying, spilling the contents onto the sand. Then her hand swung to the side as if in fright, and she knocked over the drink that was on the bar in front of her.

The bartender reacted quickly, grabbing up the glass. Melanie dropped to the ground to collect her strewn items.

Lawrence watched her, intrigued and mortified.

Melanie looked terror stricken. She kept glancing at him as she picked up the contents of her purse, as if she expected him to charge over to her.

And there was no doubt that a part of him wanted to do exactly that. Go over to her and demand the answers to the questions she hadn't given him after standing him up at the altar. But the other part of him—the part filled with too much pride to belittle himself after she'd made it clear she didn't care about him—kept him rooted to the spot.

Melanie finished hurriedly putting the items into her purse, not even dusting off the sand first, then threw another nervous glance in his direction, as though she feared he was approaching her at that very second. And that was what got to Lawrence. The idea that she was afraid of him. Even when she had broken his heart, she hadn't needed to fear him. All he had wanted were answers, and even though she hadn't given them to him, he hadn't lost his mind and hounded her. He had simply let her be.

He watched as Melanie rebuffed a hotel worker's help in getting to her feet. She quickly stood, then turned in the opposite direction from the path where he was standing, and hustled out of the bar area toward the beach.

And that's when he made the impromptu decision to follow her. He had initially come to the bar to pick up a couple beers for him and his buddy, Shemar, but that would have to wait.

Nine months had passed and, yes, his relationship with Melanie was over. But still, he had to know.

She looked over her shoulder once more as she tried to flee, and her eyes widened when she realized he was coming after her. The reaction irked him. She had known him—known his heart—yet she had let every insecurity come between them and prevent them from getting married. Now, she was looking at him as though she thought he would rush her and throttle her.

Lawrence picked up his pace, jogging. Nearing the water now, Melanie suddenly stopped. She wanted to get away from him, but she wasn't about to dive into the ocean to make her escape by swimming. Not the Melanie he knew, anyway.

She quickly scanned the area to the left. Endless beach. Then the right. Same thing. He caught up to her in time to hear her whimper.

She took a step to her left, but Lawrence put his hand on her shoulder, stopping her. "Hey," he said softly. "You're seriously not even going to say hi to me?"

Turning, Melanie looked up at him, and he could see the trepidation in her eyes.

"For God's sake, Mel. Why are you looking at me like I'm some sort of crazy stalker? If there's one thing you knew about me, it was that you didn't have to be afraid of me. Yet the look on your face would make a person think you're scared I'll hurt you."

To emphasize his point, he looked toward a couple a short distance away. Indeed, both the man and the woman were staring in their direction, clearly a little too curious about Lawrence's interaction with Melanie.

"Oh," Melanie said, following his line of sight to the couple in question.

"Yeah," Lawrence said, unable to hide his irritation. "After everything, I figure the very least you can do is say hello when you see me, not run scared. I don't deserve to be treated like *I'm* the one who hurt *you*."

There. He'd gotten that off his chest. Because if anyone should be running scared, it was him. Melanie was the one who had trampled all over his heart.

He sure as heck hoped that she hadn't avoided him because of an unfounded fear that he would become some sort of nutcase. She owed him a conversation, an explanation, and that was *all* he had wanted. If she'd been able to tell him that she didn't love him and didn't want to marry him, as much as it would have hurt, he would have wished her well and moved on.

But she hadn't told him anything, and that had him stuck emotionally. Unable to truly move on.

"I—I—I'm sorry," Melanie stuttered. "It's just—I didn't expect to see you here."

"That makes two of us."

"I'm here for Richelle's wedding," she explained.

"Ah. So Richelle's getting married again?" Lawrence processed the information. He remembered all too well that it was Richelle's own failed engagement that had led to Melanie's doubts about whether or not any marriage could be successful. That and the fact that her father had never been able to stay faithful to her mother.

"Not *again*," Melanie clarified. "This will be her first marriage. Since her wedding to Vern last year didn't actually happen."

"Yeah, I know what that's like," Lawrence couldn't help saying. When Melanie's lips tightened, he asked, "She getting married to Roy? The football player?"

"Yep," Melanie answered, not looking at him. Instead, she was searching the beach. "And, ah, there they are. They told me to meet them, so, uh, I'll see you around."

Lawrence's eyes narrowed. "You'll *see me around?*"

"What do you want me to say?" Melanie asked, sounding exasperated.

"I want to know why," Lawrence said. "That's what I want to hear from you. Tell me why you left me."

Melanie withered beneath his hard stare. But Lawrence didn't avert his gaze, because she deserved to wither. She deserved to feel even a morsel of the pain she had caused him to feel.

"This isn't the time," she said.

"Then when is the time?" Lawrence asked. "Let's set a date. Mark me in on your calendar and put it in that phone of yours so you won't forget. We're in Fiji, where you can't hide behind your work. Maybe now I can get some answers."

"Lawrence, stop."

"Stop?" he countered. "So that's just it? You break my heart, you humiliate me in front of my family and friends, and I don't have a right to know why?"

"I didn't say that."

"No, you didn't say anything. You just stood me up and never even gave me a courtesy call to say you were sorry, at the least."

Melanie's bottom lip trembled. And once again, there was the look of fear in her eyes. But he could see now that it wasn't the kind of fear that said she was afraid he would hurt her. Rather, it was the kind of fear that came when you were caught in an uncomfortable situation you didn't want to be in.

But dammit, she owed him closure. She owed him answers, and then he could forget her forever.

"We were supposed to get married," Lawrence went on. "We were supposed to be husband and wife. Only you didn't show up. You made an executive decision to change the plans we had for our life together. Fine—maybe you're not sorry about how you handled the situation, about how you hurt me. But at the very least, don't you think you owe me an explanation as to why?"

"I—I can't do this. Richelle…she's waving me over."

"Richelle isn't going anywhere. We're on island time."

Melanie was shaking her head. "I—I'm sorry, Lawrence. I—I am. I know I never told you, and, yes, you deserved an apology, so I'm telling you now. I'm sorry. Just know that."

And before he could say another word, she quickly turned, desperate to be able to escape him, and all but sprinted on the sand over to Richelle and Roy.

Leaving Lawrence standing there like a fool.

Much like he had stood like a fool at the altar of the church on their wedding day, waiting for his bride-to-be who would never show up.

Chapter 3

"*Was that Lawrence?*" Richelle asked, gazing beyond Melanie's shoulder to look in the direction of the stretch of beach near the island bar.

Now beside her friend, Melanie finally released a pent-up, frazzled breath. "Yeah."

"You've gotta be kidding me!"

Melanie's heart was beating frantically, and she felt light-headed. She was in a state of shock.

"Why is he *here?*" Richelle went on, a sense of wonder in her tone.

Melanie threw her hands up in frustration, and then dropped down onto the lounge chair beside the one where Roy was sitting. "Hell if I know."

"Wait," Roy said. "That was Lawrence—your former fiancé?"

Melanie nodded.

"I didn't realize you guys were talking again."

"We're not."

Roy looked confused. "But you must have told him you were going to be here."

"You think I invited him here?" Melanie asked, her tone incredulous. Then, realizing that her reaction was too harsh, she said, "Sorry. I didn't mean to raise my voice. It's just that…I haven't spoken to Lawrence in nine months. I have no clue why he's here."

"I was just gonna say, if you want to bring him to the wedding, it's cool with me."

Melanie's eyes widened. *Invite him to the wedding?*

"Roy, honey," Richelle began, placing her hands on Roy's shoulders. "You said you were going in the water, right?"

Roy looked over his shoulder at Richelle, who smiled sweetly at him, then at Melanie. And he seemed to get that Richelle was shooing him off so that she and Melanie could have some privacy.

Roy stood and dutifully took his shirt off. "Yep."

Richelle gave him a quick kiss, and then he headed into the turquoise-blue water. Richelle sat across from Melanie on the second lounge chair.

"Wow," Richelle said, and then chuckled softly. "We come all the way from New York to Fiji and *Lawrence is here?*"

Melanie looked up from the sand and met Richelle's gaze. Her friend's eyes were dancing with excitement. "You don't have to sound so happy about it."

"I don't think that's a coincidence," Richelle went on. "Come on, you don't think it's a coincidence that he's here?"

"It's a disaster, that's what it is."

"You didn't tell him accidentally, did you?"

"Accidentally?" Melanie looked at Richelle in shock. "How could I tell him accidentally if I haven't spoken to him in nine months?"

"I'm just wondering if he saw the news about the wedding on your Facebook page, or on Twitter."

"I unfriended him, but even if he had access, I never said where we were going to be. I've been very careful about that."

"Well, maybe he heard about the wedding through a mutual friend, and he decided he'd head to Fiji to get a chance to talk to you. I'm sure he still wants closure."

"Lawrence isn't the kind of guy to get on a plane and come all the way here for the sole purpose of talking to me. If he'd wanted to talk to me, he would have done so in New York."

"If you're certain that he didn't find out about the wedding, then it sounds like fate is making a major play."

"Fate?" Melanie countered. "It's simply a coincidence."

"Coincidence?" Richelle shook her head. "No, it's more like the universe forced the two of you together. I sense a reconciliation in the making...."

Melanie's jaw dropped. "Don't say that. Don't even start on that."

"Why not? I always thought you and Lawrence—"

"We're over. He never even called me after the wedding, remember?" Melanie swallowed painfully, remembering how a part of her heart had hoped that he would reach out to her. Reach out to her and beg her to take him back, beg her to come to her senses.

"You mean the wedding where *you* stood him up?" Richelle said, giving her a pointed look.

"Obviously, he wasn't too torn up over it," Melanie insisted. "Because he said nothing to me. Not a call, not a text message, not an email."

"Because you stood him up—" Richelle stressed.

"He didn't reach out to me, and I didn't reach out to him, which makes it very clear that both of us knew we were heading down the wrong path. It was better to leave things as they were than fight for something that wasn't supposed to be."

Richelle rolled her eyes. "It's more like you broke his heart, and he was too hurt to talk to you," she said. "Everyone has to have their level of pride."

"Don't take his side," Melanie said, pouting.

"This isn't about sides, Mel. You're my friend, and I love you, but I've never once told you that I agreed with you if I didn't. Remember how I reamed you out for putting Nair in LaRita's shampoo in tenth grade? I still loved you, but I told you that you were wrong to get revenge like that. You should have just reported her for bullying you."

"She never bothered me again, now did she?" Melanie countered, smiling slightly with the memory of how the tables had turned on LaRita. Once half-bald, other students had started bullying her, and Melanie's life had gotten a lot easier.

"You got what you wanted, but you didn't do it the right way," Richelle said. "Just like with Lawrence. If you didn't want to marry him, fine. But you shouldn't have stood him up at the altar like that. It was wrong. You can't turn around and blame him for not trying to talk to you after that."

Melanie swallowed uncomfortably. She knew that no matter what she said, Richelle was right. Melanie couldn't shift any blame onto Lawrence for her actions.

It was just that she never expected to see him again. Least of all not here, in Fiji.

"What did he say to you?" Richelle asked.

Melanie sighed. "That he wanted an answer. That I owed him one for how I humiliated him on our wedding day."

"And you said?"

Melanie hesitated. Then she shook her head.

"You avoided him," Richelle surmised. "Of course."

"It's a big enough shock that he's here in Fiji, for God's sake. I'm supposed to have a serious conversation like that on the spot?"

"Mel." Richelle *tsked*. "What are you going to do? Avoid him for the rest of the trip?"

"I didn't say that."

"You didn't have to. I know you. You're afraid to face him. And I understand why. But please, hon, don't run scared while you're in Fiji. If it's truly over between you and Lawrence, what harm will come from talking to him? And what if it's not really over...."

Richelle got to her feet, grinning devilishly as she did. Then she pulled off her bathing suit cover, dumped it on the lounge chair and jogged into the water to join Roy.

Leaving Melanie to ponder Richelle's words.

"Was that Melanie?" Shemar asked when Lawrence slumped onto the lounge chair beside him.

"Yeah." Lawrence's tone was clipped.

"She's here?" Shemar asked, disbelievingly. "We come all the way to Fiji and *she's here?*"

"Tell me about it, bro. That about sums up my luck."

"Unbelievable." Shemar made a face. "Guess that's why you didn't get our beer."

"Oh, sorry. I was distracted."

"So, what'd she have to say for herself?" Shemar asked, his tone sounding cautious.

"That she's here for a wedding. You remember how her friend Richelle started dating that quarterback who used to play for the Giants?"

"Vaguely."

"Well, Richelle's marrying the guy. Here. In Fiji. Of all places."

"Don't sweat it," Shemar said. "If there's a wedding happening, sounds like Melanie will be busy. And so will we. You probably won't run into her again."

Lawrence gritted his teeth as he stared out at the water.

This was an island paradise, the exact type of place he would have loved to come with a special woman in his life. But he'd come with Shemar instead to golf, snorkel and scuba dive.

And now Melanie had appeared and had already turned this trip upside down. Lawrence had six more days here—six days he was supposed to be spending purging Melanie from his system. Yet how could that happen now?

Shemar stood and clamped a hand down on Lawrence's shoulder. "I know that look, Lawrence. But like I said, don't sweat it. It's a big resort. You don't have to see her again if you don't want to. I'm going to get those beers. You need it."

Shemar was Lawrence's best friend. He'd been his best man for the wedding that never happened. He'd been there in the aftermath of Melanie's no-show and had consoled him with tough talk about how he was better off not having married her because clearly Melanie wasn't the woman for him. Shemar had assured him that there were many other fish in the sea, and that there were thousands of women in New York City who would appreciate a guy like him.

"We're stockbrokers, man," Shemar had told him. "We make a ton of cash. You know how many women appreciate men like us? They'll be coming out of the woodwork for you, bro. Trust me."

There were problems with Shemar's theory, of course. The first one was that Shemar himself was still single, despite the fact that he saw himself as a hot commodity. The second problem was that the women who tended to be interested in them simply because of their careers were shallow. That breed of woman was more intrigued by their healthy bank accounts than by who they really were.

And it was easy to find the gold diggers when out with Shemar. He loved to flaunt like a high roller, buying drinks for beautiful women, waving cash at the bar, the whole nine yards. It was no surprise to Lawrence that women ended up being more interested in what Shemar's money could buy them, than in the man himself.

None of that fazed Shemar, though. He enjoyed dating a series of beautiful women, enjoyed wining and dining and impressing them. And ultimately, leaving them when he got bored.

It was that kind of mind-set Shemar had tried to impart onto Lawrence, but without luck. Lawrence wasn't like Shemar. He couldn't move from one monogamous relationship to the next with ease. Shemar had set him up with a few girls back home after his disastrous wedding day, but Lawrence had ultimately compared all of them to Melanie.

Which was ridiculous. What was the point in comparing any woman to Melanie? She wasn't the ideal woman. Certainly not the ideal woman for him.

He was still dealing with the pain of heartbreak. Lawrence's funk was the reason Shemar had suggested they get away. Far away. They both loved the water, and Shemar had suggested Fiji for diving, snorkeling and water sports like kayaking. Lawrence had readily agreed.

Shemar had also joked that maybe they'd find some lovely ladies at the resort whom they could spend time with. He had hoped that would be the answer to Lawrence forgetting about Melanie once and for all.

And now, incredibly, Melanie was at the very same resort. Was fate playing some kind of cruel joke on him?

"Here you go, my man," Shemar said.

Lawrence looked over his shoulder to see Shemar extending a bottle of Fiji Gold beer.

"Thanks." Lawrence accepted the bottle and took a pull of the light-tasting ale.

"We've got just about an hour before Ratu comes to take us out on the dive," Shemar said. "I'm gonna head to the room, get changed. You?"

Lawrence stood. "Sounds like a plan."

And though he didn't want to, as he started to walk away from the beach with Shemar, Lawrence threw a glance to his right, in the direction where Melanie had run off to.

He saw Richelle and Roy in the water in the distance, but he didn't see Melanie.

She was gone.

But whether he could physically see her or not, she was back in his thoughts.

There was no doubt about that.

Chapter 4

Try as Melanie did to get a good night's sleep, she couldn't. Not with the exchange between her and Lawrence playing in her mind over and over again. Instead of feeling relaxed and at ease—as she initially had once on Fiji—her body was consumed with nervous tension.

She hadn't seen Lawrence for the remainder of the day, but as she'd gotten dinner, and enjoyed a traditional Fijian show on the beach as night fell, she had been consumed with worry that Lawrence would make an appearance at any given moment.

He hadn't, but she was still cursing fate and whatever joke it was trying to play on her by having Lawrence show up on the very island paradise where she had hoped to soothe her still-hurting heart.

The first thought that came to her mind as she got up that next morning was that she would see Lawrence again. In fact, she was half-paralyzed with the fear that she would run into him sooner rather than later.

"Ticktock," Richelle chastised her. "We've got to get going if we're to make it for breakfast."

If not for Richelle, Melanie might be tempted to hide out in the room. But she knew that was an insane idea. She hadn't battled her fear of flying long distances, traveled through how many time zones and gotten on a seaplane, only to stay in the room—despite how incredible the view from here was.

No, she had to leave the room sometime. For one thing, there was no room service, which meant Melanie had to go to the restaurant in order to eat if she didn't want to starve to death. She and Richelle were going to enjoy breakfast on their own this morning since Roy, his brother, cousin and some other family members had gotten up at the crack of dawn to scuba dive. Richelle had opted to pass on the excursion, because she and Melanie had a spa appointment later that morning. Today would be a day for the two friends to relax and enjoy whatever the resort had to offer.

Now, if only Melanie knew that Lawrence had left the island…then she could truly relax.

"Mel—"

"I'm ready," Melanie quickly said, pulling her hair into a ponytail as she looked in the bathroom mirror. "My beach bag is set. Call for a golf cart."

Melanie and Richelle had donned bathing suits with summer dresses atop them, since they didn't want to have to head back to their rooms to change. They'd also decided to pack small bags with towels, sunscreen and reading material. Thanks to Richelle's work as an editor for a publishing house in New York, she had a number of novels for Melanie to choose from.

Minutes later, the golf cart arrived with a man named Henry, who already knew them by name because he'd driven them around the previous day. They rode the golf cart to the Fijiana, a restaurant overlooking the pool and the ocean. Melanie took in the stunning decor only briefly—then surveyed the place to see if Lawrence was anywhere in sight.

He wasn't.

"Table for two?" a smiling woman asked them when they approached the restaurant's entrance.

"Yes," Richelle said.

The woman led them to a table close to the pool as a band played lively island music for the diners. Melanie took the seat that faced the ocean as well, and as she looked out at the view, she sighed happily. This place was truly stunning.

"I love how the pool looks as if it leads right into the ocean," she said. "Maybe we can hang out at the pool instead of the beach until our eleven o'clock appointment?"

"Works for me. A couple drinks poolside? No crazy schedule? I'm going to hate to leave this place." Her eyes narrowed as she stared at Melanie. "You left your phone in the room, right?"

"Yes. And you didn't sneak one of your author's manuscripts into your bag?"

"Not a chance," Richelle said. "I'm thrilled to be able to use my free time to leisurely read a novel I'm not working on. I think I'm going to read that time-travel horror everybody's raving about.

"But since I am getting married, maybe I should read something romantic."

"Whatever you want," Melanie said, lifting the menu. But Richelle suddenly frowned, so Melanie set the menu back on the table and asked, "What is it?"

"Here I am, worried about which novel to read." She shook her head. "Shouldn't I be doing something else?"

"What do you mean?" Melanie asked.

"Everything just seems so easy and peaceful and beautiful, and I feel like I should be a stressed-out bride. Am I missing something?"

"That's the reason you came here, right? Because you didn't want the stress. Because you wanted a simple yet incredible Fiji wedding." Melanie smiled. "So here we are. And if your biggest decision right now is which novel to read, be grateful, not wary."

Richelle drew in a breath and nodded. "You're right. I don't know why I keep expecting disaster."

"Probably because, between the two of us, we've had two failed weddings," Melanie supplied. "But this one's different. This one's gonna happen. Don't you worry."

The waitress arrived and offered coffee, then took their orders. They both opted for a plate of fresh fruit and omelets. As they waited for the breakfast to be prepared, they enjoyed the sounds of the Fijian music and the tranquil setting.

"Here you go," the waitress said cheerfully. "A plate of fresh fruit."

"This looks amazing," Melanie said, eyeing the splendid-looking display of pineapple, papaya, kiwi, oranges and strawberries. And as she glanced up at the waitress to say thanks, she saw Richelle's eyes widen.

The waitress walked away, and Melanie asked, "What is it?"

But by then, she felt *his* presence behind her. And she knew.

"Melanie. May I talk to you for a second?"

Melanie shivered. She felt a tremor through her entire body at the sound of Lawrence's voice. And then her eyes fluttered shut.

"Mel, it'll only be a few minutes."

Richelle speared a piece of pineapple with her fork and got to her feet. "Why don't you sit here?" she suggested. "By the way, great to see you, Lawrence."

Oh, my God, no! Don't leave, Richelle—don't leave me!
With her eyes, Melanie tried to implore her friend to stay put,
but Richelle was already walking through the restaurant toward the far edge of the pool.

And then, Lawrence lowered himself onto the seat Richelle
had vacated.

Melanie could hardly breathe, as her throat had suddenly
constricted. The inevitable meeting with Lawrence had come
sooner than she was prepared for.

As if she would ever be prepared for it.

Melanie tried to swallow, but couldn't. There he sat, looking as fine as she had ever seen him, staring at her in this
beautiful restaurant with a backdrop of palm trees and the
perfect ocean. And as her heart began to hasten, all she could
think was that this was exactly where they *should* be right
now. The two of them together here in this restaurant. On
this gorgeous island. But not by chance. Because if things
had worked out for them nine months prior, they would be
here as husband and wife, together on this trip to Fiji for
Richelle's wedding.

Which was exactly what she didn't need to be thinking.
"Good morning," Lawrence said casually, as if their sitting
together like this was entirely normal.

"Lawrence, this is a bad idea."

"Actually, I think it's a good idea. It's the one way I know
to get the answers I need from you."

Melanie's jaw flinched.

"I know you, Mel," Lawrence continued. "And you're not
going to want to make a scene. So with me sitting here, you're
not going to jump up and leave, or go into hysterics or anything like that. I figure this is my best shot at finally having the conversation we should have had nine months ago."

Nervously, Melanie glanced around. The other diners were
all absorbed in their own lives. Their own relationships. Most

were couples, and they all looked happy and carefree and deeply in love.

"I know that yesterday it was a shock for you to see me," Lawrence said. "Trust me, it was a huge shock for me, too. And when you left me standing on the beach, I told myself that I didn't care why you stood me up. But I've had a night to reflect, and I can't lie to myself any longer. I've cared since September 15. Here I am at this resort, and here you are. And if there's any chance I'm going to enjoy the rest of my vacation, I need to know why. For my own peace of mind, for me to have closure, I need to know why you left me at the altar without even letting me know that you were having second thoughts."

Melanie picked up a piece of pineapple and put it into her mouth, buying time. She chewed the morsel, but couldn't savor the sweet taste. All the while, Lawrence's eyes bore into her.

The moment she swallowed, he said, "I'm waiting."

Then he picked up a strawberry and popped it into his mouth. Casual as could be.

"What's the purpose of this?" Melanie asked in a low voice.

"You owe me," Lawrence said. "Or do you think that it was actually okay to leave the man who loves you and tell him absolutely nothing? Leave him to guess and explain to his family why the woman of his dreams was a no-show at their wedding?"

"Fine." Melanie shifted uncomfortably in her seat. "I just— I just didn't think it was going to work long-term. I figured it was best to walk away before tying the knot."

"Not good enough," Lawrence said.

"That's my answer."

He folded his arms and placed them on the edge of the table.

The waitress returned then with the two plates of omelets. Her eyes widened in surprise when she saw that a man had replaced one of the women.

"Oh," she said. "The woman who was here?"

"Will be back momentarily," Melanie said. "Please." She gestured for the waitress to put the food on the table, which she did.

"Actually," Lawrence said, lifting Richelle's plate. "Our friend is right over there." He pointed to the far end of the pool, where Richelle sat with her feet in the water. "Now, see my buddy at that table there? Can you set our friend up at his table so she can enjoy her meal there?"

"Sure," the waitress said, shrugging. "No problem."

Lawrence grinned at her. "Wonderful. Because the two of us—" he eyed Melanie "—we'll be a while."

Melanie raised her eyebrows at him.

"And whatever this omelet is," Lawrence went on, "I'll take one, too. It smells delicious."

"Certainly."

Horrified, Melanie watched as the waitress walked over to Richelle with the plate of food. Then watched as she gestured toward Shemar's table. Richelle then got to her feet and made her way over to where Shemar was sitting, eyeing Melanie with a puzzled expression as she did.

"Now," Lawrence began, "where were we?"

Melanie gaze met his. "Seriously, Lawrence."

"Think of it this way. Once you explain it to me, I'll be able to move on. Then, if we see each other around here again, you won't have to worry about me hounding you for an answer."

Melanie drew in a frazzled breath. "You want an explanation? Okay. You and I were on different pages, Lawrence. That's why I realized I couldn't marry—"

"Bull," Lawrence said, cutting her off.

"If you want an answer, then you—" She stopped herself

when the couple at the table across from them looked at her. "If you want to hear what I have to say," she went on in a calmer tone, "then you need to listen."

"I'm happy to listen." Lawrence's jaw stiffened. "But I want the truth."

"I don't know, Lawrence. Like I said, I'm sorry for what I did. I know I took the coward's way out. It's just…we didn't agree about everything."

"Who does?"

"And I was afraid," she pressed on. "Afraid those differences were going to lead us in different directions."

"Really?" Lawrence looked flabbergasted and hurt.

"You thought I worked too much. And I know it annoyed you that there were a lot of things you wanted to do that I was afraid to try. Like swimming."

"We are different people," Lawrence said. "I didn't expect you to be a carbon copy of me."

"Yes, you said that. But I just… Come on, Lawrence. We wouldn't be the first couple to drift apart because of differences like that. And then there was that job offer I had on that series in Los Angeles. You weren't happy that I was considering it."

"Not so unhappy that I thought it meant the end of our relationship. If I had to live without you for a while, I would have managed."

"I know," Melanie said softly. "I know it's easy to think that issues are surmountable when you're in love, then suddenly, everything changes. What if I got a wardrobe job on a set in another part of the country or even in another part of the world—one that would take me away for weeks or months?"

"Did I ever once say that I didn't support your career? From the day we met in that men's clothing store—where you were doing some shopping for a film, and you gave me advice on the suit I was picking out—I knew what you did for a living. And I've always supported it."

"I know. But…"

"But you were looking for reasons to walk away," Lawrence said, his tone sour. "Sure, we got involved, but ultimately, you never could let down your guard with me. I thought I'd made it clear how much I loved you, wanted to be with you, wanted a life with you. But you…you couldn't get past what your father did to your mother. He told your mother that he left because she wasn't a homemaker, and you, at the end of the day, you believed I would do the same thing."

Melanie's heart began to pump a little harder. Lawrence had so easily torn away the layers of her excuses and hit the very core—something she didn't even like to acknowledge to herself. Because Melanie had spent years believing that her father wasn't a typical man. And then, there she was, on the morning of her wedding, and suddenly paralyzed with fear that Lawrence would hurt her the way her father had crushed her mother.

"Nothing's impossible."

"Wow." Lawrence shook his head. Though he had come up with the very reason for her bailing on him, he seemed stunned to hear her verify his hypothesis. "Wow."

Melanie glanced down, feeling bad for how her words had clearly hurt him. At her core, she had definitely believed that Lawrence was a family guy, one who would value her and not up and leave.

That was why she had fallen for him, why she'd agreed to marry him. But in the end, she just couldn't go through with it.

"Why didn't you call me?" Lawrence asked when she faced him again. "After all we meant to each other, after we were about to get married, you didn't think you owed me the courtesy of a phone call?"

"I was afraid of how you would react."

"Nothing would have been harder than the reality I was left to deal with. Being stood up at the altar and facing all the wedding guests who wondered what the heck was going on. My family and yours. Having to explain to them that the wedding was off. Having to be consoled by people when I didn't even understand what was going on."

"I'm sorry," Melanie said.

Lawrence pushed his chair back and stood. "Yeah," he said dully. "Thanks."

And then he walked away, and Melanie knew—by the tone of his voice, even though she had explained her actions—her apology nine months after the fact was too little, too late.

Chapter 5

Hours later, Melanie still felt ambiguous about her meeting with Lawrence and how he had left her. He'd wanted answers, saying that he needed closure, and she'd given them. She even hoped that, by finally talking to him about their failed wedding day, she herself would feel better. But while Melanie had watched Lawrence's back as he'd walked away from her table—moments before the waitress had returned with his omelet—the last thing she had felt was closure.

Still, during her spa session with Richelle, she'd talked tough. "I feel good," she'd said as she and Richelle had lain on side-by-side massage tables, overlooking floor-to-ceiling windows that faced the stunning view of the ocean. "We talked, I explained my feelings, and now he understands. It's silly that I avoided him for so long, because the truth is, talking to him today helped me get closure, as well."

"Closure?" Richelle asked, her voice ripe with skepticism.

"Yeah. He deserved to know why, and I'd been running from

that for months. That's why I was so stressed. Because I never talked to him and gave him answers. I guess I thought he was going to flip out, and I couldn't deal with that. But our talk went well, we resolved things, and now all the stress is leaving my body."

That's what Melanie had said as the skilled masseuse had worked the kinks out of her neck and back, but hours later, she felt some of the tension in her neck return. That's where she really felt her stress. She was still thinking about Lawrence, remembering that crushed expression in his eyes. And she was definitely feeling guilt over the fact that she knew she had hurt him.

"I didn't even ask Lawrence how long he was staying in Fiji," Melanie said now, leaning in to whisper to Richelle hours later, as they sat on chairs on the beach for the evening's entertainment.

"Why does that matter?" Richelle asked.

She shrugged. "Just curious. I know you don't believe me about having closure, but if he shows up here tonight, I assure you I'll be able to go over and have a friendly chat with him. He and I can be friends now, Richelle."

The fire illuminated Richelle's face, making it extremely easy to see exactly what she thought of Melanie's theory. "Hogwash."

"What?"

"You do realize that you haven't stopped talking about Lawrence all day?" Richelle pointed out.

Melanie's stomach tightened uncomfortably. "Richelle, let's just enjoy the show."

"Hey, I'm not the one who brought up Lawrence. *Again.*"

Roy returned from the bar then with the two piña coladas Melanie and Richelle had requested. He handed a drink to each of them, then sat beside Richelle and slipped his arm around her shoulder. The entire wedding group seemed to be enjoying the traditional Fijian warrior show, with men in grass skirts and donning swords doing some sort of ritualistic dance. It was spectacular. But with each minute that passed, Melanie felt increasingly alone.

Beside her, Richelle was caught up with Roy. Leaning into him. Giggling at words he whispered into her ear. It suddenly struck Melanie that once the wedding was over, and even before that, she would be largely left to her own devices.

She surveyed the crowd of hotel guests. So far she hadn't seen Lawrence and Shemar. She wondered if he was avoiding tonight's festivities on the beach because of her.

But he had no need to. He had gotten the answers he'd wanted. Even if he didn't like them.

About ten minutes later, Melanie caught sight of his face through her peripheral vision as he sifted his way through the crowd. Instantly, her heart slammed into her chest at the mere glimpse of him. She felt that familiar, fierce attraction she'd felt even the first day she had laid eyes on him. He was absolutely gorgeous.

You let him go? people had asked. *But he's so hot.*

Perhaps it was because Lawrence was so hot that Melanie had felt even more insecure. She was a beautiful woman, and he'd told her so often, but women were often dogged in their determination to steal a man like Lawrence. That's what Vern had claimed when Richelle had found out about his affair.

But right now, as she took in his sexy torso draped in a white cotton shirt, and his firm behind clad in denim, she felt a purely carnal pull of lust for him.

He was alone and looking for a place to sit. She swallowed, wondering if this was the time for her to put her money where her mouth was and get up and go over to him. Invite him to sit in the empty seat beside her.

And she was just about to rise when she saw him turn and gesture to someone behind him. Craning her neck to see whom he was beckoning over, her stomach tensed violently. Because walking toward Lawrence was not only Shemar, but also two olive-complexioned women dressed in short, tight dresses.

They were gorgeous. The kind of women who oozed sexuality.

"What's he doing with them?" Melanie asked, her heart beating faster than normal.

She didn't realize she'd spoken the question aloud until Richelle turned to her asking, "What was that?"

Melanie glanced at Richelle, saw that even as she was trying to talk to her, Roy was nuzzling his nose in her neck.

"Nothing," Melanie said, swallowing. "Nothing."

"Stop it!" Richelle chastised Roy playfully. Then said to her, "Sorry, Mel. Oh. *Oh.* I see. Looks like he did get his closure after all."

Melanie gaped at Richelle.

"What?" Richelle asked. "You said you two are friends now, didn't you?"

Melanie grimaced, then put on a brave face. "Exactly."

"Then what's the problem?"

"Nothing," Melanie said. "He's entitled to talk to whomever he likes. We're not together."

But despite Melanie's words, her stomach sank when she looked at Lawrence with the women and saw one in particular laughing and touching his arm.

"Wow," Melanie muttered. "She's *so* not his type."

"Obviously, he's had to get a new type," Richelle said. "Since you dumped him."

The words stung, even though they shouldn't. But before Melanie could think of a reply for her friend, Roy was stroking Richelle's face, and she was turning back to her man, and no longer paying any attention to Lawrence or either of the two women who were no doubt trying to seduce him.

The crowd erupted in applause, and Melanie jerked her gaze forward. Out of duty, she put her hands together and clapped as well, though her mind wasn't on the show at all. Her mind was on Lawrence, and how he was now flaunting his single status in front of her.

Several moments passed and she glanced over her shoulder and saw that Lawrence, Shemar and the two women had taken seats at the far back of the small seating area. He was sipping some sort of green cocktail concoction in a tall glass.

Melanie couldn't help scoffing. "Since when did Lawrence drink froufrou drinks?" she asked.

Richelle placed a hand on her arm, and Melanie faced her. "Mel, you say you've moved on. That you gave him answers and closure. And that you yourself got closure, as well. So what do you expect?"

"You seriously don't think there's a part of him doing this for my benefit?"

"Why would he need to? You dumped him nine months ago. As you've said all day, he's single and free to date whomever he wants. I suggest you do the same. Roy told me that Edward is interested...."

"You're joking, right?" Melanie asked. She had picked up Edward's glaring interest, but he was totally not her type.

"Why not?" Richelle challenged. "He seems nice enough. A little awkward, yeah, but certainly a nice guy."

"This isn't about me dating anyone else. I'm not about to get caught up in some island romance. Unlike Lawrence, it seems."

"Seriously, Mel—why do you care?"

Melanie swallowed. "Because—because he's *flaunting* the fact that he's moved on in front of me. Don't you think he should exercise a little tact?"

"Is that what bothers you?" Richelle asked. "That he's flaunting someone new in front of you? Or are you really bothered by the fact that you're not with him right now?" She raised an eyebrow, an exclamation point on her question.

Melanie tried to tamp down on the unsettled feeling in her stomach, on the sensation of bile rising in her throat. She knew she had no right, after all it was she who had let him go.

It was just that seeing him move on so quickly… She didn't like it.

The show was over, and people were now going up to the warriors and posing for pictures with them.

"I know you better than you know yourself sometimes," Richelle said. "And you know as well as I do you didn't dump Lawrence because you didn't love him. You dumped him because you couldn't stand the idea of getting hurt one day. But you can't expect a guy you've dumped to worry about how you might react to the fact that he's met someone new. If you're upset because you still love him, then why don't you fight for him?"

Melanie tightened her jaw as she looked at Richelle. "It's over."

"Then get over it."

Richelle's blunt response left Melanie stunned. Her stomach twisting painfully, she couldn't think of a thing to say.

"Sorry, Melanie," Roy said, getting to his feet and taking Richelle's hand. "I'd like to borrow my fiancée, if you don't mind."

"Of course." Melanie forced a smile.

Roy helped Richelle to her feet, and the two walked off wrapped around each other toward the shoreline.

A lump formed in Melanie's throat as she watched Richelle and Roy. Perhaps she was coming down with something.

Yeah, right, she said to herself. The only thing she had come down with was a case of the blues.

She dared a glance behind her again, and saw that Lawrence, Shemar and the women were walking away from the beach.

Yeah, she had the blues all right. And perhaps a major case of jealousy.

As Melanie got up, a feeling of defeat came over her. One that didn't make sense. She'd dumped Lawrence, and even when they'd spoken today, she hadn't thought of asking for his forgiveness so that they could reconcile. So why, as Richelle had asked her, did she care?

She turned from looking in Lawrence's direction and felt a spate of alarm when she saw that Edward was walking toward her, a huge smile on his face.

"Hey, Melanie," he said, adjusting his glasses as he reached her. "It's a beautiful night, isn't it?"

"Yeah, it is."

He glanced up. "Have you ever seen so many stars?"

"No." Melanie looked at the sky. "It's incredible."

He was still grinning when his eyes met hers again. "The night is young. Feel like taking a walk on the beach with me?"

"Actually, I'm not feeling well." Which wasn't a lie. "I think I'd better rest up, since tomorrow will be a busy day."

"You're getting sick?" Edward asked, concern in his expression.

"Probably still the jet lag," Melanie said to allay his concern. "I'm sure I'll feel better after a good night's rest. But thanks, anyway."

"Oh, sure." Edward sounded disappointed. "Maybe another time."

Melanie didn't reply to his suggestion, just offered him a smile. "Good night, Edward."

Then she turned and headed toward the path that led to the main lobby, her eyes frantically searching. When she didn't see Lawrence on the lit path, she then surveyed the darkened areas.

She didn't see him anywhere.

And she began to feel an enormous ache in her heart. Because as she made her way toward the lobby, she couldn't help wondering if one of those women had offered to spend more time with Lawrence tonight.

And if he had said yes.

Chapter 6

The next day was busy with the final details before the wedding. One of Roy's cousins was going to act as the photographer, and Roy had made arrangements with a local videographer to capture the event. The wedding planner from the resort went through all these details with the bride, groom, maid of honor and best man.

How many Fijian touches did they want for the wedding, if any? Did they approve of the stretch of beach allocated for the special event? Was the reception menu okay?

Melanie was intrigued when the wedding planner mentioned the option of the bride and groom wearing traditional Fijian tapa wedding costumes. These special wedding garments would have to be made on the day of the ceremony, mere hours before the event. Formed from the bark of a mulberry tree and hand painted, the tapa costumes would be all raw fiber, and wrapped around the bride and the groom, creating the look of long and full skirts on both. Though charming and definitely a uniquely Fijian touch, Richelle and Roy had passed on that idea. Roy wanted to wear the tuxedo he'd brought, and Richelle wasn't going to pass up the opportunity to wear the designer gown she'd purchased from an upscale fashion house in New York.

Late in the afternoon, the bridal party had a fitting to make sure none of their outfits required adjustments. Then came discussions about the choir that would sing during the bridal procession. And on went the last-minute planning, with Richelle and Roy approving every aspect for their special day.

After a day that was spent finalizing the details, the wedding party got together for a lovely dinner at one of the resort's famed restaurants. It was an opportunity to spend some quality time together as a group before the big day, and was followed by the wedding rehearsal.

Richelle was overcome with emotion for much of the day, and Melanie couldn't help remembering how jittery she had been on her own wedding day months earlier.

"And lastly," Roy said, now that everything had come to a conclusion, "I'd like to thank you all for being here to make our day that much more special. I know Fiji was a far trek, and I appreciate you committing the time to be here. It wouldn't be the same for Richelle and me without you all."

Richelle had been dabbing at her eyes during Roy's thank-you speech to the wedding party, and now she pushed her chair back, uttered an "Excuse me" and headed in the direction of the restrooms.

Melanie quickly got up from her own chair and followed her friend. By the time Richelle was shouldering the restroom door open, she was crying.

"Hey," Melanie said as she stepped into the bathroom behind her. "What is it, hon?"

Richelle lifted a thick paper towel from a basket on the

sink. She wiped at her eyes before speaking. "I just… Is this really happening? Am I really getting married?"

Melanie walked toward her. "Yes, this is really happening. You're marrying the man of your dreams. Don't you worry about a thing, okay?"

"I'm not making a mistake, am I?" Richelle asked.

"A mistake?" Melanie gaped at her. Then she placed her hands on her shoulders. "No, honey. Of course you're not making a mistake. Not at all. You and I both know that Roy is the one."

Richelle sniffled. "Everything happened so easily. I can't help thinking that the other shoe is going to drop…and that I'm going to be devastated."

"No, no, no, no." Melanie shook her head. "Don't you go thinking like that. If there's one thing I'm absolutely sure of, it's that that man loves you. He'd do anything for you. Don't start doubting your love."

Richelle blew her nose, then said, "But you did. You doubted Lawrence's love for you."

Melanie exhaled sharply. "I know. And perhaps that doesn't make me the best person to give you this pep talk now. But from the outside looking in, I can tell that Roy is the real deal."

"I told you the same thing about Lawrence," Richelle said. "But you didn't listen to me."

Melanie's stomach twisted as she remembered how Richelle had tried to convince her to go through with her wedding, but she hadn't been swayed. There had been a huge part of her that regretted not listening to her dear friend.

"And now Lawrence is here, and I don't know. Is it a good sign? A bad sign? Your wedding didn't happen, and now the guy you were supposed to marry is here in Fiji. Maybe Roy's going to stand me up and my marriage won't happen, either."

As Richelle began to cry now, Melanie pulled her into an

embrace. "Are you kidding me? Roy stand you up? There is zero chance of that happening. Lawrence being here isn't a good sign or a bad sign where your wedding is concerned." Melanie paused. "You said something about fate…and maybe you're right."

Richelle eased back to look at Melanie, her eyes wide. "You really think so?"

Again, Melanie felt her stomach tightening. She had run from Lawrence months ago, but seeing him again, she knew he was still in her heart. "I don't know," she said honestly. "I do know that I've been hoping to see him all day. Last night, you called me on my claim that I'd gotten closure, and you were right. I was lying. To myself, mostly. All I keep thinking about is how Lawrence was with that woman, and now I haven't seen him all day." She paused. Swallowed. She hadn't wanted to burden Richelle with her thoughts, not on the eve of her wedding. "Maybe it's too late for me and Lawrence, but you and Roy…that's an entirely different story. He adores you. Absolutely. And in your heart, you know that. Seriously, sweetie, you have nothing to worry about."

Richelle dabbed at her eyes again, but the edges of her lips began to curl. "You're sure?"

"Of course I'm sure. And there's one thing you ought to know by now, I wouldn't lie to you."

Satisfied with that, Richelle nodded and finally smiled. "I do know that." She breathed in deeply. "Okay. I can do this."

"Girl, you didn't drag me on a plane—and heck, a seaplane—to *not* do it."

That elicited a chuckle from Richelle. "That's for sure. Okay, I'm going to do this."

"You're going to do this."

"And it's gonna be great."

"It's gonna be *amazing*. And you're going to be happy forever. I'm absolutely certain of that."

Richelle threw her arms around Melanie's neck. "Thanks, Mel. Thanks so much."

As Richelle eased back, Melanie couldn't help thinking about the advice she'd just given her friend and wondering why she hadn't been able to apply it to her own life.

Instead, she had let Lawrence go.

There was a sudden knock on the bathroom door, then Roy called out, "Everything okay in there?"

"I'm fine," Richelle said. She glanced at herself in the mirror, fluffed her hair and then went to the door. Melanie watched Roy pull Richelle into his arms the moment she went through the door.

"I was worried," Roy said.

"I'm sorry, baby," Richelle said. "I just needed a moment."

Roy glanced at Melanie as she exited the bathroom, too, and his gaze held hers a beat too long. Then he said to Richelle, "Don't scare me like that again."

Melanie knew exactly what he feared. That like Melanie had done, Richelle was contemplating not walking down the aisle.

"Everything's fine," Melanie told him, offering him a re-assuring smile. Then she continued on, leaving the two of them alone.

And not just for their sake, but because she needed to be alone with her thoughts of Lawrence.

Melanie drew in a shaky breath as she remembered a few days earlier when she had first set eyes on him in Fiji. As her eyes had traveled up that magnificent body... Good Lord, what a shock! And while she had been absolutely stunned to see him—mortified, actually—her body had also been elec-trified. It had been as if she had touched a live wire.

Even as she'd tried to get away from him, the one thing she hadn't been able to escape was how utterly incredible he looked. One glimpse of him had been enough for her to realize just how much she had missed him.

She had talked to Richelle about closure. She had told herself for nine months that she had dodged a bullet by not marrying Lawrence. But now, as she sauntered back into the restaurant, hugging her torso, all she felt was conflicted and uncertain.

Melanie recognized herself in the Richelle who had been sobbing in the bathroom. The difference was, Richelle was going to go through with her wedding. She wasn't running scared. She trusted her love for Roy.

Why hadn't Melanie been able to trust Lawrence's love?

She was far from convinced that she'd made the right decision. In fact, she couldn't stop thinking that she'd made the biggest mistake ever when she'd let Lawrence go.

Chapter 7

Melanie didn't see Lawrence at all the rest of that day, but she spent much of the night dreaming about making love to him, and awoke in a state of arousal. Quickly, she glanced at the other side of the bed, and found it empty. For which she was glad. She didn't want to think that she'd done anything to embarrass herself with Richelle there to bear witness.

She glanced around the room, and then saw that Richelle was standing on the patio overlooking the ocean. Melanie got out of bed and went outside to join her.

"Hey," Melanie said brightly, shading her eyes from the sun with one hand. "Morning."

Richelle didn't face her. She continued to look forward at the vast turquoise waters. "You stand here, being still, taking the time to see what's around you, and you realize you are one small part of a big world. A beautiful world." She faced Melanie. "How can you be afraid in a place like this? Everything is calm, peaceful. It's stunning, isn't it?"

"If ever there was a description of paradise, this is it," Melanie said.

"It's a perfect day." Richelle sniffled and reached for Melanie's hand. "Absolutely perfect."

"Yes, it is. It couldn't be more perfect."

"My wedding day." Richelle sighed contentedly. "It's finally here."

"You ready?"

"Absolutely." Richelle beamed. "I'll never be more ready."

A surge of emotion washed over Melanie as she remembered the contrast of how she had felt on the morning of her wedding. Crippled by fear.

Melanie squeezed Richelle's hand. "Then let's go do this."

As Melanie, Richelle and the rest of the official party began to get ready, Melanie was able to push thoughts of Lawrence aside. She was too busy to obsess over him, and it was time for her to be there for Richelle as her maid of honor.

With Richelle's makeup and hair done and sleeveless princess-style dress on, Melanie's eyes filled with happy tears. "Wow, Richelle. You look gorgeous. Seriously, you are the most beautiful bride. Ever."

Richelle's chest heaved with a shaky breath. "Thanks, Mel."

Richelle, Melanie and the bridal party were in a special wedding *bure,* from where the wedding procession would begin. Melanie and Richelle were side by side in front of a standing mirror framed in bamboo wood, staring at their reflections.

"You're the princess you wanted to be," Melanie said. "A princess on your fairy-tale day."

Melanie was wearing a beautiful red dress made of satin that swooped low over her breasts, and hung to the floor. The two other bridesmaids were wearing similar dresses.

The gown defined Melanie's shape, and she found herself thinking that if Lawrence could see her now, he wouldn't be able to resist her.

"The flowers on my veil don't seem right," Richelle said, pulling Melanie from her thoughts.

"Here," Melanie said, and adjusted the crown of white flowers so that it was symmetrical. "There you go. Better?"

Richelle checked out her reflection, and nodded. "Thank you. I guess we should finally take the official pictures. David has been patiently waiting."

Moments later, David, the photographer, was taking photos of the bridal party. When Melanie wasn't in a photo, she stood to the side and watched, not sure she had ever seen Richelle smile so brightly.

While Richelle and Roy had declined to dress in the style of a traditional Fijian bride and groom, they had opted for other touches native to Fiji. Richelle wore a lei of fresh flowers around her neck in addition to the veil adorned with flowers. Soon, the choir would begin singing wedding songs. And Melanie especially couldn't wait to see Richelle escorted to the beach by Fijian warriors.

"Those pictures are going to be amazing," Melanie said when they were done. She fussed with the curls hanging at the side of Richelle's face. "And you're glowing. Everyone should get married in a place like this. It just seems so right. I look around here and the setting is so romantic, so meant for love."

Richelle sniffled. Her eyes were moist again. "Do I have everything I need? I have something old, something new, something borrowed—"

"You have everything," Melanie assured her. "But most importantly, you have your man waiting out there on the beach, thrilled about making you his wife."

"You're right. I have the man of my dreams, and I have

my best friend here." She grinned at Melanie. "I have everything I need."

"Are you ready?" the wedding planner, Maria, asked.

Melanie looked at Richelle, deferring to her. Then Richelle nodded and said, "Yes. Tell them to start the music."

Moments later, the cheerful sounds of the Fijian choir drifted from the beach to the wedding *bures*. And the wedding procession began.

Though Melanie had had no idea how a wedding in a tropical location would play out, that moment exceeded every dream she could have had. As she made her way barefoot in the sand toward the beach, her heart skipped a beat as she saw Roy beaming with pride and expectation.

I should have had this moment, she told herself, trying to hold back the sudden urge to cry. *I should have had this moment when I got to see Lawrence standing at the altar, excited to see me as his soon-to-be bride.*

Somehow, Melanie kept it together as she took her place on the bride's side of the altar. Once the last bridesmaid made her way down the sand, the sounds of the choir became softer and more romantic, and the guests were beckoned by the wedding planner to stand.

Everyone looked on in anticipation. And after several seconds, the bride emerged. Six men dressed as Fijian warriors, with green skirts made of the leaves of banana plants, carried her to the beach on a bamboo raft. Cell phone cameras began going off. David quickly began to take shot after shot.

It was magical. And when the bride and groom exchanged their personal vows, there wasn't a dry eye among the guests.

The wedding was simple, yet beautiful. The music of Fiji enthralled everyone during the wedding and continued to do so at the reception. A band was playing and a smaller choir was singing an array of happy, love-inspired songs as the meal and speeches came to an end.

Roy was at the microphone, addressing the small group of wedding guests. "Honestly, this day would not have been as special without all of you here. So thank you."

The guests clapped and cheered.

"Now, I don't know if you all know the story about how Richelle and I got together," Roy went on, and at the center of the wedding table Richelle playfully groaned.

"I don't know why he keeps harping on about that," Richelle said.

But Melanie smiled as she prepared to hear the story for the umpteenth time.

The guests began to laugh.

"You never know when Cupid's arrow is going to hit you." Someone cheered. "When I saw that fire in her, even as she gave me a piece of her mind, I was hooked. I knew that I had to get to know her. And thankfully, she allowed me the chance. Because that was it for me. And here we are in Fiji, and I've made this incredible woman my wife," Roy concluded.

There was exuberant applause to Roy's closing statement. The applause only got louder when he went back to the table, where Richelle rose to meet him, and the two shared a long, passionate kiss.

Richelle and Roy's love was a testament to the fact that people could find their happy ending. As the wedding party moved to the sand to dance under the stars, Melanie beamed with happiness for her friend.

Just like Richelle had said that morning, the day had been perfect. The skies remained clear and the weather not too hot. But even a torrential downpour would not have soured the mood for Richelle and Roy.

A DJ began to play American love songs, and Richelle

and Roy started their first dance to "I Found Love" by BeBe Winans. As they gazed into each other's eyes under the moonlight, Melanie felt that familiar pang. She had four more days here. Four more days when she certainly couldn't be the third wheel with Richelle and Roy. Now legally husband and wife, they were going to begin their honeymoon. Melanie knew she wouldn't see much of them, if any, before she left Fiji.

Another slow song began, and the guests made their way onto the sand dance floor.

"May I have this dance?"

Melanie turned around to see Edward standing there. All day she had been busy with her duties as maid of honor, and had been able to avoid him for the most part. But now, there was no putting him off.

He was a nice guy. There was no real reason to avoid him. "Sure."

They danced, and he held her close, and on a night like this, Melanie was all too aware that these were not the arms she wanted to be in.

She wanted to be in Lawrence's arms.

"Thank you, Edward," Melanie said after that dance. "Will you excuse me?"

Edward seemed surprised, but he didn't object. "Sure. I'll be here."

Melanie first went to the restroom, where she checked out her reflection and touched up her makeup. Here she was, looking beautiful with her hair and makeup done, and in a dress that flattered her figure. This was the day she wanted Lawrence to see her.

With Lawrence on her mind, she exited the restroom and headed toward the beach away from where the wedding celebration was taking place. She wanted some time alone. She began to walk along the water's edge, pausing to dig her toes into the sand. Behind her, a lively tune was now playing.

Melanie strolled, holding her dress up so the hem wouldn't get wet. She was doing what Richelle had done that morning before her wedding. Taking time to simply enjoy the environment around her.

Melanie had only been walking alone for a couple minutes when she heard a male voice call out, "Hey."

That voice… Her pulse began to race. She turned, her eyes searching the stretch of beach. And in the distance, she saw him.

It was Lawrence.

Her heart began to pitter-patter in her chest as he walked toward her.

She stood rooted to the spot. Waited until he caught up to her. And when he did, she looked at him, felt that familiar jolt of white-hot heat when her eyes could fully take in his face.

How did you let this man go? she couldn't help asking herself.

"Hey," he said again when he reached her.

"Lawrence."

"What are you doing out here by yourself?"

"I went for a walk." She paused. "What are you doing here?"

"I…" he began, and then paused. "I knew it was the day of the wedding. I came by to see you."

"Oh." Melanie was excited, though she tried not to show it.

His eyes swept over her. "You look…you look beautiful."

"Thank you." But as nice as it was to hear Lawrence say that, Melanie felt a rush of doubt. "I haven't seen you for a couple days. I guess you've been keeping busy with your new friends…."

"My friends?" Lawrence asked, but a moment later, his

eyes registered understanding. "Wow, I came out here to see you, and that's what you have to say to me?"

"One minute I saw you with them at the beach, the next minute, you'd disappeared."

"And you think…"

Melanie's shoulders drooped. This wasn't what she had planned to talk about the next time she saw him. What was she doing?

"Forget what I just said," Melanie told him. "Obviously I gave up any rights to you a long time ago."

Something flashed in his eyes. Hurt? "What you saw was me and Shemar being friendly with two women. No big deal." He paused. Held her gaze. "The truth is, I wish I could get involved with someone else. Shemar keeps telling me that I need to start dating again. But damn it, all I keep thinking about is you."

Butterflies began to flutter in Melanie's stomach, but she said nothing.

"Do you know I came here to try to forget you once and for all?" He laughed without mirth. "Instead, I get here and you're at this resort. Of all places. Talk about a kink in my plan."

"If I had known…"

"If you had known, what? You would have avoided coming here? That's how uneasy you are at the idea of seeing me?"

Melanie said nothing. Because every time she opened her mouth, she was saying the wrong thing.

"I always believed that you loved me, Mel. But I guess I was wrong."

"Of course I did!" she said immediately.

"Then prove it."

Melanie looked up at him in confusion. "What?"

In a flash, Lawrence took her by the shoulders and brought his lips down on hers. He kissed her in a heated, almost angry fashion. As his tongue tangled with hers, he slipped his hands around her waist and pulled her close.

She sighed against him. His kiss... It was like coming home. Coming home when there was a celebration going on. Because the sensations she felt were hot and thrilling, like fireworks going off in rapid succession.

Lawrence eased his lips from hers. "God, this is what I wanted to do since the moment I saw you again. It's what I wanted to do every day for the past nine months."

A lust-filled sigh escaped Melanie's lips, and then his mouth was on hers again. Her hands were moving up his back now. She dug her fingers into his shirt, needing to feel more of him. Re-familiarize herself with his magnificent body.

She hadn't felt this alive in a very long time.

And as his tongue twirled with hers, creating the most delicious sensations, and as her body overheated, she acknowledged that this was the truth. Since the day she had dumped him by not showing up for the wedding, a part of her had been dead.

But that part had just come roaring back to life.

Chapter 8

All too soon, Lawrence broke the kiss and stepped back, leaving Melanie feeling dazed and confused. She stared up at him with narrowed eyes, not understanding why he had stopped just as things had gotten decidedly hot.

"What— Why are you stopping?" Melanie stammered.

Lawrence took another step backward. "I've wanted to do that since I first saw you again," Lawrence repeated, too dispassionately for Melanie's liking. "Maybe that's my own way of getting closure."

"Closure?" Melanie nearly choked on the word as she said it. "You—you kissed me for *closure?*"

"Good night, Melanie."

"Good night?" Melanie repeated, totally baffled.

But he was already turning, already starting to walk back toward the hotel.

Melanie scrambled after him. "I don't understand. You

follow me out here, you kiss me like that—and then—and then—"

"And then nothing." Lawrence paused. "You don't trust me, remember? I'm a man, so I'm bound to cheat. Right?"

Melanie didn't want to think about what she had said to him, the words she had used to push him away. Because right now, she wanted to be lost in his kiss again. The sensations she had just experienced were overpowering and so delicious that nothing else mattered.

"You're right, I was wrong to mention those women," Melanie said.

Lawrence raised an eyebrow as he looked at her. "You don't get it, do you?"

"What I'm saying is that, right now, it doesn't matter."

"It might not matter for you, but it matters for me."

Lawrence began to walk again. Melanie was hot and bothered and utterly frustrated. She continued after him. "Okay, I don't believe you slept with that girl from the bar. I'm just saying that, even if you did, I don't have a right to be upset. I pushed you away."

Lawrence stopped, looked at her. "Great. See you around."

Melanie was at her wit's end. He couldn't leave her like this!

Holding up her dress, she ran in front of him and stopped him by putting her palms on his chest. Her heart was beating hard. She smoothed her hands over his firm, hard muscles and drew in a shaky breath. Oh, how she had missed this.

"Lawrence, I don't understand. You come out here on the beach with me, and you kiss me like—"

"You needed to let me go, and I needed closure."

"Then why stop at just a kiss?" she asked. "Why don't we… Why not make it a night of real closure? One last time."

She knew she sounded desperate, and she was. That kiss… She wanted more of him.

Lawrence placed his hands over hers, and Melanie's heart began to beat more rapidly. But then he lifted her hands from his body, removing rather than caressing them, and the night air around her seemed to suddenly chill.

"No," Lawrence said.

"No?" Melanie said, her voice sounding like a little cry.

"You don't understand, Mel. I can't do what you want. I can't make love to you without emotion and just go on."

"Why not?" Melanie asked, one last desperate attempt. Again, she was aware that her words had come out wrong. But she didn't want to argue, to bring up the past. Because she was certain that once they fell into bed together, everything else would fall into place.

"Because I'm not the kind of guy that you made me out to be," Lawrence said, holding her gaze. "I never was."

Melanie swallowed.

"It's okay, Mel. Now that we don't have the pressure of a relationship between us, we can be friends."

Friends?

"Like I said…I'll see you around."

And with that, he walked away from her with long, fast strides.

Melanie watched him, feeling as though her heart was breaking.

All over again.

Walking away from Melanie had been one of the toughest things that Lawrence had ever done. To see the look of lust in her eyes, to know that she wanted him in her bed… It would have been so easy to simply say yes. Say yes and end the nine-month dry spell with the woman he still loved.

But he couldn't do it. He wouldn't do it. He wanted all with Melanie, or nothing.

And he had a plan. Sort of. The kiss had been calculated.

To give her a taste of what she had walked away from. And if a part of her still loved him, then she would now be remembering that love.

He knew that she wanted him physically. But he wasn't about to start a booty-call relationship with the woman he had once planned to marry.

Oh, no. He wasn't going to do that. But if she loved him, he was willing to try and work things out.

Because the truth of the matter was that he had come here, halfway around the world, to escape the memories of Melanie. And yet she was here. Making forgetting her impossible.

And maybe, just maybe, there was a reason why.

Fate?

Shemar would tell him he was an idiot, but he couldn't help how his heart felt. When he and Melanie were together, snuggling in bed, or talking about their hopes and dreams, he saw a passionate woman he wanted in his life forever. So if fate had any hand in trying to give them one more chance at love, he was willing to take it.

But the ball was in Melanie's court. She had to show and prove now that she wanted the same thing.

And if she didn't... Well, then he would be able to move forward with a sense of closure.

Melanie had a night of tossing and turning and sweating. But mostly, she spent the hours thinking of Lawrence when she was awake and dreaming of him when she was asleep.

She couldn't forget the kiss they had shared, nor could her body. And knowing that Richelle was spending the night making love to her new husband only had her feeling more alone in her beautiful resort *bure*.

Melanie was still hot and bothered the next morning. And confused. Why would Lawrence kiss her like that, claiming it was for closure, and not want to take it to the next level?

Of course, she knew she was speaking as a woman whose body hadn't been touched in nine months.

Though she was barely rested, the sun was shining and she was in paradise. She wasn't going to sit in her room and mope. Besides, staying inside would ensure that she didn't see Lawrence.

Maybe once he saw her again, in the sexy gold bikini she'd packed, he would change his mind about sharing her bed.

What's gotten into me? she asked herself. She wanted to bed the man she had left at the altar. It wasn't natural.

She got up, got dressed, packed a beach bag and took a golf cart to the restaurant for breakfast. She knew she could contact Richelle's family, see about spending time with them now that Richelle and Roy would be honeymooning. But she preferred to enjoy the morning breakfast alone and then head to the beach or the pool.

She entered the restaurant and looked around with a fluttery stomach, wondering if she was going to see Lawrence. But he wasn't there, at least not from where she could see. She didn't even know when he was leaving. For all she knew, he had left the island already.

She continued to look for him as she was escorted to a table, and not seeing him, she felt a wave of disappointment. Then she felt stupid. Maybe the kiss Lawrence had laid on her hadn't been about closure, as he'd said, but about a sort of payback. One last hot kiss designed to make her remember just how good they'd been in bed—and drive home the point that she would never have him again.

Priya, one of the waitresses she had come to know, greeted her with a warm smile. "Good morning, Melanie. Would you like some coffee?"

"Please."

Priya filled her cup and asked if she was dining alone.

"It's just me," Melanie said cheerfully.

"I hear the wedding was beautiful," Priya said. "Maria is very pleased with how everything turned out."

"She was a fabulous wedding planner," Melanie commented. "Everyone was thrilled with how the day went."

"Maybe you will come back here one day for your own wedding?" Priya said, her voice rising on a hopeful note.

The very mention of marriage made Melanie's stomach tickle. *Right now, she should be in bed lying in Lawrence's arms, recovering from a night of wild lovemaking.* But to Priya, she said, "Perhaps. But for now, I would love to try the strawberry crepes this morning."

"Excellent," Priya said and headed off.

Melanie's gaze wandered to the view surrounding the restaurant. It truly was magnificent here. But what was she going to do for four days on her own?

Reaching into her beach bag, she found her novel. She opened it to the page where she had left off, and then saw the shadow of a body approaching her from behind. She looked up, hopeful.

And saw Edward.

"Morning, Mel," he said, smiling brightly at her. Then added, "You don't mind if I call you Mel, do you?"

"No, it's fine."

"You're not dining alone, are you?" he asked.

"Richelle's married now, so it's just me."

"Dining alone…it isn't right. Let me join you."

"Oh, I'm sure you have company already. Don't worry about me. I was planning on enjoying a quiet breakfast, so I'm perfectly fine."

"Actually, I came here hoping to see you."

A beat passed. A beat in which Melanie tried to think of an excuse to send him away.

But then she shrugged. What harm would it do? It wasn't that she didn't like Edward, she just didn't have any romantic inclinations toward him. But a simple friendly breakfast couldn't hurt. "Sure, join me."

"Great." Edward took a seat at the table across from her. Melanie slipped her book back into her beach bag, knowing that she couldn't very well read with Edward here.

When she raised her head to look at him, she wondered if she'd made a mistake by saying yes to him. His eyes practically twinkled with an obvious attraction to her.

"I know I've told you this before, but you are absolutely beautiful. And while we haven't spent a lot of time together here on this island, I was thinking, hoping, we could change that. Oh—and by the way—the company I work for has an office in New York. I'm thinking I could transfer there."

Melanie blinked as she stared at him. Had he just gone from *A* to *Z?* "I'm sorry. I'm confused."

Edward chuckled nervously. "Oh, I guess I'm not making myself clear. I'm trying to say that I'd really love to get to know you better, and I'm even willing to move to New York to do so."

Wow. He *had* gone from *A* to *Z!* The man had barely sat down, and now he was planning a future centered around her?

"Edward, where is this coming from?"

"You must feel it. The romance. Just being here inspires romance. And you're single, I'm single. Not too many more available people out there." He chuckled. "I'm just kidding. I know you must have your pick of men. But obviously you haven't met the right one." He paused.

Melanie was stunned speechless.

"Am I coming on too strong?" Edward asked. "I don't mean to. My family says I do that all the time, that I scare women away. But what I'm trying to tell you is that I really, really like you. I don't think there's any point in playing games. I don't know how you feel about that."

"I agree with you. I don't agree with playing games, either."

Edward beamed. "See, something we have in common!" Then he added, "Also, I want you to know that I would never cheat on you. I don't believe in it. I'm a one-woman type of man."

Melanie didn't doubt that. Not for a second. Then when she looked up, her heart began to thud hard in her chest. Lawrence was walking past her table.

"How many kids do you want?" Edward was asking. "I'd like at least two."

Melanie cringed, hoping Lawrence hadn't heard that part of their conversation. But he looked over his shoulder at her. His eyes met hers, and then volleyed to Edward, and when they landed on her again, she saw understanding pass over his face.

"You do want children, right?" Edward was asking. "Though I guess I'm getting ahead of myself."

Melanie watched Lawrence place a hand on Shemar's shoulder, then lean in to whisper something into his friend's ear. Then she heard Shemar say to the hostess, "We've changed our mind. We'll come back for something to eat later."

And just like that, the two of them turned and started walking toward the restaurant's exit.

"Oh, my God," Melanie uttered.

"What?" Edward asked.

"He heard what you were saying," she said more to herself. "And now he thinks—" She craned her neck to see where Lawrence was going, and saw that he was indeed leaving. And this time, he wasn't stealing one last glimpse of her.

"Mel?"

She turned back to Edward. "Edward, I think you're a really nice guy. Truly, you're a sweetheart. But my heart is with someone else. Maybe if it wasn't, we could see what might develop between us. But like you said, I don't believe in games. So I can't lead you on. I'm in love with someone else."

Edward's eyes widened in surprise. "Oh. The guy who just walked out of here?"

"Yes."

"Ah." Edward nodded in understanding. "I saw him come into the wedding reception last night, looking around on the beach. I guess he was looking for you?"

"We used to date," Melanie explained. "We were engaged, in fact. It's a coincidence that he's on this island at the same time we are."

Priya arrived with the plate of food at that moment, and looked confused when she saw Edward.

"Priya, can you put my food in a to-go container?" Melanie said without preamble. "Quickly, please?" She wanted to try to catch up with Lawrence.

"Oh. Of course."

"Thank you."

When Priya walked off with the breakfast plate, Edward asked, "But if you were engaged, you've obviously broken up since. Why? Did he cheat on you?"

"No," Melanie said, and had no doubt of the verity of her answer. "It was my fault," she went on. "I was scared. So scared things would fail that I pushed him away."

The words that fell from her own lips shocked in a way she didn't expect. Richelle had told her the same thing, and Melanie had denied it. But now, the idea that Lawrence had misconstrued what he'd heard and might write her off forever suddenly made her actions nine months ago as clear as day.

She had been running from the idea of experiencing any pain, but that hadn't protected her heart. Because here she was, feeling a pang so deep that she knew she was prepared to do everything in her power to win Lawrence back.

And if she didn't… She couldn't even begin to imagine how painful that would be.

She rose and got her beach bag in order and slipped it over her shoulder. Priya hurried back to her with the container, plastic utensils, a bottle of Fiji water and the bill.

Melanie signed the bill to charge the food to her room. Then she turned back to Edward, who was watching her. "I'm sorry, Edward. I know I said we could have breakfast. But I have to find Lawrence. I think he heard what you were saying, and he's going to assume… I—I have to make things right. I hope you understand."

And showing just how nice of a guy he truly was, Edward offered her a smile. "Of course I do. Good luck."

She smiled back, and squeezed his hand as a sign of gratitude. "Thank you."

"And, Mel?"

Melanie had taken a couple steps, but now turned to face him. "Yeah?"

"I don't believe in coincidence."

Hearing Edward say the words held even more significance. Again, Melanie grinned at him.

Then she hurried out of the restaurant, in search of Lawrence.

Chapter 9

When Melanie stepped out of the restaurant, she rapidly looked left and right, and didn't see Lawrence or Shemar anywhere. Darn it, she needed to find him!

She walked along the path for a bit, and saw a golf cart way off in the distance. Could Lawrence be on it, heading back to his room?

He'd been wearing a T-shirt and black swimming trunks. Maybe he was going to the beach. If he were on the golf cart in the distance, she would never catch him. She might as well head to the beach and see if he was there. And if he isn't, she would leave a message for him at the front desk.

Melanie made her way to the stretch of pristine beach, where half a dozen couples were lazing around on lounge chairs. Some people were frolicking in the water. She didn't immediately see Lawrence, but searched the beach for an available chair. Maybe if she just waited here...

And it was while she was walking toward two available

chairs that she saw him. He'd been swimming at least sixty yards out. His head emerged, and he treaded water for several seconds, and then disappeared under the water again.

Melanie watched the water as she set her bag down. A good ten seconds passed before Lawrence's head popped up again, this time much closer to shore. Finally, he stood tall and began to walk to the shoreline. Beads of water glistened on his magnificent body. He looked like a god.

Melanie took a tentative step toward the beach, and then paused midstep. She simply stared at him. And thought about how foolish she had been to all but throw him away. And just like the night before, she felt lust burning in her belly. Lust she knew she would never feel for another man.

Not while Lawrence was in her heart.

"Go already," she told herself, trying to force herself to approach him. But she was afraid. Afraid of what to say to make him realize that she didn't simply want sex, which is how she had come across the night before.

She saw Lawrence beckon to someone, and followed the direction where he was looking. Shemar was sitting on a lounge chair several feet down the beach from her.

Suddenly, Lawrence was turning and diving back into the water, and in no time at all, he was at least twenty yards out. From behind her sunglasses, Melanie watched him swimming laps in the ocean, clearly having no intention of stopping yet. And she wished she had the guts to just get out there and join him.

What's stopping you? she asked herself. *Just go in the water.*

She inhaled deeply. Nothing ventured, nothing gained. Lawrence wasn't going to seek her out, not after what he'd overheard in the restaurant. And not after his comment the night before about finally getting closure.

So it was up to her. She had to prove to Lawrence she still wanted him, and hope that he gave her another chance.

Lawrence turned and began swimming toward the shore again. But he was heading in the direction of where Shemar was seated.

Casually, Melanie glanced toward that stretch of beach. And then her eyes rounded in horror. The two women who had been flirting with Lawrence at the bar the other day were starting toward the water.

Melanie's stomach twisted painfully. And then she didn't think—just acted. She threw off her bathing suit cover, and all but sprinted into the water. The two women were heading toward Lawrence from an angle on the right, which gave Melanie the advantage, because he was closer to her. She jogged toward Lawrence, the water splashing around her legs and making noise. It was then that Lawrence's eyes moved from the women to her. And widened with surprise.

She grinned widely and waved at him as she moved with determination. A quick glance to her right and she saw the other women, steadily making their way in his direction. It was like a race for her, one she was determined to win.

She was out of breath when she got to him—trying to run while waist deep in water was extremely hard. But she said as brightly and as casually as possible, "Hey."

Lawrence didn't blink as he stared at her, clearly stunned by her appearance.

"Hey," he echoed, a question in his tone.

"The water's lovely, isn't it?" Melanie asked, barely able to catch her breath.

"Yeah," he agreed.

"I was watching you for a bit. You're a really strong swimmer."

"Yeah, you already know that."

"Yes, true. But this is the first time I've seen you swim in a large body of water."

Lawrence studied her, and Melanie got the distinct sense that he didn't know what she was going on about. Heck, she didn't know, either.

Once again, she looked toward the two women. Were they both after Lawrence's affection? Were they a package deal?

Melanie took a few steps forward, closing the distance between her and Lawrence even more. The women paused, finally seeming to notice her.

Satisfied, Melanie took yet another step toward him. "Remember you told me you would teach me how to swim one day?"

"Yeah, but you were never interested."

It was true. Her fear of the water had gotten the better of her. But she said, "This water is so calm and peaceful, I feel safe in it."

"Mel, what's up?" Lawrence asked, clearly wanting to get beyond the idle chitchat.

"About last night," Melanie started. She shuffled her body so that it was in the direction of the line of sight of the women. "I want to apologize for how I came across."

"No need to apologize," Lawrence told her. "I kissed you, and understandably, that stirred something. In both of us."

"But I think I came across as sex starved," she said with a laugh. Then, realizing that perhaps she was making it seem as if she was far from sex starved, she said, "Not that I've been with anyone since you. That's not what I'm saying—"

"I have no issue with how you acted last night," Lawrence told her. He began to move to his left. "Friends, right?"

"No!" Melanie screamed, to which his eyes cut to her. She forced a chuckle. "I—I had something I wanted to ask you."

She didn't even know what she would say, she only knew that she didn't want him leaving her and going over to those two women.

"What is it?" Lawrence asked.

Melanie hesitated. Then her mind came up with something. "Obviously, Richelle has gotten married. Which pretty much leaves me to my own devices for the rest of my stay here. How long are you staying here, by the way?"

"Five more days."

"Excellent!" Melanie said a little too excitedly. "I'm here for three more days, four counting today. And I was thinking… maybe we could do something. Maybe we could go out boating or something."

Lawrence's eyes narrowed in suspicion, as if he had just witnessed her become a different person in front of his eyes. "You? You want to go boating?"

"On a kayak. They have them here at the resort."

"I'm aware of that."

"Well, you competed in the Olympics as a kayaker. Maybe you wouldn't mind taking me on a tour.…"

Melanie's heart was beating at the suggestion she never in a million years would have made before this moment. But she wasn't about to retract her statement.

Nothing ventured, nothing gained. And what was life if it was always spent in a blanket of security?

"You want to go on a kayak? With me?" The tone of Lawrence's voice said he couldn't believe she had asked him to do that.

The truth was, she hadn't been thinking. But if she had to get into a kayak and fight her fear of water in order to prove she wanted another chance with him, then that's what she was going to do.

Forget Lawrence looking at her as if she had just sprouted a second head.

"You always told me that I needed to get over my fear of water. And what can I say? In Fiji, I'm inspired." She threw another glance in the direction of the women and saw that they were finally making their way back to the shore.

"Why don't you ask the guy you were at breakfast with? From what I heard of your conversation, he'll probably be upset to see you out on a kayak with me."

"Edward is one of Roy's cousins, and he's just a friend."

"You were talking about how many children you wanted."

"*I* wasn't talking about that. Edward was. Obviously, he has a crush on me."

"You looked pretty cozy to me."

"Looks can be deceiving. There is nothing going on between Edward and me. In fact, after you left, I made it clear to him that I wasn't interested in a relationship with him."

Lawrence folded his arms over his brawny chest. "Let me get this straight. You're telling me that things looked one way, but things aren't really as they seemed?"

Melanie's shoulders drooped. "Touché. And you're right. I jumped to conclusions about you and those women," she said with yet another glance over her shoulder. "I'm starting to realize that I've been wrong about a lot of the assumptions I've made."

Lawrence stared at her, seeming to study her. Then he said, "I'm not sure spending time together is a good idea."

"Friends," Melanie said. She knew that they had to spend time together so he could see the change in her. It wouldn't help to simply blurt it out, because he would doubt it. "That's what you said, isn't it? That we could be friends now? Well, why not start today? Spend some time together and get to know each other again? Put the past truly behind us before we leave this island."

Lawrence wasn't so sure about this idea. Not because he didn't want to spend time with Melanie, but because she was talking that nonsense about being friends.

Yes, he'd said that to her the night before, but he hadn't

been serious. He couldn't settle for being Melanie's friend. Not after having been prepared to spend his life with her.

But the truth was, he was happy to be in her presence, happy to be simply laying eyes on her. Though he felt a stirring in his groin as he checked out her narrow waist and full hips. And, man, those bountiful breasts... They looked especially appealing in that gold bikini top.

How had he had the power to resist her last night when she had all but begged him to take her to bed?

Lawrence swallowed, and glanced away. He had to stop the direction of his thoughts before he embarrassed himself.

"Are you sure you want to go kayaking?" he asked her.

"I can't say I'll be much help, but I want to try."

Lawrence nodded. "Then how about we go over to that island?" He pointed, "The one where they filmed *Cast Away?*"

"That far?"

"Why not?"

Lawrence saw the fear in Melanie's eyes and expected her to rescind her offer. But to his utter surprise, she steeled her shoulders and said, "Okay. Let's do it."

"Are you sure about this?" Lawrence asked yet again as he helped fasten Melanie's life vest around her. His fingers had brushed against her skin here...and there...and each time she'd felt a jolt of heat.

"Yes, I'm sure."

"Because I don't want you freaking out once we get farther to sea."

"I trust you." Melanie drew in a deep breath as she met and held his gaze. "An Olympic kayaker? If I'm not safe with you, then I'm not safe with anybody."

"That was thirteen years ago," he said, barely looking at her as he donned his own life jacket. She was certain he didn't need one, but either was smart enough to opt for safety, or he wanted her not to feel self-conscious about having to wear hers.

"It's not like you're over-the-hill at thirty-five, Lawrence. You're still in great shape."

"I expect you to help me however you can. Go on, take a seat out front."

He took Melanie's hand and led her into the kayak, then helped her get settled. He had already chosen a paddle for her that he believed would be a good length, and he settled it across the boat in front of her.

"So you know, I have to be back before noon," Lawrence said. "Twelve-thirty at the latest. I've got an excursion planned in the afternoon. So we won't have a ton of time on the island once we get there. But enough time to hang out a bit and explore."

"That'll give us over two hours," Melanie said optimistically.

"Including rowing time. But we should make it in twenty minutes if the water stays calm."

Twenty minutes of paddling... Melanie worked out, but could she handle that? When she wasn't a big fan of the water in the first place?

Suddenly, she wasn't sure she knew what she was getting herself into. The only thing she did know was that she wanted to get to the island and be alone with Lawrence.

Lawrence led the kayak far enough into the water that it wouldn't get stuck on the sand, and then maneuvered himself into the boat behind her. He did the first bit of paddling, getting the boat in the direction they needed to be going in order to make it to the island. Then he gave Melanie instructions about how to paddle in strong and steady strokes. "Right paddle in the water, now the left. Good. Just like that. You'll get used to it. There you go."

They kept the same pace for a while, Melanie digging

deep to do her part to keep the kayak moving forward. Her muscles were getting tired and her movements slowing, but she did the best she could.

"Take a break if you need to," Lawrence told her. "I know it's not easy work."

Melanie was happy to hear him say the words, and rested the paddle in front of her. Taking a deep breath, she ventured a look over her shoulder, and was startled to realize that they'd already gone a far ways from the beach.

They were almost halfway to the island, which, with how tired she felt, seemed a million miles off. But the shore where the resort was, was nowhere near close enough to easily get back to.

As the saying went, there was no turning back now....

Melanie picked up her paddle and began to row again. Her arms were burning, but she pushed through the pain. She wasn't about to complain. This trip to Fiji had already offered her a few new experiences. And she hadn't died while doing any of them. She was trying to be a new person, one who didn't let fear rule her life.

Which was why she didn't object when Lawrence had loaded snorkel gear onto the boat, telling her that they could do some snorkeling once they got to the island.

As they finally neared Monuriki, Melanie looked behind her, at the resort in the distance, and was amazed.

But Lawrence wasn't directing them to the closest shore, as she thought he would. Instead he was venturing past that portion of the beach and around a curve, which would take the resort out of their sight.

Melanie continued to help paddle, and as the kayak rounded the corner, she checked out the island in front of them, with a perfect beach and thick trees.

"Oh, my God," she suddenly uttered.

"What?" Lawrence asked. "Are you afraid?"

"No," she told him. "Look beside the boat. Look at all those zebra fish!"

Lawrence looked down. "Oh, wow. The fish are plentiful here. Can you pass me the bag of bread?"

Melanie rested her paddle across the boat, and then passed Lawrence the small bag of bread that was resting on her lap. He began to throw morsels into the water, and the fish multiplied. They surrounded the boat in a frenzy to get food.

"This is amazing!" Melanie said, taking it all in with a sense of wonder. She never would have experienced this if she hadn't had the courage to fight her fear of the water.

"It is. And it's even better when you put on a snorkel mask and get into the water."

"I'm in awe. This is so…". She looked around, surveying the ocean and the shoreline of the small island. "This is so incredibly beautiful. For so many years, I've been afraid to get in the water. I've been missing so much."

"I'm glad you suggested this."

She turned then, slowly and carefully, so that she was facing him as well as she could over her shoulder. "I'm glad I came here, too." She held his gaze. "And I'm glad I'm with you."

"Mel…"

"No. Don't say anything. I just want to be still with you out here in this beautiful place." She remembered Richelle's comment, about realizing how we were one small part of a big, beautiful world. And that's exactly how Melanie felt now.

Lawrence said nothing, and Melanie looked forward again. For a long moment, they were still, and all that Melanie could think, even surrounded with all this beauty, was how much she had missed being with this man.

"You ready to head to the beach?" Lawrence asked.

"Yes," Melanie said quickly.

"I'll hold the bread for now."

"Okay."

Melanie picked up her paddle and started rowing again. She felt the adrenaline rush that racers must feel when they got close to the finish line.

She saw the movement of the tree leaves, and then a flock of red parrots took flight. "Lawrence, look!" Melanie cried.

But in her excitement, she rocked the boat. As it began to tip, Melanie panicked. Instead of trying to keep her body upright, she reached to the right instinctively, as if to embrace her fall.

And then Melanie screamed as she realized the kayak was capsizing.

Chapter 10

Melanie's scream was the last thing Lawrence heard before the kayak turned over in the water. Lawrence had tried to teach Melanie the basics of how to prepare for a kayak roll so that they could turn the boat upright naturally. But once Lawrence came back around in the boat, he saw that Melanie was no longer in it.

"Lawrence!" she screamed. She was about five feet from the boat, and being kept afloat with her life jacket, but she was panicking.

"It's okay, Mel. You're okay."

"Help me, please!"

"Just swim toward me. I'll help you back onto the boat."

"I can't!"

Lawrence was going to try to tell her that she could, but he could see the panic in her eyes and knew it would be pointless. He had to get in the water and help her.

Lawrence slipped out of his seat and jumped into the ocean.

* * *

I'm gonna drown, I'm gonna drown!

That was the thought racing through Melanie's mind as she flailed her hands in the water.

She was so full of fear that she didn't even see Lawrence jump into the water, but now he was beside her. She felt his arms and grabbed at them.

"No," Lawrence said sternly. "Let me hold you."

Melanie drew in a deep breath and tried to relax. And she noticed that she didn't immediately begin to sink, which had been her irrational fear. Just then Lawrence's arms wrapped securely around her.

"It's okay, Mel. It's okay."

Her heart was racing frantically, but she concentrated on the strong arms of the man she had once loved so fiercely. The man she had let go because she was afraid he would hurt her.

But he wasn't hurting her now. He was holding her, reassuring her, whispering words of comfort to make sure she knew she would be okay.

"I've got you, baby. You're okay."

Baby. A slip of the tongue? Regardless, the word gave her butterflies despite her fear.

And though Melanie was still afraid, she looked Lawrence in the eye. And she saw the truth of his words. That he would never let anything happen to her.

"Okay," she said.

"Try to breathe easily," he told her. "Salt water is wonderful. Look around. See how calm it is? Without any real effort, you can stay afloat. And you've got a life vest. You're not going to drown."

"Okay. I'm not going to drown."

"That's it, babe," he said. "Good, let the panic go."

Melanie felt infinitely safer, but she was still frightened by the experience of falling overboard.

"How does the water feel?" Lawrence asked.

"Huh?" Melanie asked, surprised by the question.

"The water. Concentrate on not being afraid and tell me how it feels."

"It feels nice." And it did. "It feels warm." She dared to look around. "And, my God, the color of it. It's beautiful."

"That's right, babe. You don't have to be afraid of it. You're protected, and I'm here, and I'm not going to let anything happen to you."

Their limbs stroked each other as they moved their feet in the water. Not by design, but every touch had meaning for Melanie nonetheless. She loved the feel of his body touching hers.

"Lawrence…" His name fell from her lips. Her heart still beat from fear, and not just the fear of being in the water. The fear of whether or not he would reject her if she told him she'd made a huge mistake by letting him go.

She slipped an arm around his neck, determined to conquer the mental shackles holding her back. Fear hadn't brought her happiness.

Then she put her other arm around his neck. And no longer hesitating, she leaned in and put her mouth on his.

For a moment, she just let her lips press against his, enjoying the feeling of sweet contact. Then with a moan, she tightened her arms around his wet body and began to move her mouth over his. She angled her head and slipped her tongue between his lips, hanging onto him as though she never wanted to let go.

It didn't take more than a couple seconds before she heard him groan. His arms tightened around her waist. And then right there in the water, they kissed as if there were no tomorrow.

And Melanie wasn't afraid. In fact, she had never felt more alive in her life.

Lawrence's hands smoothed from her waist down over her bottom. He dug his fingers into her flesh as he pulled her against him. Melanie gasped as she felt his erection press against her upper thigh.

Lawrence broke the kiss suddenly, and Melanie looked up at him in surprise. "We need to get back to the boat," he explained. "Get out of this water."

Melanie had all but forgotten that they were in the middle of the ocean. Being in Lawrence's arms was all that had mattered. Now, looking over at the drifting kayak, she felt a jolt of anxiety. "I don't know, Lawrence. I don't think I can get back in." Her chest shuddered. "I'm gonna make the boat tip, and—"

"It's all right," Lawrence said, his voice calm and soothing. "You trust me, right?"

A beat passed. Then Melanie nodded, looking Lawrence directly in the eye. "Yes, I trust you."

"I'm going to lead you to the boat. Then I'll position you on it near the tip."

"What?" Melanie asked, confused.

"You're too afraid to get back in, and we're close enough to shore. I'll let you sit on the boat while I swim it to the shore."

"You can do that?"

"Don't worry. I just want to get you to dry land as soon as possible so you're comfortable."

Lawrence got onto his back, secured his arm around Melanie's waist, and swam with her to the boat. Once there, he released her and instructed her to hold on to the side of it while he collected the oars. With that task complete, he came behind her, and said, "Okay, reach and grab the rope that's at the other side of the boat and hold on. I'm going to give you a boost to get you up. I only want you on there with your stomach positioned over the boat so your weight is evenly distributed over the front. Understand?"

"I think so."

"All right. On three, I'm going to give you a boost. One, two, three."

Melanie tightened her hands on the rope and heaved her body while Lawrence pushed her up. His hands moved from her waist to her bottom as he helped her secure her center over the kayak.

His hands lingered over her bottom, perhaps too long. Melanie looked over her shoulder at him, feeling a rush of excitement as she did. "Is this okay?" she asked. "Am I supposed to be like this?"

"Yeah," he said, and Melanie could hear a hitch in his voice. "That's perfect."

Lawrence swam to the back of the kayak and proceeded to lead it to shore. There was nothing for Melanie to do but hang on for the ride.

And hang on she did, noting that she was far less anxious than she would have been even a week ago out on a boat like this. She wasn't entirely unafraid, but she wasn't worried, because she was with Lawrence.

And more than that, in the position she was in with her butt upward, and after having kissed Lawrence, she felt a sexual charge. Was he checking her out, thinking about making love to her?

When they got to the shallow end of the beach on the small island, Melanie eased herself off the kayak. She grabbed hold of the rope and started to pull, helping Lawrence maneuver the boat onto the sand. With the front end of the boat on dry land, Melanie stood back and watched as Lawrence got the back end secured on the beach. She took a moment to shamelessly look at him, at the way his muscles tightened with each strong move.

Her body thrummed with arousal. She wanted to make love

to Lawrence, to feel his hard body against hers. She wanted to moan and scream his name.

"I'm proud of you, Mel," he said, breathing a little heavily. "That was a far trek. But you did it."

Melanie said nothing. Just started walking toward Lawrence and unfastening her life jacket. He dropped down onto the sand, exhaling harshly as he looked out at the ocean before them. Only when Melanie reached him did he look up at her, finally seeming to understand that she had approached him with a purpose.

"Mel?"

She threw off the jacket and tossed it onto the beach. Then she went down onto the soft sand beside him. As his eyes widened with curiosity, she climbed onto his lap, wrapped her arms around his neck and began kissing him.

Raw carnal lust surged through her body.

No, it was more than lust. It was the sense that she was supposed to be with him. The sense that he was the missing piece of the puzzle in her life.

For several glorious seconds, they made out, the kiss they shared slow and deep. But then Lawrence turned his head to the side, saying, "Damn, Mel. I don't know."

"You don't?" she challenged. "You don't know that you want this?"

She began to stroke the back of his neck above his life vest, and felt him quiver beneath her touch. She knew how much he loved to feel her nails on his skin.

"We don't have a lot of time here," Lawrence said.

"Oh, I think we have enough time." She softly kissed his lips. "Don't you?"

"Sex is easy," he told her. "But—"

Melanie softly kissed his lips again. "No buts. Please. There's no one else here. At least, there are no other boats on the beach, and I have every reason to believe we're alone."

She stroked him more, this time trailing her fingertips around to the front of his neck. He let out a low rumble. "Don't deny me."

She knew the moment he had succumbed to her seduction. Because he moaned softly, then wrapped his arms tightly around her waist. He planted his lips on hers and dropped backward onto the sand so that her body was fully on top of his.

His tongue delved into her mouth with a sense of urgency. It swept over her tongue, twisted with it. Then he gently bit her bottom lip before suckling it between his full, sensuous lips.

His hands smoothed over her bottom, skimmed the sides of her bikini. Again, Lawrence groaned. Then, swiftly, skillfully, he was flipping her onto her back on the sand and positioning himself on top of her.

He broke the kiss, and Melanie inhaled a much-needed breath. She looked up at him and he down at her. His eyes were filled with want, but she could see the conflicting emotions on his face.

She reached up and framed his cheek. He turned his face into her hand and closed his eyes. When he opened them, his gaze held hers for a beat, and then moved downward, heating her skin as they took in her breasts, and then her legs, which were bent at the knee.

Moments later he was kissing her again, another hot, breathless kiss, while his fingers went to the base of her throat and trailed down her skin to the hollow between her breasts.

Arching her back, Melanie purred. And then she whimpered in disappointment when Lawrence stopped touching her.

But he was only easing up to take off his life jacket, which he did in record time. Then he stretched out on the sand beside her and kissed her again. First, her lips. Then her chin.

Then the base of her neck. Melanie held her breath as his fingers played over the mounds of her breasts before slipping beneath the fabric. She released her breath on a sigh of pleasure when he found her nipple.

"Oh, baby," Melanie rasped.

In a flurry, Lawrence dragged the one side of her bathing suit over her breast, exposing her nipple. And then his mouth closed over it, and he was suckling her. Slowly at first, his tongue twirling over the hardened tip. He was laving her with hunger. Sucking her nipple hard.

He reached for the other side of her bikini top and pulled it down harshly. His lips moved from one nipple to the other, where he trilled the second one with his tongue and teased it with his teeth and lips.

Melanie slipped a hand around the back of his head, holding it in place as she savored the pleasure his mouth was giving her. He tweaked one nipple while suckling the other one, and Melanie, who hadn't been touched by a man in nine months, knew it wouldn't take much more for her to climax.

Lawrence eased back. "I want you naked."

Light-headed from pleasure, Melanie got to her knees. She fumbled with the back of her bikini top until it loosened. With Lawrence's eyes steadfastly on her body, she got to her feet and began to pull the bikini bottom down her thighs.

"Melanie," he uttered. "You're even more beautiful than I remember."

His words were like a potent aphrodisiac. He got onto his knees, moved toward her, and curled his hands around her thighs. An electrical shock of pleasure zapped Melanie as she realized what he was about to do. They were on this small island, and they were alone. Yet she had never been intimate with Lawrence in an open space before now.

She felt like an exhibitionist.

It was exciting.

His tongue flicked over her center, and her knees buckled. His fingers tightened on her skin and his mouth continued to move over her. The sensations were dizzying, amazing, intense. Lawrence's tongue worked its magic, not relenting until her entire body began to quake with the onset of her climax.

He gripped her hard as she rode the wave of pleasure, as she cried out his name in this beautiful private place. Then he gathered her in his arms and settled her on the sand and stripped out of his bathing trunks.

Naked, he stared down at her. "You're gorgeous."

"So are you." Catching her breath, Melanie got onto her knees and reached for his thighs. She stroked his flesh, heard him moan. And when she looked up at him, into his lust-filled eyes, she saw his vulnerability and felt a surge of power.

She pleasured him the way he had just pleasured her, until he stepped backward and eased down onto the sand. "Climb onto me," he told her, lying on his back.

Melanie did, straddling him. He wrapped his arms around her and urged her upper body down. Their mouths found each other's and began a slow, sensual kiss. And as their lips mated, Lawrence gently guided his member inside her.

Melanie cried out as he filled her. The feeling… It was exquisite. But it wasn't just the physical sensation overcoming her. It was the emotion swelling in her heart.

She and Lawrence were one with each other. One with nature.

Nothing had ever seemed more right.

Chapter 11

For the entire ride back to the main island, Lawrence felt like a new man. Like he had been recharged in a way that had been critical for his well-being. Emotionally and physically, he was on a high. He didn't even feel the burn of his muscles as he paddled at a fast pace to get back to the resort as quickly as possible to make sure he had time to get ready for his excursion with Shemar.

He'd spent more time on the island with Melanie than he had planned, foregoing the snorkeling for making love not only on the sand, but also in the water, and then in the brush along a path leading into the trees. He hadn't been able to get enough of her. And the seclusion of the private island made the tropical paradise truly seem like their very own personal love nest.

Making love to Melanie had been phenomenal. Nine months he had gone without a woman's touch. Without the touch of the woman he loved. And though he knew she still had the power to destroy him, what he'd just experienced with her had been worth the risk of more pain.

Hearing her cry out his name, seeing the look of rapture on her face, nothing had been more satisfying. And the fact that they were on that small island alone, free to run around naked and do what came naturally, had been a huge thrill.

Lawrence wanted nothing more than to take her back to his room where he could make love to her without having to worry about the discomfort that came from getting naked on a beach. Sure, they'd had the ocean to themselves to wash off their bodies. And the experience of having sex in the open, totally unrestricted, had been organic and highly erotic. But he craved the comfort of his bed to finish giving it to her with every ounce of energy he had left.

If only the seaplane was coming later in the afternoon. Then Lawrence could take her to his room for at least an hour. But it was wishful thinking, because he and Shemar were scheduled to go to the main island of Nadi and hike through the Koroyanitu National Heritage Park. Shemar wouldn't be happy if Lawrence canceled at the last minute.

No, as much as Lawrence wanted nothing more than to continue in his bed where he'd left off with Melanie on the island, it would have to wait until later.

"What's this excursion you're going on?" Melanie asked.

"Shemar and I are heading to the main island on a sea-plane. Where the national airport is. We're going hiking."

"Ah, a seaplane. I took one to the resort."

"You?" Lawrence asked disbelievingly. "You got on a sea-plane?"

Melanie glanced over her shoulder at him. Playfully, she splashed water at him with her oar. "Yes, I did," she said with a measure of pride. "And it was terrifying, and I could hardly breathe. But in so many ways, it was amazing."

"Wow," Lawrence commented. "I thought for sure you would have taken a boat over here."

"Why do you seem so surprised? I'm out on a kayak with you, aren't I? I've been doing a lot of things outside my comfort zone on this trip."

"And?"

"And...I've been having a great time."

Her words held meaning, and Lawrence knew that in part she was referring to their experience of making love. His groin tightened with the desire to touch her again, but as they were nearing the shore, he knew what he should do—wait until tomorrow to see Melanie again. The plan hadn't been to simply bed her and move on. He wanted her back in his life. He'd just given her a taste of what she'd been missing, and maybe now she needed to spend a night alone, thinking of him, reflecting on what she wanted in order to determine if she wanted him back in her life, as well.

He needed to pull back, give her time to figure out what was in her heart.

And if she decided that one last tryst was all she wanted...

Lawrence didn't want to contemplate that, but if she broke his heart again, then he would have to accept her decision and move on. And this time, he wouldn't look backward, no matter how hard that would be.

"Speaking of new experiences," Lawrence began, "have you gone into the village to experience a kava-making ceremony?"

Melanie paused her paddling and looked over her shoulder at him. "Someone prepared kava for us to drink at the wedding reception, but I haven't been in to town to experience it."

"Then how about tomorrow? You want to go with me?"

"Sure. I'd like that."

"Great. How about we meet at the main lobby for ten?"

"Sounds like a plan." Melanie began to row again. "What are you doing tonight?" she asked, her voice tentative.

"I'm not sure. But I'll be gone for hours with Shemar. I'll probably be tired when we get back to the resort."

"Oh. Right. Of course."

Lawrence knew Melanie well enough to get that she was trying to ask if they could spend the night together. After an incredible time spent on the island, he could understand why she wanted more. He did, as well.

It would be all too easy to plan to meet her later and enjoy every moment naked in bed with her. But he was going to exercise restraint.

"Ten o'clock in the lobby," Lawrence reiterated.

"Ten o'clock. I'll be there."

Finally, Lawrence and Melanie reached the shallow waters of the beach. As Lawrence maneuvered himself out of the kayak, he noticed a woman rushing toward the kayak. It took a moment for him to realize that it was Richelle.

"Oh, my God," Richelle said as Lawrence began to guide the kayak to the shore. "That really *is* you. Melanie Watts out on a *kayak?*"

"Hey, Richelle," Melanie said casually.

Richelle gave Melanie a knowing look. Then her gaze went to Lawrence. She raised an eyebrow. "Hello, Lawrence."

Lawrence nodded. "Richelle."

"How nice to see the two of you out *together.*"

"Where's Roy?" Melanie asked attempting to cut off her friend's thoughts.

"He's over there." Richelle gestured behind her. "Can I borrow Melanie once she gets out of the boat? Just for a moment?"

"She's all yours," Lawrence said. "I'm heading out with Shemar, so I've got to get back to my room."

"Perfect." Richelle smiled sweetly.

Lawrence helped Melanie out of the boat. She looked up at him, the expression in her eyes saying she wasn't ready to say goodbye. "Tomorrow," he told her. "Don't be late."

Melanie nodded. "I won't."

He smiled down at her. "Good. See you then."

"I can't *believe* you!" Richelle said to Melanie as she walked with her down the beach once Lawrence was out of earshot. "You and Lawrence...out on a kayak? I said to Roy, that looks like Melanie. And my God, it *was* you. I could hardly believe my eyes!"

"We went over to the island where they filmed *Cast Away,*" Melanie explained, as if her getting on a kayak was no big deal.

"I could barely get you on a seaplane. And you willingly got in a kayak with a man you said you wanted nothing more to do with?"

"I didn't exactly say that...."

Richelle rolled her eyes, guffawing. "Who are you, and what have you done with my friend? Don't get me wrong, I like the new you." She lowered her voice, though no one was close enough to overhear them. "Come on, Mel. You and Lawrence on that island? Were you alone?"

"Yes."

Richelle squealed. "Oh, my God. Obviously, you reconnected. Tell me everything."

"Let's just say, we had the island to ourselves. And...it couldn't have been hotter."

Melanie blushed, remembering how liberating and exciting it had been to make love to Lawrence on the island. She hated that he was heading off with Shemar now, instead of back to her room.

"You got on a boat and went to a deserted island with

Lawrence to make love! Girl, you are changing before my very eyes!"

"You told me that I've been afraid of so much, and I took those words to heart. So I got in a kayak and trekked across all that water." She told Richelle about how the boat had tipped. "I panicked, of course, but Lawrence was strong and calm, and he was there for me, holding me. In his arms, I felt safe."

"And then you thanked him appropriately."

"Richelle!" Melanie playfully swatted her arm.

"Good. I'm happy for you. I was worried that you would be bored for the last days of your vacation. But you're in good hands now so I don't have to be concerned."

A smile touched Melanie's lips. "Yeah. There's something magical about this place. I love it here."

"Maybe there'll be another wedding?" Richelle said hopefully.

"Oh, I wouldn't say that." And Melanie's stomach fluttered. "I mean, it was just sex."

"Mel, seriously. You're here, he's here, and you've reconnected for a reason," Richelle said sternly. "But if you hold back on him, I don't know if you'll get another chance with him."

Melanie shrugged. "I don't know that this *is* about another chance. I don't want to get my hopes up, only to—"

"So you'd rather hide behind your wall in hopes of protecting yourself from getting hurt?" Richelle made a face. "You just finished telling me that you haven't been letting your fear hold you back from trying new experiences. Don't let your fear hold you back from telling Lawrence how you feel."

Chapter 12

It was one thing for Lawrence to tell himself that he needed to harden his heart. It was another thing to put it into practice.

Fifteen minutes after ten o'clock the next morning, Lawrence was still waiting for Melanie to meet him in the lobby. And he was starting to fear that he should have kept his guard up. Because it was looking like she wasn't going to show.

Just like she hadn't shown on their wedding day.

As each second passed, his heart sank. It was becoming pretty obvious that she'd spent the night deciding what she wanted and had come to the conclusion that she wanted to move on in her life without him.

Pain ripped through him with the thought, as raw and intense as the day of his foiled wedding. One incredible morning with Melanie, and he was back to being completely vulnerable again.

Of course she's not going to show. Why am I even surprised?

Lawrence glanced at his watch. Ten-seventeen. Exhaling sharply, he turned, ready to head back to his room.

And there she was, hurrying toward him on the path leading into the lobby. Her lips curled in a bright smile as their eyes connected.

Lawrence's lips parted, and a long breath whooshed out of him. She was here.

She was a vision of loveliness in a white dress with her hair pulled into a ponytail. Her ample bosom looked enticing, and her feet were especially sexy in gold wedge sandals.

"Sorry I'm late," Melanie said, warmth emanating from the smile on her beautiful lips. That smile had always been Lawrence's undoing.

"No problem," he told her, speaking casually, as though he hadn't just been experiencing a world of doubt and pain.

"So, do we call for a taxi? I can't wait to head to the village. This is going to be fun."

"I don't think I can do this," Lawrence muttered, the words falling from his lips on their own.

"Pardon?" Melanie asked.

Lawrence cleared his throat. And then he spoke clearly. "I can't do this, Mel." Suddenly, he was sure. He couldn't hang out with her, act as though they were a couple if they weren't. "You and me… I—"

"You don't want to go into town?" Melanie's eyes narrowed in confusion.

"I shouldn't have suggested this. I'm sorry."

"Lawrence, I don't understand."

"You do understand," Lawrence said, and it hurt him to say so. "Nine months ago—" He stopped abruptly, exhaled sharply. "You made your choice."

"No!" Melanie said. And then she stepped toward him and placed her hand on his chest. "Lawrence, please. I think…I think it's time we had a talk."

"Mel, I don't—"

"In your room, or mine," she pressed on. When he said nothing, she continued in a lower voice, "A real talk, Lawrence."

On one hand, Lawrence wanted to walk away from Melanie the way one tore off a Band-Aid. Quickly, so there was as little pain as possible. But on the other hand, the way she was looking at him, with those wide, pleading eyes…it was hard to say no to her.

And there was another reason he couldn't say no. Because where Melanie was concerned, his heart seemed unable to give up hope.

"All right," he said, knowing that it would be now or never. "Let's talk."

A short while later, Melanie and Lawrence were alone in his bungalow on the beach. Shemar had been there when they had arrived, but after a short chat with Lawrence, he grabbed some snorkel gear and headed to the beach.

Not before giving Melanie a look, though. The kind of look that told her just how he felt about what she'd done.

"This is a gorgeous room," Melanie said, trying to lighten the intensity of the mood. It was a stunning *bure,* larger than the one she was in, with a considerable patio that even boasted a private plunge pool. She looked around at the beauty of the patio, with the pristine beach as a backdrop. Shemar had disappeared down the beach. "I thought my room was special. But this…it's magnificent."

"You said you wanted to talk."

Turning, Melanie faced Lawrence, who was standing just inside the patio doors. His arms were folded over his chest, which spoke volumes.

"Yes." Melanie started toward him, and then stepped past him into the next room. The sofa bed was open and unmade, and the king-size bed, while unmade, at least had the comforter pulled over it in a neater fashion. Melanie knew without having to ask that's where Lawrence slept.

And just looking at the large bed, and at this incredible room, situated in this magical island resort, she wished desperately that she and Lawrence were here together.

She sighed softly and began to speak. "I look at this romantic place, and I can't help thinking that we should be here together. Wishing that we were. I know it's my fault that we're not," she pressed on when Lawrence opened his lips, as if to speak. "And I am sorry, Lawrence. I screwed up. I hurt you. Heck, seeing the way Shemar looked at me—with anger—was hard. I know what he's thinking. He hasn't forgotten that I hurt you, and he's wondering if I'm going to do it again."

"Are you?" Lawrence asked.

"You can't possibly think that."

"I don't know what to think. The first thing you did when you saw me was run."

"Are you forgetting yesterday?"

Melanie saw Lawrence's Adam's apple rise.

"And then there was yesterday. But that could have simply been the sex. Something familiar and easy for both of us."

"You're wrong. That wasn't what it was for me. I didn't come to meet you this morning just because I want more hot sex."

"You say you look at this room and think we should be here together?" Lawrence began. "Well, it's all I've been able to think about since I saw you again. That I want you in that bed with me." He gestured to the king-size bed with a jerk of his head. "The two of us naked. Barely seeing what the island has to offer because we can't get enough of each other."

His words caused Melanie to feel a sexual charge. "Really?"

"But every time the thought comes to me, I remember that

we *should* have had that. *Would* have had that. If you hadn't thrown it away."

A moment ago, she'd been feeling a sexual charge. Now, her stomach fizzled.

"Yesterday," Lawrence began. "God knows I wanted yesterday. But the morning after, I find myself wondering what it means."

"It means something," Melanie told him. "It wouldn't have happened if it didn't mean something."

"Given our history, how can you expect me to believe that?"

Lawrence's words stung. But he was right. What had she given him to go on that he could have faith in? They'd had wonderful sex before, yet she had still left him standing at the altar.

"I want you back," Melanie said, knowing that she had to lay her heart on the line. "Yesterday was about me wanting you in my life again. Let's just say it's become crystal clear that I made the biggest mistake of my life when I walked away from you."

Lawrence turned away from her and strolled into the living room. Melanie followed him, her heart tightening as though someone was squeezing the life out of it.

"How can I trust you?" he asked.

His voice had been soft, the question earnest. And it caused a surge of emotion within Melanie that she wasn't prepared for. Because she truly felt a sense of fear. Fear that she had lost Lawrence forever.

"I've changed," she said softly. "Lawrence, this trip for me has been a life changer in a lot of ways. I've stepped out of my comfort zone. I've faced some pretty big fears. And..." She paused, swallowed. "And I found you again."

"You had me. You didn't want me."

"Yesterday, in the water, when you were with me, I'd never

felt safer. I knew without a doubt that I could trust you with my life."

"But not with your heart," Lawrence said, and she saw his jaw flinch. "And that's what mattered most to me."

Melanie swayed as her eyes fluttered shut. Thinking about the fears that had sent her running always brought her pain. But she knew she would have to expose her vulnerabilities if she was going to have a chance of winning Lawrence back.

"Lawrence," she said, and already her eyes were filling with tears. "When my father left my mother, she became broken. I learned very early that love has the power to destroy. My mother hasn't been the same since he left. Her smile used to light up an entire room. And when my father left, it was like a part of her died. I never realized how much that shaped me. When I saw my parents together, they looked happy. But my father ended up having an affair anyway. As much as I always wanted to get married myself one day, I guess a seed of fear and distrust was planted in my soul. I knew all too well that people could be happy together, and one partner could still devastate the other."

"Yeah. Tell me about it."

His comment had the effect of dousing her with cold water to wake her up. Until Lawrence uttered the words, she'd never seen him in the role of her mother in the story she was telling. She had always seen herself in that possible role, but she had actually become her father, hurting a man who truly loved her.

"Then there was Richelle. Here she was, engaged to be married, and happy. Or so she thought. Then she learned of Vern's affair. What he did affected me deeply. That seed of fear, the doubt…it started up again. Fiercely. Lawrence, all I could see on our wedding day was the huge risk of me being hurt…and I…suddenly I couldn't take that risk. You think it didn't hurt me to leave you? God, it was the hardest thing I'd ever done. But I convinced myself that the pain would be far greater down the road."

"You should have talked to me."

Tears spilled down Melanie's cheeks. "Yes, I know. But I couldn't. I knew what you would tell me. I knew you would tell me that you loved me. But Lawrence, I was frozen with fear inside." She brushed at her tears. "The crazy thing is, I wanted to protect myself from pain. And I know now how stupid a decision that was. Because the truth is, standing right here, knowing that you might tell me that you want nothing more to do with me again—you have to know how much my heart is hurting. And hurting mostly because I realize just how much I hurt you, something I never wanted to do. I love you, baby, but I also know that I have no right to tell you that. Not after what I did."

He wasn't taking her in his arms. He wasn't telling her that he forgave her. The agony was unlike anything Melanie had ever known.

She wrapped her arms around her torso, turned toward the window and let her tears fall freely. She'd lost Lawrence, and she had no one to blame but herself.

Suddenly, she felt arms encircling her waist from behind. She gasped as Lawrence's hands pressed against her belly. Then, he was pressing the side of his face against hers and raising one hand to wipe at her tears.

Relief flooded Melanie, and more tears fell. And as she cried, he kissed her cheek. Then he turned her in his arms and planted his mouth on hers.

A heavenly sigh escaped her. The kiss was deep and slow and full of meaning.

Melanie gripped the collar of his shirt and surrendered completely to him. It was amazing how much she had missed this. How much she would never tire of this.

Finally, she eased back to catch her breath. "I love you, Lawrence. I love you."

He looked down at her, held her gaze a moment before speaking. "You love me?"

"God, yes. My doubts...they weren't about you. They were about me. And I'm sorry." Another beat passed, and now Melanie was the one who needed an answer. "Do you still love me? Do we still have a chance?"

Lawrence's hand went to her face. He gently caressed it before speaking. "I've never stopped loving you."

She grinned, the warmest of feelings filling her entire body. "I'll never hurt you again," Melanie told him. "I promise."

"Then why don't we get married? Right here, right now?"

Melanie held her breath as she stared at him. "You want to get married here? To me? In Fiji?"

"We were supposed to get married nine months ago. I want all with you, or nothing. And if you feel the same, let's make it official."

A laugh bubbled in Melanie's throat. She had never been so spontaneous.

"But our families..." she began.

"Will probably be relieved to hear the deed is done," Lawrence said, and then smiled. "And this way, we wouldn't have to endure anyone waging bets on whether or not the wedding was actually going to happen."

"Oh." Melanie scowled playfully. Then she grew serious. "Lawrence, I leave in a couple days. Can we really pull this off?"

"We can extend our trip, can't we? If we do this, we'll need a proper honeymoon, after all."

"You're not joking, are you?"

Lawrence shook his head. "Seriously, Mel. Why not?"

Why not? This trip had already been about adventure,

about facing fears. And here she was with the man she loved, and she knew she didn't want to let him go again.

Most importantly, she wanted him to know that she was totally committed. That she wouldn't leave him standing at the altar again.

"Yes," she said. And she started to laugh with excitement. "Let's get married!"

Lawrence grinned from ear to ear before wrapping his arms tightly around her and bringing his mouth down onto hers. His warm tongue swept through her mouth with wide broad strokes, eliciting the greatest of pleasure. Then, with their lips still locked, he began to walk backward, leading her toward the king-size bed.

His mouth moved from her lips to her neck, and Melanie's body flooded with heat. His lips teased her skin, and then his teeth pulled the strap of her dress down one shoulder.

"What about Shemar?" Melanie managed to ask on a rapturous moan. She didn't want Lawrence to stop, but she also didn't want them to be interrupted.

"I told him to stay busy for at least a couple hours," Lawrence supplied. He urged her backward onto the bed and lay beside her. His hand went to her thigh, where his fingers gently trilled her skin. "I didn't get to make love to you properly at the beach."

"I beg to differ."

"Still, I like the idea of you being in my bed. No sand. Just you and me."

Melanie's entire body flushed at his comment. "I like the sound of that. A lot."

He kissed her hotly, but briefly, then said, "Take off your clothes, baby."

Melanie eased up on the bed and began to strip out of her dress, while Lawrence shed his shirt and pants. Her eyes drank in the sight of his muscular body.

Unclothed, they came together on the bed on their knees, their hands exploring while their tongues mated wildly. Lawrence stroked her nipples, making them harden. And then he lowered his face to her breast and drew a nipple deep into his mouth.

Melanie's body exploded with sensation. Lawrence pleasured her with his tongue and lips for a long time, not relenting until she was digging her fingers into his skin and moaning his name. Only then did he finally capture her lips with his again, settle himself onto her body and enter her with a slow delicious thrust.

And as they made love, the energy between them was different than it had been on the private island. Yesterday had been as much about satisfying a carnal need as it had been about reconnecting.

But today…this was about rebuilding the foundation of their relationship.

This was about solidifying their unending love.

Epilogue

Days earlier, when Melanie had helped Richelle get ready for her wedding, she had never imagined that she, too, would marry the man of her dreams on this lushly beautiful island.

And in the place where they had come together again, where it seemed as if fate had truly given them a second chance, it only seemed fitting.

"You look gorgeous," Richelle told her, tears filling her eyes as she spoke.

"You think so?" Melanie asked.

"Yes. I love the traditional wedding gown on you. You totally made the right choice!"

Melanie checked her reflection in the mirror, amazed at how radiant she looked in the tapa costume. Unlike Richelle and Roy, Melanie and Lawrence had opted for a fully traditional Fijian wedding—which included the tapa wedding costumes for both the bride and the groom. They had been touched by the magic of Fiji, and for them, it was the right choice to make the spirit of Fiji a part of their wedding.

"In so many ways, I love this dress much more than the one I designed for myself," Melanie said. Hand painted by local women earlier today, it wasn't the kind of dress she would ever have created for herself.

And yet, it was absolutely perfect.

"I'm just so happy for you," Richelle said. As her matron of honor, she too was dressed in traditional Fijian wedding attire. "Who knew, when I had to beg you to agree to Fiji, that we would come here, and you would reconnect with Lawrence?" She beamed. "Now I'm married, and you're getting married, too…and everything feels right."

Melanie nodded, joy washing over her. "I'm so glad my foolish actions didn't cost me the man I love forever."

"He's a keeper," Richelle said.

"That, he is."

"Oh, you hear that?" Richelle said. "The choir has begun to sing." She gripped Melanie's hand. "Are you ready?"

Melanie drew in a deep breath. "I'm ready."

Richelle gave her a hug, then left the wedding *bure* to begin her walk down the aisle to the beach. Then, the warriors helped Melanie onto the raft.

They lifted her into the air and carried her down to the beach. This was a small, quaint wedding. Other than Shemar, Lawrence's best man, Richelle, and of course the minister, only Roy and some of the hotel staff were in attendance as guests.

But that didn't matter to Melanie, because her eyes were only for Lawrence. He was beaming with love and pride as he took in the sight of her.

When, at last, she was helped off the raft, he took her hand and whispered, "You're beautiful, baby. Absolutely beautiful."

Melanie's eyes misted. Nine months earlier, she should have married this wonderful man in a big church in Harlem, with all her friends and family present.

And yet here, with the stunning beach backdrop, barefoot in the sand, this intimate wedding held much more appeal for her. Because she didn't need the world to hear her proclaim her love for Lawrence. She needed only him.

"Melanie Avery Watts, do you take this man to be your lawfully wedded husband?" the minister asked.

"I do." Melanie smiled at the man she loved, tears of happiness finally falling down her cheeks. "I definitely do."

And minutes later, after they'd shared their personal vows and the minister pronounced them husband and wife, all Melanie could think, as Lawrence's lips met hers for the first time as her husband's, was that this was perfect.

The perfect day. The perfect wedding.

The perfect man.

And the perfect start to the rest of their lives.

* * * * *

THE WEDDING DANCE
Carmen Green

Chapter 1

The walls of Jay Smith's office were covered with photos of him and every world-class athlete of the last ten years. Since joining CNN's Atlanta office eleven years ago, he'd made it his business to become the Color Commentator to know. Athletes *wanted* to be interviewed by him. So why, in what could only be described as a professional man-cave, was he staring at a ballerina dancing on his computer screen?

His coanchor, and friend, Ashton Bolton, was standing over his shoulder watching the woman, Vivian Franklin, swing and sway across the dance floor in quiet concentration. She broke out in some popular hip-hop moves, adding the Dougie, and then did a few things that made both men rear back and look at one another in awe.

"Damn, man. She's hot." Quiet admiration streaked the baritone chords of Ashton's voice as he glanced at the office door as if they were viewing porn on the company computer. "How'd you hear about this Vivian woman?"

"I found her on Twitter. She's an award-winning dancer. Classically trained, sidelined by an injury—her career seemed over. But after choreographing a dance for a wedding party that went viral, she's smokin' hot. I want her."

Ashton and Jay watched the end of the dance, and then Ashton picked up the controller and started shooting hoops. "So what do you want her to do for you? Teach you how to dance? 'Cause she don't look like a miracle worker to me."

Jay grabbed the controller he'd been using to play the Xbox basketball game and blocked the shots Ashton had been making. They began a heated game of one-on-one. Their *NFL Lineup* show was going on the air in ten minutes. They had twenty more minutes to goof off.

"When Troy and Destinee asked me to be the best man at their wedding," Jay began, "I thought, no problem. Show up at a couple dinners, make a couple speeches, do the wedding thing and I'm done. But after going to six weddings last year, I realize now I have to bring my A game."

"Man, you turn everything into a competition. Six guys in this office got married, and now you have to best them. You don't. They're not worried about you."

Jay threw up his hands. "My wedding—" He stopped himself. "*This wedding* has to be the best, if I'm involved. We have to have the best wedding dance. Not some whacked-out, old-time Electric Slide, shake-your-booty thing my grandma made up. I'm talking first-class, top-of-the-line, choreographed stuff that knocks people's socks off!" Jay banged on the controller knocking down four three-pointers.

Ashton answered by blocking his next two shots. "And you think Ms. High-Class-Ballerina Franklin can help you?"

"Definitely." Jay stopped with the controller to study the face of the woman who looked like she was staring back at him. She sat on the floor, one leg folded beneath her, both hands braced on the floor in front of her. Her eyes were deep chocolate-truffles brown and her skin this soft-baked brown sugar that intrigued him. Her hair was pulled back into this bun caught low and tight at the nape of her neck, and her earlobes were bare.

He normally went for women who were the total put-together package. Tall, slim, with big earrings and long polished nails. But this woman was without nail polish, earrings and makeup, and still she made him want to strip her of her leotard and tights…and handle her. Jay was impressed.

This was a character she was playing. A role she'd taken on to convince people that her artistic performance was true. He patted his gut. Well…*sold.* He'd bought her entire act. hook, relevé and passé.

Those were the only two dance moves he remembered since taking the NBA-mandated dance class for agility and balance.

"Dude, quit looking at her so hard. You don't know her like that, and you don't even know if she's going to say yes." Ever the voice of reason, Ashton butted into his fantasy.

"She'll do it."

Jay dialed her number from the contact information that was on the bottom of the screen.

Uninterested, Ashton began to do his mouth rotation warm-ups. *"Waah-oooo. Waah-oooo."*

"Shut up."

"Hello?" The voice tickled his eardrum.

"Vivian Franklin, please. This is Jay Smith."

Jay stood and began adjusting his clothes. For the next two hours he'd be on the air talking about sports. But that wasn't what had propelled him out of his seat. It was the directness of her tone and his surprise that she'd answered.

The woman on the phone hesitated. "Ms. Franklin is unavailable, Mr. Smith. What is this regarding?"

The voice on the speakerphone was slightly rough and low, like the person on the other end had a cold. Jay felt his brow tick up. This was her. He'd put money on it. "I viewed Ms. Franklin's video online, and I want her to teach me how to dance."

There was a slight hesitation. "No." The phone went dead.

Ashton's laughter was slow to come but long to end. "You sounded like a real pervert."

No lights blinked on the phone. "She hung up on me!" Jay exploded. "I *bet* that was her. How do you run a business by hanging up on people?" He was stunned.

Ashton pretended to pull up his pants, mimicking him. "*I want you to teach me how to dance.* You're a nasty man."

Jay would have laughed if the fool hadn't been talking about him. Grabbing his jacket, he didn't put it on. Who the hell did she think she was hanging up on? He had a championship ring! "I didn't sound like that."

"Yes, you did. Forget it, man. She shot you down. We're live in fifteen minutes. Make up a dance. It's going to be funny anyway because you're the only black dude I know who ain't got an ounce of rhythm."

"Why do you think I was calling what I thought was a professional?" He picked up the phone then slammed it down again, replaying his movements in his head. He *had* been adjusting his clothes. Maybe he had sounded slightly pervish.

Jay dialed her number again and got voice mail. "Ms. Franklin, this is James 'Jay' Smith, anchor of *NFL Lineup* for CNN. I called a minute ago and asked you to teach me to dance, but what I need is for you to teach a dance to a *wedding party.* I'd like to invite you down to our studio, here at CNN, just so you're comfortable in knowing I'm not a perv."

Ashton shook his head.

Nervously, Jay wiped his forehead. The feeling was totally foreign to him. He was an award-winning broadcaster.

Nerves hadn't struck him since he'd met the members of the 2012 Women's Olympic Soccer Team.

"Vivian, I didn't mean that. What am I saying? I mean it! I'm not—" He punched his palm with his fist. "Just come down here so you'll know I'm a stand-up guy, and not trolling the internet for women. I hope to hear from you." He left his number along with the time for the meet tomorrow, and then headed for the studio.

Ashton sat in his coanchor chair, allowing himself to be prepped by the makeup team. "She'd be a fool to come here after that message."

Jay kept his eyes closed. "Yeah, I know."

Chapter 2

Pouting, and none too pleased, Vivian allowed herself to be pulled into the CNN building because her best friend, Kerri Vaughn, was in love with Jay Smith's coanchor, Ashton Bolton.

Mr. Smith had left her three more messages last night apologizing for his previous messages, clarifying his message and the last one, restating his earlier messages. The man was a control freak from the word go.

The only reason she'd come was because she'd heard Ashton in the background telling him to give up, and because Kerri had insisted Ashton was the man for her.

Who was she to stand in the way of true love?

"I'll buy you a steak if we leave right now."

Kerri rolled her eyes and kept walking toward the security officer while Vivian matched her friend's long stride. "I'm a vegetarian today," she told Vivian, then turned to the guard. "Excuse me. Can you tell me how to get to Jay Smith's office? Here's the security pass he emailed Ms. Franklin."

Security escorted them to the bank of elevators and sent them up.

"Will you relax? He sounded like he was nervous as all hell, but when you watch him on TV, you wouldn't think anything rattles him."

"I don't watch sports talk shows."

"I'm a sports nut," Kerri gushed, making Vivian smile as they glided toward the sixteenth floor. Her feet were in perfect third position, a stance she'd become accustomed to standing in since she was six. "Ashton is gorgeous, and can you believe he's single?" Kerri continued.

"No. I can't believe a man I don't know is single."

Kerri, who was two years older than her twenty-five, regarded her with amusement.

"You're always snarky when you're scared. Pretend this is a performance, because then you would be quiet and composed."

Suitably chastised for her bad mood, Vivi pulled the pins from the bun in her hair and felt her tresses fall past her shoulders. She swiped it behind her ears, then shifted the dance bag on her left shoulder. "I'm sorry. I won't take this out on you. We're just meeting so I can say no in person. Don't leave my side, Kerri."

The doors opened and dropped them off in a sports haven.

Photos of sports legends were everywhere, some in tall thick frames, others looping around on various screens.

Vivian linked arms with Kerri and they turned to see a man buttoning his jacket.

James Connor Smith—Jay—reminded her of a Jaguar car. Sleek, classy and…pretty. Were his eyebrows arched?

One inched up under her scrutiny.

Green eyes rimmed with black studied her with an intense fascination. Why, she wondered, didn't she like him?

"You don't like me," he said. His voice was clear and crisp, Southern, yet educated.

"You're full of yourself."

Kerri gasped and pulled at Vivian, but Jay didn't break eye contact.

"That's all right. My niece didn't like me, either. I had to win her over when she first met me."

For some reason this amused Vivian, and as hard as she fought a smile, she lost. "I think I'd like your niece."

His mouth was full and smug, his lips thick, confident. His jaw was hard and round and relaxed. Usually she made men nervous. She was eyeballing him hard, yet he hadn't backed down.

"Woman, what are you looking at?" he demanded and Vivian finally backed up.

The crack in your shiny veneer.

"We can speak in my office." He gestured down a long hallway, but she stepped aside so she had to follow him. No way was she going to allow him to watch her butt all the way up the hall.

"Where's Ashton?" Kerri asked. Vivian gave her a rag-doll shake that nearly loosened her back teeth, and she fell silent.

Jay turned at the commotion, but it was over in a flash.

"He's in his office." Jay stopped at a door, knocked and kept going. "He's coming. Right this way, ladies."

Escorting them into his office, Vivian's arm was locked on Kerri's as they stared at the room. It was very interesting and smelled of cologne. There were sports journals, biographies, health magazines and newspapers everywhere. Everything had sticky notes on them. Including the video games.

"Do you have a secretary?" she wondered aloud. It was a nightmare. There was no place to so much as sit.

Jay laughed. "No. She quit. The cleaning lady empties the garbage and I…uh, use a Swiffer when it gets really bad in here." He moved a bunch of papers off the guest chair in front of his desk and set them on the floor behind his chair.

"Have you thought about buying the Swiffer company and moving them in?"

"You're funny. I like that."

The question on Kerri's face was obvious. Where was her seat?

"Oh!" he exclaimed. "You can have my chair," he told her.

"Awesome," Kerri said, not really meaning it.

Vivian chuckled as Kerri tiptoed around the desk and sat. "Why do you have so many toys?"

"Boys and toys go together," Vivian and Jay answered at the same time.

Their gazes met and held.

Just then Ashton walked in and Kerri unfolded from the chair like a hothouse orchid. "Kerri Vaughn," she purred.

He took her in.

Vivian read loud and clear his appreciation for her long, lean and lovely friend.

"You look hungry," Ashton stated.

"I am," she said, and walked out with him.

"Kerri? Kerri?" Vivian said softly, but Kerri didn't answer.

"She'll be back. He won't go far, I promise."

"I don't even know you. How can you promise anything?"

"Well, get to know me. I need your help anyway."

"So I gathered from your numerous messages. I believe I gave you an answer already."

"No, you gave a stranger a message. I want to show you something. Come on."

"Where are we going?"

She hadn't perceived the sense of danger, but one never knew. He could be crazy.

"Around other people. I want you to be comfortable with me."

"But what if Kerri comes back?"

"Promise, we'll be back before them."

There was that word again. Speculatively, Vivian eyed the interviewer and decided to give him a little rope.

Jay's tour ended at his boss's desk with Ross Lincoln telling Vivian that Jay was a practical joker, he gave terrible wedding presents, ate out of everyone's lunches in the refrigerator and never chipped in on the monthly birthday cakes.

Jay could do little to defend himself. Ross was charmed by Vivi's beauty as was everyone who'd met her on the fifteen-minute-turned-half-hour tour.

The five guys surrounding her admired the view.

"You sound like a really terrible guy. Used gift cards for wedding gifts? Tacky."

The guy who'd told that urban legend walked by, laughing.

"Why did you tell that lie on me?" Jay demanded, his hands in his pockets, a smirk on his face.

"Lie? What lie? I plead the fifth." His rival continued to walk by. He'd lost the show to Jay two years ago and was still a little bitter.

"I want that baby stroller back that I bought you and Tiera," he told Rajid.

"Sorry, dude. We sold it. What?" the man smirked, observing the shock on Jay's face. "It was really nice, and we already had one."

The guys drifted away, and Jay and Vivi strolled back to his office. "I was trying to make a good impression."

"I'm completely sure you didn't," she said, laughter in her voice. "Do you really eat out of people's lunches?"

"Lunch in this building gets expensive," he joked. "Are—are you judging me?"

He half closed the door and made room on the couch behind the guest chair she sat in. Vivian had to turn her chair to look at him. "No, I just think you're a greedy—"

He grabbed his chest. "That hurts. Right here."

She laughed. "Go to the food court. I'm sure there's one in this huge building."

"I already told you—too expensive. Those guys were terrible character witnesses. And my boss, Ross, he likes to tell lies."

Regarding him, her gaze slid from joyful to peaceful. She was simply fine in that elegant way women weren't anymore.

"So now that you know I'm not a serial killer, will you teach me to dance?"

Her slender shoulders slid up and down. A little pout tipped her lips up, and her eyes slid left and right.

Jay waited for her body to stop reacting. "I'm that revolting? I've left you speechless. It's hard for me to do that. This doesn't happen to Jay Connor Smith."

"Jay, I don't have a lot of time. I've got a big obligation coming up, and I don't want to commit to something I can't fulfill."

Vivian had crossed her legs and clasped her hands together. She was shutting down.

He clapped his hands and closed the door. "Okay. I wasn't going to go here, but you forced me."

"Jay, open the door."

"Not until I'm done." He handed her his wireless phone. "Hold on to that. You can call security if I get out of line. But you forced this out of me, so if anything bad happens, it's your fault."

This time when she pouted, it was with attitude. "What are you talking about?"

"Obviously you need a dance demonstration."

Her pout pulled inward, but she said nothing.

Jay turned on his internet radio to the hip-hop station, and he started bopping his head. "Yeah, this is good. Right?"

"It's *your* audition. Do your thing." She folded her arms.

"Okay." He smiled. "I can go old-school and do the Running Man." He started running, and she grinned and nearly hit herself in the face with the phone. "You're laughing, but this is the dance. I'm doing it. I bet you don't know this! Or the Dirt Off Your Shoulder. Hey! The Moonwalk! Or the Snake! This is good! I'm good, right?"

She burst out laughing. "Please tell me you don't dance like this anywhere people can see you?"

Jay danced all around his office. "Yeah! All the time. I saw you do this," he said as he moved crazily from side to side. "Come on. Do it."

Vivi threw up her hands. "No, thanks."

Jay grabbed them and tossed the phone on the couch. "Don't be such a proper girl. Have fun! Throw your hands up!"

"Like this?" Vivi copied him.

"It's not as good as mine."

Her hands flew to her hips, and she glared at him.

"What?" He kept dancing. "I'm being honest. You gotta be free, you know? Like that shimmy thing I saw you do on the computer. That's freeing."

"I wasn't shimmying, you ding-dong. I was belly dancing. You don't even know what you're looking at."

"Your shoulders were moving."

Vivian's hips started moving, but so did her shoulders, and he saw the magic in her moves.

"Damn," he said, holding the word so long it sounded like a song. "Now Cabbage Patch," he encouraged her.

They were dancing when they spotted the shocked faces of Ashton and Kerri at the door. They stopped instantly, embarrassed.

"Can you gouge my eyes out, Ashton?" Kerri asked.

Ashton felt around on top of Kerri's head. "I've already gone blind. Help me to my office."

The door closed once again, he and Vivian looked at one another.

Jay cut off the music while she straightened her already straight dress. "So can you help me?"

"After what I just saw, we're going to have to practice a lot. You can't dance—at all."

"What was I just doing?"

"Having a seizure."

Jay sat his out-of-breath self in his chair and reached in the mini-refrigerator behind the desk for a bottled water. He handed Vivian one and got another for himself.

"When was the last time you went to the gym?"

His thoughts ticked back to the four broken dates for racquetball over the past two weeks, and he reflected on the reasons why. He'd been working. "It's been about a month."

"When's the wedding?"

"In a month."

Her hands flew to her temples. "You expect me to take nondancers and turn them into dancers overnight?"

"Yes."

"How many people?"

"Three couples."

Her mouth fell open. "Any kids? I can't teach kids and adults, too. Not at this late date."

Jay was shaking his head. "No kids. Not even in the wedding."

"What about the bride and groom? What kind of time can they commit to the rehearsal? We need to practice *at least* eight to ten times."

"It's going to be a surprise for them."

"A surprise." A sardonic laugh fell out of Vivian, and she scratched her brow. He wondered if that was her thing to do when she was a little uncomfortable. "Does the happy couple like surprises?"

Jay waited until she looked at him. Something told him she hadn't had too many good surprises in her life. "They love surprises. I wouldn't do this if I wasn't sure it would be okay. Troy and I have been best friends since the eleventh grade, and he's marrying his childhood sweetheart."

"Lovely."

"Okay, then. Do we have a deal?" Excited, he got to his feet and came around his desk.

"No. We haven't discussed my rates, which are $125 an hour. Twice a week for eight-or-so weeks and that could get expensive."

He sat on the corner of his desk. Eyeing Vivi, he chugged his water. "Troy did me a favor a long time ago. I think I can give him a knockout wedding dance. And a Crock-Pot."

"Okay then. We have a deal. If we're going to keep things a secret, why don't you have everyone come to my studio? It's on Memorial Drive near Rockbridge. North side of the street. Can't miss it. Big sign that says Dance Studio."

"In the hood?" he asked her.

Vivian only smiled. "Hey, rent is affordable. Don't worry. I've never been jumped."

She shouldered the huge dance bag she had placed on the floor when she had first come in and moved her elegant body in front of his. Her perfume lingered. "First practice is to-morrow at 7:00 p.m. I don't do late, so everyone must be on time, and they come prepared to dance. That means no loose jewelry, but comfortable clothing and dance shoes. If they don't prepurchase them, they can get them at the studio. We can't mess up the floor, or I lose my deposit."

"Got it. Anything specific for me?"

She smiled at him. "Go to the gym tonight. And in the morning. See you tomorrow evening."

Chapter 3

Vivian hadn't known what to expect—of course, not handsome men dressed in dance tights and leg warmers. But she had at least expected professional athletes, so the entrance of these former athletes shocked her. One man looked positively ready to give birth. He introduced himself as Harv. He was thick from his neck to his very full ankles. The other man had on sweats and an iPod plugged in his ears.

He walked up, shaking strawberry-blond hair from his eyes. He extended his hand. "Elliott."

Vivian met his firm grip. "Vivian. Nice to meet you. Any dance experience?"

"Ten years. Don't tell these guys, but my mother was a dance teacher. I've forgotten just about everything but how to stretch. Go easy on me." His smile was easily seductive. "Where are the ladies? I know my wife, Idalia, will be here on time. You can set a clock by her."

Vivian shrugged. "Not sure, but we'll get started in two minutes even if they're not here. I'll be right back."

Vivian took a deep breath when a woman walked in with spiked heels on, crossing the floor.

"Miss, please remove your shoes. It messes up the floor."

"I'm not dancing barefoot." The prima donna kept walking.

Vivian stepped in front of her. This woman was the typical snobby beautiful woman. She was tall, had gorgeous wavy brown hair and was born of mixed parentage. She'd probably danced up until high school, and Vivian was sure she'd try her on a few things.

What she didn't know was that Vivian had run into women like her all her life, and making this woman stay in her lane wasn't a problem.

"Take off your shoes or pay to have the floor resurfaced. The last time it was six thousand dollars."

"Shoes off," the woman said, peeling the stilettos from her feet. She walked on her toes to Elliott. "Where's my man, Jay?" She cut her very superior eyes at Vivian.

She thought that mattered to Vivian and didn't know how much it didn't. Doing the job and getting paid did.

"Do I look like your personal assistant?" Elliot looked bored. "Nobody is going for your crap, Naderia. Just because you talked your way into being the maid of honor doesn't mean everybody is up for your childish bull. Beth might baby you, but I don't have time for your mess."

"Don't bring it over here, either," Harv commented from the floor as he tried to touch his toes.

"Nobody asked you, Harvey," she snapped. "It's only fair for me to be the maid of honor, and since Destinee favors loyalty, and I've been her friend the longest, it's only natural that she selected me. *And,* she wants everyone in her wedding to be in relationships. So *her* best friend and *Troy's* best friend are the perfect match," she practically sang. "Whether we are or not is not her concern. Destinee is delicate because she just lost her mother, and we're not going to do anything to upset her. We'll pretend until the wedding is over, and by then, Jay will want me back anyway."

"You're stupid," Elliott said under his breath.

"Keep your opinion to yourself. Jay and I have hit a rough patch, but that's not Destinee's concern. We're all doing this for her. Because we care about *her*. Once I put little Ms. Over Here in check, my day will be perfect."

"You could be nicer. That's all I'm saying," Harv said, watching the manipulative woman.

"So could she. She *is* getting paid."

Hurrying back from the bathroom, Vivian watched Naderia interact with the men. They all seemed to dislike her. All she could say was that Jay had expensive and high-maintenance taste. Figures. Vivian walked to the corner of the room, re-arranged the perfectly arranged music and tried to quell her temper. Naderia was just one snotty woman, but she could be handled. Dancing was hard work. But there was nothing to say; they would need to deal with each other.

Besides, as a dancer, Vivian had dealt with some of the worst bun-headed bitches in the business. Naderia would be in a corner chewing Xanax and calling her therapist when Vivian got finished with her. Vivian popped her neck, releasing some tension.

The rest of the women filed in, dance shoes in their hands, Jay behind them.

"How's everybody?" he asked, his eyes bright, a smile on his face. Vivian stayed where she was and allowed the group a chance to get their greetings out of the way.

She heard the men giving him the rundown, but she was determined to have a good class.

He was heading toward her, but she was having none of

his feel-good nonsense. Naderia was his woman. She was leaving that whole mess alone.

"Everyone face the mirrors." She put on Michael Jackson's "Wanna Be Startin' Somethin'" and two of the women grimaced.

"Not that old crap," Naderia complained.

"Shoulder shrugs," Vivian called out, taking center floor and everyone fell in line, following along. "Step Ball Chain. Five, six, seven, eight," she called, and started to the right, seeing who could keep up and who needed a little more time. "Jump, one, two, three! Sway," she ordered and the group followed. "Ladies, arms out. Hip action. Guys," she said, getting them ready, "jump on. *Yee-hah!*"

The music built and they started over. Soon Vivian was making calls, and they had the dance down pat. At the end of the song, which had played through twice, she assessed the group.

Most were sitting on the floor looking like they were ready to pass out. Elliott was still on his feet along with Jay, who was doing his best to keep Naderia from undressing him.

A woman, who she believed was Harv's wife, Beth, was near Naderia shooting mean looks at Vivian.

"Good evening class, I'm Vivian, your dance instructor. I've been dancing all of my life and have danced professionally for ten years. I've danced on Broadway, and in two musical movie productions. I'm also licensed to teach dance. I've choreographed something I think is fun and will be a treat to see."

"You didn't say it was easy," Harv said. He was lying flat on his back, dripping sweat and wheezing. "You're a very talented woman. I didn't think I could sweat like this anymore. We just learned a dance. Let's do that one."

Vivian made her way through the land mine of bodies on the floor and leaned over him.

"You're right. Surprises are supposed to be a lot of fun. You can't do the Warm Up dance for a wedding. Plus, that song is twenty years old. I don't want people to think anything I do is crap. Anytime you get that feeling, I can raise my game. I just want you to be able to raise yours. Okay?"

"I didn't say that," Harv said. "I've had enough of taking on women for two lifetimes." He patted his stomach and the class laughed.

"Come on," Vivian encouraged him. "I don't want to work with cold muscles. Everyone to the barre."

She walked to her troubled child. "Naderia, there are jazz shoes on the shelf for thirty dollars. You have to have the proper attire to be on this floor, and you can't be barefoot. You can use a credit card to pay for them. But you'll need to go get them right now."

Naderia stared her down until Jay clapped his hands. "I'm paying $125 an hour twice a week for this, Naderia. You got the email just like everybody else. If you didn't buy the shoes beforehand, buy them now or go home."

Vivian kept her shock at bay. That was a harsh way to talk to his girlfriend, especially in front of everyone, but Naderia took it like a real woman. She got her purse and bought the shoes without saying a word, rejoining the class when she was finished.

The no-nonsense clip in Jay's voice had shaped everyone up. The women stopped whispering and Harv wasn't lying on the floor anymore.

Apparently when Jay meant business, people listened.

Vivian wondered how his and Naderia's relationship was at home, but she wasn't going there. What they did past dance class was none of her business. This job was. It was going to pay her rent for the next two months and give her the chance to audition for *Porgy and Bess* in New York City.

"Let's go, ladies," Vivian encouraged, raising the energy in the room.

The rest of the women, Beth, Harv's wife, and Idalia, Elliott's wife, moved to the barre. For women in their mid-thirties, they didn't move too badly. Only Beth worried Vivian. She was holding her leg.

"Your hamstring okay?"

"I didn't know I had one. We're getting familiar with one another." Chuckles echoed in the room.

"I won't work you too hard tonight."

Beth shook her head vehemently. "Don't you dare back off. This is the first exercise me and Harv have had since we got married. He's pregnant this week because he can't keep his big mouth shut about other people's sizes. So now he's learning an uncomfortable lesson by wearing a manufactured pregnancy belly."

Vivian gave a conspiratorial nod. "Okay. Let's learn what a plié is."

After fifteen minutes of ballet warm-ups, Vivian was sure she'd covered the muscle groups needed so nobody would pull or strain anything.

"This is all well and good, but what's this dance look like?" Naderia demanded, staggering to sit down although she'd been told sitting was forbidden.

"I'm glad you asked. Up! There's no sitting."

"Oh, my gawd! We ain't on Broadway!" Naderia snapped.

Jay watched Naderia and rolled his finger, signaling Vivian to go on.

"The music will be a medley of hip-hop, some old-school for the mature folks, a touch of classical and R&B. Nothing too nasty. Nothing too funky." Sensing a hesitant vibe she looked to Jay. "That's what your email said."

Four of the students looked at the others, and there were

various shrugs. "I kind of agree with Naderia's hesitation," Beth said. "Well, let's see it before we shoot it down."

Vivian took a chair into the center of the floor. "The men will start on chairs, sitting backward like this." She posed with her elbow pointed toward the floor, her chin on her fist, legs open. Then she jumped up, twirled the chair around and came out stomping. "This is the Atomic Dog dance."

Then she slid to the right and acted as if she were taking her partner's hands. She waltzed, and then executed two lifts that had the women gasping and the men smiling. She shimmied and Lambadaed, Cha-chaed and shook her bottom in a Beyoncé fashion until the dance was over.

Then she showed them again, to the music, and one last time with Jay as her partner, lifting her when she said *up*.

"The only thing I don't know is the type of dresses you'll be wearing."

The women looked surprised, then Idalia chimed in, "Naderia is the maid of honor."

"It's only right," Naderia remarked. "Jay and I are together."

"How does everyone feel about the dance?" Vivian asked, catching her breath.

This was the second time she'd choreographed for novices and she wasn't sure accepting hadn't been a mistake. There were too many personalities in this room, and if the dance didn't come out right and it got out onto the internet, that could be bad for her.

"I like it." Idalia swung her arms, repeating some of the movements. Her husband, Elliott, who sat on the chair, hopped up, doing the Stomp dance. The couple clasped at the right time and began to waltz. Their synchronicity seemed to make Naderia jealous.

"I like this part," Elliott commented, oblivious to the woman's scorn.

"I like everything but the lifts. I hate being picked up, but my dress is going to be long, so maybe I can get away with doing a small one." Beth crossed her arms, appearing angry.

"You don't have to do a high lift. You could bend your knees and rise on your toes and make it look like a lift." Vivian showed Beth what she was talking about but was stopped by Harv.

He'd been reclining on the floor and sat up. Struggling, Elliott and Jay helped him to his feet. "We're doing the lifts. I've been a pregnant man for four days because I shot my mouth off at the wrong time to the wrong person. We all get a little embarrassed, but we deal with it." He caressed his wife's back. "We'll walk later and get really serious about Weight Watchers. But as of right now, we're doing the lifts."

Beth cozied up to her man and kissed him.

Elliott, the best dancer out of all of them, and Idalia looked at one another and nodded once. "We're in for whatever. I think we should add something soft at the end, then invite the bride and groom to join us."

Vivian nodded enthusiastically. "Elliott, that's a great idea. I can do something really sweet. I've got something in mind." Vivi turned. "Jay? What do you think?"

Smoky green eyes with chocolate-colored flecks gazed back at her. His opinion counted more than anything. "Sounds fun. Let's get started. I've got other things to do tonight."

"I think Jay and I need to be out front a little more. We're the best man and maid of honor," Naderia repeated, draping her arm around Jay's waist.

Vivian flicked her fingers in the air. "I choreographed a dance that doesn't have any stars. If you want headliners, it's going to cost you."

"If you want something special, then *you* pay for it. I like the dance the way it is," Jay told her. "Besides, it's not about me and you. It's about Troy and Destinee."

"Yeah, but, this is our five minutes of fame, for all the expense and time it's taken to be in this wedding. For the women especially."

Idalia looked appalled and showed her frustration by walking away from the group. Elliott's sarcastic laugh made Naderia suck her teeth.

"You look really good from my point of view," Beth said, stroking Naderia's ego.

"I do?" Her shoulder dipped, soaking up the compliment. She eyed herself in the large mirror before them.

"Yeah, you and Jay look better than me and Harv. Let's try it again," Beth suggested.

Everyone could see the social worker was using her skills to avert a meltdown and it was working. Naderia took her position and arched her back like a swan. There was no denying her obvious beauty.

She favored a younger Vanessa Williams without the sophistication. She had the pretty skin, flowing hair, a killer smile and a smoking body. But her personality was like one of those women on the *Bad Girls* TV show, and Jay didn't appear too interested. Who could blame him?

Dance class was concluded, and they'd gone over their time, but Jay signaled Vivian that he would take care of the additional fees, and she started the music. Naderia who had been lazy during practice, suddenly had perfect lines. She and Jay looked like couple of the year.

There was a seductive quality about them that teetered on the edge of legal, but the dance moves changed so quickly they didn't allow for the law to be broken. Jay's facial expressions helped. He was a comical crowd-pleaser. He played to his audience and, when Naderia tried to take things a little too far, he knew how to back things off and not lose his balance. The other two couples joined in, and afterward Elliott and Idalia showed them an ending they'd been working on at home. It was quite a show.

Naderia shocked everyone by caressing Jay's jaw and kissing him tenderly on the lips.

Idalia softly gasped while Beth grinned. "I knew there was something there."

Jay shook his head. "There isn't."

Cooled by the gentle rejection, Naderia sucked in her lips. "Don't get it twisted. I always get my man."

Vivian backed away from the friends to give them some privacy.

"Hey, dancer."

The hair on the back of Vivian's neck stood up at the warning in Naderia's voice.

She didn't even bother to turn around. "I thought you'd had enough for the night, Naderia."

"While Jay and I are working on our relationship, you need to stay out of my way."

"What?" Vivian said, turning around with confusion across her face.

"Naderia," Jay and Elliott warned.

"You'll regret it. I promise you. I've got friends in every state in the union. All over New York."

Vivian laughed and waved her hand. How many times had she heard that? "Good night, Naderia."

The woman was ridiculous. Besides there was nothing going on between her and Jay.

Chapter 4

By the third night of practice, Jay wanted to strangle Naderia. She was making life unnecessarily difficult for everyone, even for her girl Beth who was always in her corner. All week she'd called his office, to the irritation of his admin assistant. She'd even phoned Ashton who'd put her on hold until she had dialed him back and cursed him out.

The woman was coming unhinged for no reason. Their relationship hadn't even been a relationship. Earlier, she'd been blowing up his cell phone, and when he'd finally spoken to her, she'd said she just wanted to say hi.

Driven to distraction, Jay had arrived early to practice to find Vivian alone and dancing. "At Last" by Etta James was throbbing through the speakers, filling his chest. So as to not disturb her, he watched from the doorway and witnessed magic again. She leaped and spun, sweeping the floor with her body, and swinging through the air. When he could no longer see her, he snuck through the door, onto the floor and into a corner against the wall, huddling like a recalcitrant child, too afraid to breathe. He had to watch her closer and witness the glory that was Vivian.

She was the personification of RAP. Rhythm and poetry. Rappers might disagree, but Vivian was rap in motion. The song was so simple, but it was an endearing love song. He wondered why she'd chosen today to dance to it.

As the music faded, her body slowed. Deep breaths made her chest rise and fall. Then he saw a single tear streak her cheek before she turned away from the mirror. He wasn't sure she was aware he was even in the room.

"Silly girl," she chastised herself aloud. Turning away she swiped her face and hurried to the music stand and cut the music.

Why was she crying?

His phone blared an NFL-themed ring tone, and her head jerked up. "Jay!"

Embarrassed, he answered. "What? You're going to be late, Naderia? Okay. Fine." He hung up. "Sorry about that." Jay took off his shoes and stood. "I hope I wasn't intruding. You dance beautifully. Like an angel. Why aren't you in New York?"

"I'm too old to dance professionally."

"That's crap. Not after what I just saw. Try again."

"I'm twenty-five. I could get a few parts, but do I want to hustle for the rest of my twenties or build a life doing something else? *Something else* is making me money. I refer people to Broadway and they're getting parts. I'm building a niche. But—"

Jay took in the stray hairs that had escaped from her bun. Those were the ones he concentrated on. "But what?"

"I got an email that there's a part in *Porgy and Bess*. I can try out for it."

"Can you sing?"

She nodded.

"Then money *isn't* what you need. You didn't come all this way to be a facilitator for others. You didn't go to all those classes all those years, endure all that pain and deal with all the rejection just to make other people's dreams come true."

"What do you know about me?"

"You're a competitor," Jay told her, stepping closer. "You want to win. You want to hear the crowd cheer for you."

"I don't need that type of adulation. I know who I am."

"Do you?"

Vivian smiled up at him and picked up a nearby chair. "Yes, I do." She walked past him. "Come on. We still have forty minutes. Let's rehearse your part."

Jay had been all set to challenge why she wasn't trying to be more than she was, but now he was getting a private lesson? He'd take her up on that offer any day of the week!

"Okay." He ripped off his workout jacket and changed into his dance shoes. He met Vivian in the center of the floor.

"Put your hands on your thighs and bounce."

Jay did as instructed. "How's that gonna look in a tuxedo jacket?"

Vivian stood up straight and finished the movement in front of the mirror and then did the arms. He watched her from behind and admired the view. Her body was firm from so much training, but she was supple the way a woman was supposed to be.

"Jay? Jay!"

"Yes?"

"Eyes up here," she said, gesturing toward her face. She was smiling at him. "Come on. Stay with me. Can you guys take off your jackets before you hit the dance floor?"

"Can you add in Mary J. Blige's 'Family Affair' to the mix tape? Give a little intro?"

Vivian nodded and added a sideways Step Ball Chain shoulder shrug that Harv liked and would get them onto the floor fast and into the chairs.

"I like that."

Jay tried it again, adding his own swagger.

"That's it, Jay," Vivian encouraged. "Now sit. Count, one, two, three and up, and go right into the Atomic Dog stomp.

That's a shout-out to the groom who's a Que. Then the music changes fast into the waltz."

Jay grasped Vivian's palms and froze. "Hold it," he said.

"What?"

She was gazing up at him.

"I feel like I'm about to crush your toes."

Her smile was quick and reassuring. "We're going to practice this tonight. You're the leader, so I'm trusting you to lead me. Put your right hand on my back. Your left goes with my right. Then you step forward on your right foot and I'll step back."

He looked down at her.

"Look forward, Jay."

"I like looking at you."

Her eyelashes fluttered. "But that isn't proper. You have to return to the promenade position." She adjusted his chin then put her hand back in his.

"But there's nothing pretty over there. It's just a wall."

A giggle that never made it out of her body trickled up her back. That was the advantage of touching Vivian. He could *feel* her emotions.

"I think you'll live. Now back, and side, up and stop." She gave instructions and Jay followed. He soon realized the shift in power of the waltz.

Really, the man was leading, and the woman was following. When they stopped, her body was a little behind his as if he was protecting her. He suddenly liked it very much.

"Let's try it again," he said. Looking at his feet, he noticed their position and straightened his legs. Vivian adjusted his face.

"Remember to look that way. Promenade."

"Just say *ugly* and I'll remember."

This time she chuckled. "Five, six, seven, eight. Right, front, left. Very good. Ow!"

Jay knew when he stepped forward he was wrong, but his

body was in motion. He couldn't jerk back fast enough. Their knees knocked together and Vivian cringed.

She grabbed her knee, but reached for his, too. "You okay?"

His hand was still around her waist but he removed it because he knew once she realized, she would probably have a problem with it. "Yeah." Kicking his leg out, his knee creaked and popped. "It's all better. Maybe we should move on. You good?"

"I've had two-hundred-pound men fall on me. I'm fine. Come on. I think it'll be fun to have the women spin you guys."

Jay laughed and gazed at her skeptically. "Funny, yeah. But realistic?"

Vivian turned to the mirror and tested her knee by executing a few turns. "It's good. Watch this. Once you guys come off the chairs, the women can brush off their shoulders. Then the waltz, then the hip-hop moves, spin, spin, Dougie, lift one, then the Charleston. Lift two. The crowd will love this. Then we slow it down a bit. Bend here, tick your arms. Tick-tick-tick-tick-tick. Good. We shimmy here. Do a slow Snake, then really slow it way down and do an exaggerated Grind. The men spin the women, and we come back together here. 'At Last' will be playing at this time."

Jay tried to keep up. He wasn't a dancer by nature. He was the side-to-side brother.

"That Dougie and spin into the Charleston almost killed me. We need a break in there. Can we shimmy in between?"

Vivian closed her eyes and moved her hips, replaying the dance in her head. She re-choreographed the steps and added the part he'd just requested. "That works." She waved him up. "Come on. We have ten minutes to try this before everyone gets here. Let's give it a go." Using the remote, she started the music and guided Jay to the chair.

Once he sat, she bumped up his chin. "When you lift me, put your hands here." Her hands circled her slender waist, but his huge paws didn't ever stay put.

Jay could see what was going to happen. She was built like the beautiful, slender actress, Zoe Saldana. If he missed Vivian's rib cage, he'd have a palm full of boob.

"Uh, okay." He tried the lift.

"Too tight." She slid down his body. "Again."

They waltzed and then went into the lift. He caught her ribs on one side and her full breast on the other. Then he lowered her and her feet smacked the floor.

She patted his shoulder. "That was better. Try it again."

"No." Jay shook his head to release the tension and frustration.

"What's the matter?" Vivian walked over to Jay who'd drifted away. She stood in front of him. He backed up and she slowly approached.

"I'm not getting it right, and I keep—"

"What?"

He backed up and she followed. Jay stopped.

"You scared of some breasts?" she argued.

Her directness confronted his embarrassment. If they hadn't been in the dance studio, if they'd been at home, if the situation had been totally different, he'd have made a meal of her breasts. "No, breasts don't scare me. It's the woman the breasts are attached to.... I want her respect. So I don't want to do anything that she might think is inappropriate, no matter where my thoughts and my hands might take me."

She picked up his hands and cupped her waist. "You have to hold me here to do the move right." She moved his hands to her neck, standing really close to him. "And here, when we dance to Tyrese. Hug me," she told him.

Jay watched her. "Okay," he said, going along with the demonstration.

In very slow motion, her body molded to his. Her face was in his neck, her lips touching his collarbone. Her breasts were crushed against his chest, and their sex met through their clothes. "When we Grind dance, we'll be this close. You can't be afraid to touch me."

Vivian slowly released him.

"Lady, you're crazy if you think you can do that to me and not expect me to want to end the night with you."

There. He'd told her what he'd wanted to say since he'd met her. He was attracted to her like crazy.

She seemed suddenly self-conscious. "A long time ago I decided I wanted a man in my life, not just in my bed. I'm still waiting for the right man."

He'd heard that before from so many women, but many didn't really know what they wanted. "How's that working for you?"

"I'm happy. Nobody is running through my life and taking the best of me. I'm not ashamed of myself at the end of the day. Come on. You're not paying for therapy sessions. Lift me, quarter turn, put me down."

Blown away by the revelation, Jay did as instructed.

Vivian kept both hands on his shoulders. "That was good. Not as much pressure on your thumbs. I feel like you're going to break my ribs."

Jay lifted her again, and again, and again. They finally got it right on the fourth try.

They high-fived and were moving back into first position when Naderia walked in.

"What's going on here? I didn't know we were having private lessons." Naderia tracked in rainwater with her four-inch boots. Her tart tone broke the mood, forcing them to make room for her disrespectfulness.

She'd been off the chain all day, and tonight her mood didn't seem to have improved. Jay wondered what he'd ever seen in Naderia. She was plain evil. Though they'd broken off their two-week affair two months ago, she'd been wanting to get back together ever since. And now they were keeping up appearances for the wedding. What a crock of crap.

He could do high maintenance. But high maintenance *and* crazy? No way.

Thunder shook the building and Jay noticed for the first time that it was raining hard.

"We just got in a little practice, Naderia. I thought you were going to be late." Vivian's hands rested comfortably on her hips.

"Sorry to disappoint you."

"I'm not."

Naderia's slit eyes and the suspicion in her pouty lips were headed right for Jay. She walked up and planted a kiss on the corner of his mouth, missing his lips. He shook her off, giving her a disgusted look.

"You need to quit playing before you get your feelings hurt."

She had wrapped her arms around his waist and was looking possessively at Vivian, who wasn't giving her the time of day. "Jay, you know you want me."

"Stop," he said calmly but sternly.

"Naderia, that's a two-hundred-dollar fine for walking on the floor." Vivian pointed to the Rules posted midway atop each wall of mirrors, as she moved the chair from the center of the floor back to the corner. She threw a towel onto the floor for the water.

"Like hell. I'm not paying!" Her curls bounced in defiance.

Vivian walked over to the stereo system and cut off the music.

Jay took Naderia by the wrist and pulled her off the floor. "You're paying. Where's your credit card?"

"Why!"

"You know why," Jay started, when Vivian walked up, her dance bag on her shoulder, her street shoes in her hand.

"Jay, I said I would do this as a favor, but I refuse to work with immature people. I have to pay if the place is destroyed. Everything is on camera. The owner fines me every time someone walks on the floor. Either she pays, or the deal is off."

Chapter 5

Vivian rarely got angry, but Naderia was a woman who took her to that level.

It was obvious Naderia was spoiled, and she was accustomed to getting her way, but not when it came to destroying other people's property.

Fuming, Vivian walked down the strip mall to the Mexican restaurant and stepped inside, wondering if she'd done the right thing.

She'd never walked out of her own studio before.

Flicking open the menu, she quickly ordered. "Chicken burrito, extra peppers, hold the tortilla. Top-shelf margarita."

"You don't want to hold the liquor, too?" Lupe asked, being facetious.

"You want a tip?" Vivian countered.

The waitress walked off, and didn't bother to bring back any chips. Instead, she brought celery sticks and salsa along with Vivian's drink.

Vivian passed the time sipping from the wide-rimmed glass and eating her sizzling vegetables and chicken.

This was the first time she'd eaten out in a while, and she wasn't even enjoying herself. The disagreement kept playing in her mind. How could she have done things differently? Sure, Naderia had been a pain, but Vivian wondered if she should have idly stood by and let her walk all over the floor and kept quiet?

She never got mad. She was a black dancer in a predominantly white business. She'd faced her share of disappointment. So why today was she so short-tempered? Was it just Naderia?

Or was it the idea of Jay and Naderia?

A tiny shot of pain stabbed through her head as the tequila helped her relax.

Despite Jay's denials, was there something going on between him and Naderia?

He acted as if there wasn't, but he was good at keeping his emotions under wraps. Naderia made it no secret that they'd been involved, and she intended for them to be a couple again.

Vivian knew she had to go back, if only to lock up for the night, and she would never walk out of her studio again. If anything, she'd put everyone else out. Starting with all high-heeled, loudmouthed troublemakers.

The door to the restaurant opened and closed, and raindrops sprinkled the bar next to her.

Jay's cologne was distinctive. "You never leave your house. Kick assholes out, but you never leave."

She chuckled. "I was just reflecting on that. Margarita?" she offered.

"Is it good?" He took hers and sipped.

She gazed up at him. "I just offered to buy you one."

"I didn't want my own."

"Are you flirting with me, Jay?"

"The dancer finally catches on."

He sat on the stool beside her and swung her way, his arm on the bar.

"What's your girlfriend up to?"

"She's not my girlfriend. We dated a couple months ago, but Naderia only hears and does what she wants to hear and do. I'm not into being hateful to women, but she's been warned to stop the lies and the nonsense."

"But?"

"But she believes if she denies we're not together, it won't be true. She's using this thing about Destinee's mom as leverage, and I suppose the rest of us are letting her."

Vivian nodded. "You must have been really good to her."

"Yeah, whatever." He sidestepped her obvious leap into his business. "She paid for the floor and left. She might be leaving the wedding party altogether. I don't care if she stays or goes. I'm tired of trying to keep up appearances just for Destinee."

Vivian nodded again. "The thing is, Jay, I'm not the high-maintenance type. I don't make scenes, I don't show off, and I don't demand attention."

Jay laughed, stroking where her arm met her shoulder. "Yes, you do."

Vehemently, Vivian shook her head. "No, I don't." She then shook off the thrill of his touch. He'd excited her earlier, and that's what had angered her about Naderia. She'd ruined their good time. The anger was returning. "I'm nothing like that spoiled woman. Stomping all over my floor. Who does she think she is?"

Jay grinned at her and pulled some cash out of his pocket. He left three twenties on the bar. "Come on, Ms. Don't Make Scenes."

"Where?" Vivian stood, and the room revolved a quarter turn. Jay caught her as she swooned. "Oh, my."

"Come on, I've got you."

They left the restaurant, and Vivian didn't mind Jay's arm around her waist. He helped her into his car and they took off. Pressed back into the seat by the speed of his ride, Vivian closed her eyes enjoying the motion. Her little Cutlass registered every bump and dip in the road. This car practically floated.

Signs from businesses seemed to float by. "I need to lock up the studio."

"Mr. Sullivan stopped by, and he locked the doors. I gave him an autograph and he was fine. I told him you were sick and had to leave in a hurry."

Vivian turned in the fast-moving Audi. The liquor was playing with her head, but not so much that she wasn't grateful. "Thank you. He could have canceled my contract."

"You can repay me by continuing to teach me how to dance." He stopped the car and parked. Hopping out, he ran around and opened her door.

"Where are we?"

"A place a friend of mine owns. Come on."

The bass beat coming from the Club Carlyle could be felt inside the car. "Jay, I'm not dressed to go to a club."

"You look fine. The people here are real down-to-earth. Come on. We're just going to dance."

"But I have on a leotard and tights, with a ballet skirt barely covering my butt."

He took her hand and guided her out of the car. "I promise. You'll be the best-dressed woman in there."

Vivian got out of the car, grabbing only her shrug sweater and lip gloss; the rain had since slowed to a mist. Her bag was too big and bulky to bring inside. She had changed into high-heeled boots upon leaving the studio but she felt that she looked like a hooker rather than a professional dancer. She ran the roller of gloss over her lips, and then Jay took the tube and put it in his pocket.

"Are you sure I'm going to be okay in there?"

By then they were at the door and Jay was fist-bumping some guy who let them inside. They walked up a long hall-way and into the club. It was deceptively large and nicely built with shiny wood floors and a marble bar that stretched to all four corners. Men and women filled the space, linger-ing here and there, while some danced.

Jay walked her straight to the dance floor, taking her by the waist.

Despite her reservations about not being dressed appropri-ately, and being a little tipsy, the music felt good and Vivian couldn't help but enjoy moving with Jay. He had become a smooth dancer in just a short amount of time. His steps were sure, and he smiled a lot as he danced. He wasn't afraid to spin and just do his thing. Without knowing it, he was doing Cha-cha moves and Lambada steps, but it was his Dougie that got her going.

Jay was masculine and sexy, and so fine that when she reached up and touched his face, it felt natural.

He kissed her palm, and they moved into a slow boxed step she hadn't taught him.

"You've got skills you didn't let me know you had."

"A man has to have some secrets."

"Yeah, we do, bruh. Your wife is gorgeous." The man dancing next to them wore a fashionable straw hat, with a black band, and his lady, a red suede skirt.

"She's—"

"Thank you," Vivian interrupted. "He doesn't care about us," she said beneath her breath.

The man continued on his way; he and his lady sliding into a Chicago Step dance move as R. Kelly belted out his tune.

The dance floor had gotten crowded with couples squeezed in real close. Vivian moved in close to Jay as the DJ slowed down the music. They didn't do the typical two-step Grind, instead, a more sensual dance done close and in sync. People watched them with approving looks on their faces.

Jay brought her to him, his hands sliding over her butt and staying there. Vivian started to back away, but he held her firm.

"Jay, people are watching."

"You're a dancer. You're meant to be watched."

He leaned his head down to kiss her then. Firm but gentle lips met hers, the pressure just right. Her arms glided around his neck, her body against his, and her heartbeat thundered, deep and throbbing, that made her want more.

She had to end this showcase of intimacy. Jay was well-known on TV, and she was not going to be remembered for being the woman he made out with on the dance floor.

Slowly, Vivian pulled away.

"Dance for me," he asked.

She wrinkled her nose. "Not here."

"You only dance when strangers are paying you?"

Jay was still holding her waist, and she could tell he was joking. Still his words stung a bit. "I should slap you."

His fingers strummed her waist. "I'd get you back some-how."

"I can't be baited, Jay. I'm a professional."

"I didn't get my full lesson tonight, and I still have to pay for it. It's in the contract."

"I won't dance alone."

"Bust Your Windows" began to play by Jazmine Sullivan, and the floor cleared a bit. Apparently men weren't exactly fond of the song.

Vivian did a series of pirouette turns, stopped and swept across the small space back to Jay. She used the words in the music to motivate her movements, playing with them and him, sliding up and down his body until he threw his head back and laughed. She was behind him, goading him, the lyrics of the song echoing through the room. The other patrons were into their little display, as Jay pretended to explain and Vivian wasn't having it.

She pretended to bust the windows, executing turns and leaps, landing with powerful blows on his imaginary car. Getting right up on Jay, she showed him why she should be in the Alvin Ailey American Dance Theater, with one of her high leaps. In the end, she unthreaded his necktie and took it with her, tossing it at his feet before leaving the floor.

The audience went wild.

Watching her, Jay stuck his hands in his pockets, put his head down and walked off to thunderous applause.

Chapter 6

The next practice started as if nothing had happened the prior week. Only Naderia never showed. Vivian pushed them hard and by the end of the night everyone was limp and weary.

Elliott shouldered both his and Idalia's bags, holding his wife's hand as they walked out. "I'm giving you a massage when we get home."

"I'm not going to complain, but you have to take off those leg warmers first."

He kissed her softly and held the door for her to walk out ahead of him.

Vivian watched and Jay started for her, but Harv got to her first.

"They're adorable." Vivian toweled her neck as Beth and Harv crowded around her.

"They're the reason the best man and the *real* maid of honor aren't walking up the aisle together. Elliott wasn't having it. Idalia is the real best friend of the bride."

Vivian looked on with interest. "You're kidding."

Harv shook his head. "No. Elliott said that's his wife, and if she's walking up the aisle with anyone, it's with him. So now we have Cruella de Ville with Jay."

"That's quite a story," Vivian said, unable to tear her gaze away from Jay. Watching him through the mirrors, he was trying the tick-tick movements, but was getting them all wrong.

"He really sucks today," Harv said, and got poked in the stomach by his wife.

"You just stopped being pregnant. Do you wanna try it again? And stop talking about Naderia. She needs a friend right now."

Vivian moved out of earshot of the bickering couple and onto the dance floor. "Bend your knee, crook your arm," she told Jay. "And move your body up, arm up, over, over, over."

She walked nearer to him, taking his arm and moving it into position. Their gazes met and held. "Come on," she encouraged in a quiet voice.

"My arm isn't remembering anything. It hurts."

"Soak in the tub of Epsom salts tonight. It was remembering fine last week. Five, six, seven, eight."

Jay watched himself in the mirror, his arms doing strange things. Vivian could see his problem. Harv and his wife, Beth, had let their bags fall off their shoulders and were watching them. Harv moved his arms, but made no move to join them on the floor.

"Jay, don't watch yourself. Watch me and do what I do," Vivian told him. "Join us," she encouraged the other two members, but they declined.

She moved into the dance and soon had Jay dancing without stopping. He lifted her and set her down, moving in and out of step with an easy flow. He wasn't quite ready to close his eyes, but he was getting there.

The fourth time, he took her into his arms, and when it

was time to let her go, he didn't. "You think I don't know what you did?" he asked, looking tired.

"What did I do?"

"You got me to stop watching myself," he answered, waving to Harv and his wife who signaled they were heading home.

Vivian waved to the exiting couple, and then turned her attention back to her dance partner.

"You're so full of yourself, you're dazzled by your own beauty. You couldn't keep your eyes off yourself." She couldn't finish the insult with a straight face. She relaxed in his arms. It was late, well past 9:30 p.m., and they were finally alone.

"I'll get you back for that comment."

Vivian thought of pulling away, but Jay probably wouldn't let her, so she didn't try. "I don't have time to play with you. I have to practice. Go home."

"Only if you come with me."

The invitation shook her up a bit. She'd thought of him all weekend. He'd told her he played basketball on the weekends. All she could think about was him in basketball shorts, on a court playing in a shirts-and-skins game. He'd be on the skins team. The idea of him with a bare chest took her breath away.

Vivian shook her head and the music stopped. "No, I'm not coming with you."

"I'll take you to dinner. You have to eat."

"I eat. I have food in my bag. Now you have to go. I'm serious. I have to practice."

"The dance you were doing the other day?"

"Nobody is supposed to have seen that. It's not ready."

Jay followed her to the music stand and started stretching his warm muscles to cool them down. "Why not? It was beautiful."

"That's the problem. It's not supposed to be. It's supposed to haunt you."

He nodded. "Well, the problem is the music. You have to choose something darker. Something heavier. 'At Last' is a love song. When you analyze the lyrics, she's talking about how she's finally found the love she's been looking for. She's been waiting for him and it's like heaven now that he's finally hers."

She gazed at him from beneath her lashes, unwilling to admit he'd just impressed the hell out of her. "I understand, but I have to use that song. They chose it. I just have to change the choreography, but I have to do that without you here. You distract..."

"I distract you?"

Her nod was brief but sure. She hated admitting anything to his probing green eyes. They missed nothing. He knew she was attracted to him. "I promise not to bother you."

"No."

She pushed him, but he caught her hands and when he did, he brought her arms around his waist. "Why not?"

"Sometimes I cry. Sometimes, I stop and sit down and think, or I roll on the floor. Dancing is not all leaping in the air and spinning around. It's a process like anything."

"Okay. I'm going then."

She pulled her arms away from his waist, squeezed his hand and let go. "Thank you, Jay."

He put on his jacket and grabbed his bag. "See you Wednesday."

"Okay. Good night."

Vivian turned on the video cameras and blasted the music, closing her eyes, reflecting on the heaviest tones of Etta's voice. Vivian leaped into Etta's breaths, and swung her body on the grooves of the sultry alto. This woman hadn't had a man in a while, though she'd yearned for one.

Yearned. The dance began there. From that wanting place. That secret little quiet spot of desire everyone had experienced at one time or another.

From there she found the soul of the dance, the true meaning of "At Last." It wasn't fast or rushed. It was poignant, tender. The singer meant love was finally there. She soared on "I" and landed, the smile vibrating up her body when the move was inside and outside of her. The dance took over until she was too weary to go on. She collapsed on the floor and grew cold.

Elongating her body, she stretched each muscle until it was properly cooled and only then did she turn down the music and turn up the studio lights.

Turning toward the door, she saw the flashing lights of a police squad car in the parking lot. As she looked closer, she saw a familiar face and hurried outside.

Chapter 7

"Somebody stole your tires? Why didn't you come back into the studio?"

Jay eyed the woman he'd just watched perform the most amazing dance he'd ever seen in his life and finally found his voice.

"I called the police instead. They just got here. I thought I should stay with the car in case they came back."

"So they could attack you?" the officer and Vivian said as the same time.

"Are you crazy?" Vivian demanded.

Vivian paced the parking lot behind his car. The flatbed wrecker truck pulled into the lot, making a lot of noise for 11:00 p.m. The driver had Jay sign some paperwork before hooking up his car and towing it away.

The officer handed him a slip of paper. "You can call this number in twenty-four hours and get your police report.

Your insurance company will probably need that information. Sorry it took so long, but we had higher priority calls to take."

Jay accepted the slip and shook his head in disgust. "Appreciate it. I'll be sure to mention you on my show."

"Don't bother," the female officer said, walking back to her squad car. She drove away, looking sad.

"I wasn't planning to dog her out."

"It's not her fault your car was vandalized, Jay. But are you hungry?" Vivian asked. "My treat."

Jay shook his head and looked at the ground. "No, I've got to get home. I'm worried about Gretchen."

"Gretchen? Is that your girlfriend? Do you need to use my phone?" she offered, disappointment filling her.

"No, Gretchen is my car. What if she falls off that wrecker? What if he steals her? We should follow him. He was driving very fast."

Vivian started laughing and didn't stop until she was doubled over.

Jay could feel stupid crawling all over himself. "What's so funny?"

"You bring your fancy car into this neighborhood and don't expect anybody to want it? Sorry, you got jacked, Mr. Big Shot. And now you're going to hang around more of the area to get double jacked? Come, let me drop you off at home. I don't want anybody to take your Rolex watch and your Prada shoes."

"You know what? You seemed really sweet when I met you, but you're mean."

Under the streetlight in the parking lot Vivian seemed to consider his words, then reject them. "I wasn't sweet, and I'm not being mean. You're being unreasonable. You could have gotten killed all because you worship a foreign car. *Gretchen?* Are you kidding?" She pointed at her Cutlass. "This car here, it's like grits. American bred and born. It's a Chrysler. Her name is Chrysler. Nobody wants her. Now get your butt in the car and let's go before you get us both killed for being out here too long."

Jay got in, pushed the seat all the way back and reclined it a bit to accommodate his size. Vivian watched him, blinking, not saying a word. She started the car. "Where to?"

He gave her directions that took her out of the city and into the suburbs.

The drive took them an hour, and when they reached the house, the gate was open. "Pull inside."

"No, I have to drive back to the city."

He nudged her thigh, and she did as he asked.

Jay leaned over and cut off the car, taking the keys. "Come in."

He got out, stretching, and then walked around the back of the car and opened her door.

She walked with him through the carport of the all-brick house. He input a code and the door unlocked. Taking her hand, he started up the stairs. "Jay, I can't stay with you."

"I know," he said.

They entered a beautiful kitchen where the wood gleamed against the glowing vanilla-scented candlelight from two jars that sat on opposite ends of a long breakfast bar. "Hungry?" he asked, hanging her keys on the key rack by the door.

"No."

"Thirsty?"

She shook her head, watching as he dug through the refrigerator and unscrewed the cap off an ice-cold bottle of water. He nearly drained it.

Then he crossed the room and put the bottle to her lips. He tipped the bottle and she swallowed.

"You must be thirsty after the way you danced tonight. You need to eat to keep up your strength. You need to be pampered, for you have such a rare talent."

Her gaze ricocheted to his, but he didn't give her time to react because his mouth engulfed hers in a kiss so consuming, all of her defenses, all of her objections, instantly fell away.

Her tongue lashed his bottom lip and the nerve endings sprang to life, sending a dazzle of pleasure up the back of his legs straight to his groin. She would be his, but not in the kitchen. Vivian moved beneath him.

He backed off her a bit and released her hair from the tight bun, watching it uncurl in his hand. "Your hair is sexy."

"Thank you." She giggled.

He took her hand and walked her to a door. Opening it, he guided her inside. "When my sister is home from college, she sleeps in here. Will you stay here tonight? Have breakfast with me in the morning. I won't bother you. I promise."

"You're used to getting your way, aren't you?"

Jay shook his head no. "I try to be persuasive, but I never force anyone to do anything they don't want to."

"Where am I? What address?" she whispered.

She pulled out her phone, typed it in and hit Send. Seconds later she received a return text message. Holding up her phone, she took his picture and sent it, too.

"Have I passed your background check?" Jay chuckled.

Vivian nodded. "I'll stay and have breakfast with you."

Pleased, Jay pulled Vivian into a hug that he wanted to last until the next morning, but he knew it had to end. "Good night."

He walked to the door and prepared to shut it.

"Hey," she said, setting down her bag on the straight-back lavender-colored chair. "Where's your room?"

His heart skipped a beat. "Four doors down the hall on the right. Visit anytime you want."

He could see when her breathing changed. Her leotard did little to hide the quickness of her chest rising and falling. "Good night, Jay."

"Good night, Vivi."

Chapter 8

Jay struggled to sleep, knowing she was down the hall. Knowing she'd been in the shower his sister had used only twice since he'd bought the house six years ago. He'd been lonely out here. Rarely even came out here, staying in his apartment in Atlanta most of the time. But tonight he wanted Vivian in his home, and when he'd left the dance studio and found his car without tires, he'd gone back in to tell her about her studio's horrible location, that's when he'd been sent to his knees.

He could only watch her from the door as she flipped end over end, her arms straight, fists balled and her face sublime. She was the story of the music. She'd jumped higher than anyone he'd known, created moves he had never seen before, and while he was no dance connoisseur, he could see greatness in the making. How he'd gotten her to agree to teach them was still a mystery to him.

Driven from his bed, he headed for the refrigerator and a

glass of water, and then he headed to the nearby den where he cut on the sixty-inch television. Sprawling in his comfortable spot, he settled in watching the sports channel, when he felt a presence.

Turning, he saw Vivian with the duvet around her shoulders. She'd chosen a spaghetti strap gown to sleep in, but it did little to hide her body. She'd obviously washed her hair, because it was no longer straight but a mass of beautiful natural curls.

"Hey, the TV too loud?"

"No," she said, coming around the couch. "My feet are cold."

He smiled, looking up at her. "Just your feet?"

"No," she whispered.

"Come here."

She sat in the corner with him, her legs across his. He covered her with the duvet, took her foot and dragged his hand over the curve of her extended arch, eliciting a sigh as she sank into the couch cushions. Her tiny gown eased up, exposing more of her thighs, and he had to work to keep his body under control. It was a losing battle.

He pressed heat into her limbs with his warm hand, and then he took her other foot and kissed it. Involuntarily, her foot jumped, but she didn't stop him as he braced her foot against his chest and worked more warmth into her body.

Rubbing his thumbs up her ankle, she pointed her toes—he wasn't sure if out of reflex so they'd slide against his arm— but he gently manipulated her calves, seeing the promised land, wanting her in that way, and hoping she wanted him, too.

He slid his hands up her slender hips and brought her into his lap. This time when their sex met, neither of them did anything. There were no dance moves imaginable to cause a great escape.

"I want you," he told her.

"I want a man who's going to care about me after tonight."

"Who did you text earlier?"

"My mom."

Vivian reached up and drove her hands through her hair.

"Don't try and tantalize me with those things." Her breasts were in his face and it was all he could do to stop himself from taking a bite from the chocolate-colored tips.

"They're breasts. Only for my man."

Jay had had enough. He would have given her the moon. He put his finger on the front of the gown and pulled. The gown slipped down and her left nipple slid into his mouth. He scooped her up and carried her to his bedroom.

Pulling the gown from her body, he stripped her bare. She was the most perfect woman he'd ever been with. She reached for him, but he laid her down and remained standing as he looked at her. She had muscles and curves, and there was no hair anywhere except her head.

Very little intimidated him, but Jay found himself wondering how to please her.

"I haven't had sex in…three years," she admitted shyly.

The words unlocked all his misconceptions about perfection. Their bodies may have looked like Adonis and Aphrodite, but he was going to give her the best night of pleasure she'd ever had.

"Do you like sex?" he asked, lying on top of her. He clasped her hands above her head.

"Of course."

"What kind of sex?"

"Is this a survey?" she asked him as she smiled.

"I don't want to offend you by doing something crazy."

She stared up at him. "The only thing that would be crazy is if you walked in here with some farm animals. Then, I would leave."

"That would be crazy. I'm not that out there."

He kissed her brows, her cheeks, her lips.

"Jay, let's just make love."

"I want to—"

"Let's do it," she whispered, her fingers releasing his. "Do everything."

Jay set Vivian in the center of the bed, the soft cotton sheets pooling around her. She didn't know what he was going to do next, but he had seductively swept her hair aside and glided his fingers down her neck and then his tongue. She was accustomed to the softer touch of the men in the dance world, so it felt good to have Jay's hands on her in a strong sexual way. He knew what he wanted when he laid her on her stomach and laved his tongue down her spine.

She'd never been bitten, but nothing was off-limits tonight. He bit her lightly on the shoulder, making her rise to meet his eager mouth.

She loved his aggression and wanted more of it. He first gave her back and shoulders a lot of attention and then made his way to her little peach of a bottom. Her gluteus was her Achilles' heel in the dance business, but she couldn't fight Mother Nature on this one. It stuck out a bit, but so what.

Jay didn't care. He was in it face-first, tongue deep, seeking the mothership connection. When he found it, he flipped her over and she cried out from the pleasure. No man had ever sought the answers to the mysteries of the universe like Jay.

Her first climax spiraled from the back of her knees and made her abdomen clinch, pulling her body off the bed.

Falling backward against the mattress, Vivian reached for him, wanting to please him, too, but he refused. "It's all about you."

He used his fingers skillfully and massaged her clit, sending sparkles of residual climax throughout her body. She thrashed against the bed. With the other hand, he opened the nightstand drawer and removed a condom. Taking a second to sheath himself, he pulled her up so that he was sitting on the side of the bed and she was sitting on him.

"Come here," he said, holding her against him. "How's that feel?"

She panted. "How do you feel?" she whispered but her words were barely audible.

"I feel great."

He stood up, impaling her, holding her.

"Why can't we do it the regular way?" she asked him.

"Because it's boring."

"With a ballerina?"

A smile split his face. "I totally forgot about that."

Gently he laid her down and then she put one leg on his shoulder causing him to slip deeper into her. "Damn, that feels good."

Vivian grinned.

He started moving inside her, varying how he was giving it to her. Her ability to grip him seemed to keep him barely on the edge of sanity.

She felt sexy and vulnerable and pretty, and she didn't want to feel any of those things. She wanted him to ravage her. Snaking her fingers up to his nipples, she tweaked them and was surprised they responded by jutting out. Rising just a bit, she grazed her teeth over his nipple and dragged her nails over the other one. His dick jumped inside her. He pushed into her harder. "Yes."

Their gazes met, and he knew just how she liked it. A ghost of a smile crossed his lips. "You little freak."

"Takes one to know one." She giggled.

The deeper he pushed, the closer she thought he was getting to her heart, but that was impossible. He turned her onto her back, burying his face deep in her valley, causing pleasure she'd never experienced in her life to take over her body.

Vivian soaked it up as she watched him please her, and when he entered her again, she couldn't believe he could have anything left. This was what she'd been wanting and waiting for. He was drenched with sweat, but all she could think of was pleasing him. He kissed with his eyes open, studying her while she was on top. He filled her to a capacity she didn't know she had.

They got real close.

"You don't like this position," he told her.

"But you do. You're visual. I want you to come the way you like to. I want to please you."

"Where have you been all my life?" he groaned, taking her waist in his hands and biting her neck.

Her body gripped him and she growled. "Oh, Jay. Do that again."

He bit her again and she squeezed with her inner muscles, gripping his nipples and biting his shoulder.

Suddenly, he started pumping into her with a force so fast all she could do was hold him around the neck.

When he exploded, his cry, she was sure, bounced off every wall in the house. They stayed locked together for several long minutes, rocking, until he loosened his grip on her. "How are you, darlin'?"

"Raw," she said honestly.

"Right," he said slowly as reality sank into him. Gently, he slid out of her and laid her on the bed. "I'll be right back."

He went to the bathroom, and she could hear water running. Vivian sat up. She could take care of herself, but before she could get off the bed, he was back with a warm and a cool cloth.

"Lie down."

An embarrassed smile overtook her. "Jay, I can do that."

"I don't mind."

Tentatively, she lay back and with great care he washed all

her folds and made sure she was clean. Vivian couldn't believe this big man. When he was finished, he kissed her clit.

She wanted to jump on his back and kiss him, but was scared to move. He went halfway to the bathroom and threw the washcloths in.

Hurrying back to bed, he hopped in and snatched the covers from the bottom of the bed. Pulling them over her, he curled up behind her and began kissing her shoulder.

Vivian couldn't help but turn around in his arms and kiss his mouth. He licked her nose, making her laugh.

"You're full of surprises."

"Oh, that's just the top of my bag of tricks. Get some rest. We've got time."

Their gazes met and held. "Do we?" Vivian wanted his words to be true. Besides fantastic lovemaking, he was a good man.

"If you want. Yes, we do."

Vivian closed her eyes and snuggled deeper into his chest. "I do want to."

The last thing she remembered were his lips on hers.

Chapter 9

Vivian hurried from the bathroom and tiptoed back into bed. Jay was still sound asleep, but she didn't care. She'd needed to go to the little girl's room and brush her teeth. Unsure of the time, she crawled back in and lay down, only to be attacked.

They wrestled for a while, until she finally gave in and sat on top of him. He kissed her long and hard, coming up for air after a sizzling good-morning kiss.

"You taste like toothpaste."

She giggled. "You're a great detective."

His fingers roamed her body, stopping to squeeze her bottom. "I love your ass. From the first day I met you, I wanted to touch it, but I knew you would have killed me."

"I'm gonna kill you now."

She pummeled him with fake punches until she was against the mattress with her hands pinned above her head.

"Jay," she said, out of breath. "What are you doing?"

While he had her immobile, he was using his strong legs to open hers.

"Wouldn't you like to know, Ms. Franklin."

"Jay Smith, are you about to—"

He penetrated her with his middle finger, invading her in a way that all of their playfulness gave way to desire. She tried to get up, but he held her there pleasing her, while this gorgeous little smile adorned his face. How could he want so much pleasure for her? Then she realized he was getting as much as he was giving.

When his second finger entered her, she cried out his name, and he bit her nipple, thrusting her into a spherical climax she'd never before experienced. She wanted him to have all the pleasure he'd given her, but she was so inexperienced. One previous lover didn't make her an expert. It made her a step above naive.

She reached for him and took him into her mouth, gagging.

Backing off, she looked at his size, and wondered how to approach him.

Sucking him in, he reached the back of her throat and she gagged again, but she didn't stop. She eased off and kept sucking and licking, bobbing up and down, until he was backing up on the bed, a growl coming from his throat.

Vivian kept pursuing him, grabbing his hand and holding him as he pulled at her, tearing her away and plunging into her. He took her with an animalistic fervor that wasn't like anything she'd ever experienced, and when she felt that familiar fever rising in her body, she rolled her eyes and arched into the most beautiful climax of her twenty-five years.

This time he escorted her into his custom-made shower where there was a wall of benches. He handed her a loofah and fresh washcloth from a nearby closet, and he left her alone. Vivian cleaned herself up and, wrapped in a towel, walked her sore body back to the guest room off the kitchen—where she had initially slept—to get some clothes.

She didn't see Jay, but knew he couldn't be far. After dressing, she left the room and found him in the kitchen accepting some groceries from a woman who waved and hurried away.

"Who's that?"

"My housekeeper, Sandy. She opened the house for me last night and lit the candles. She lives over in my guesthouse with her husband, Mike. I didn't know if you like coffee, so I got tea *and* coffee."

"You didn't have to. I know you need to get back to the city. I don't mind driving you. I have to get back, too." Vivian was anxious to return to the city and her house so she could think things through. She liked being with Jay, but she had no idea what was expected of her now. She needed to get out of here.

Looking in her bag, she searched for her keys. "I'm not hungry, and I'll just take my coffee to go, if you don't mind. Are you ready?"

"Don't worry about me. Ashton can take me to get my SUV. It's in the city getting detailed."

Unable to find her keys, Vivian looked around the counter and tabletops. "Have you seen Ashton lately?"

Jay shook his head, starting the coffee. "I don't have to-go cups because I eat at the table, and so are you, woman. Ashton's been incognito because he's been all up some girl's butt. He'll get over it soon enough."

"That girl would be Kerri. I can barely get her on the phone." The kitchen island was between them.

Then without warning, an ache filled her that she had possibly made a mistake. Doubt began to creep in. What if she never saw him again? He'd said all the right things in the heat of the moment, but what if they'd been just words? This was exactly what she'd wanted to avoid. What if he, too, would *get over it soon enough.*

"Come here," he said.

Her heart fluttering, Vivian made her way to him. "I hope Ashton isn't planning to get over Kerri soon. She really likes him." *I really like you.*

Jay pushed his fingers through her hair. "What are you doing tonight?"

Vivian felt all tingly again. "Rehearsing. That's all."

Their eyes met. "All night?" he asked.

"No." His fingers grazed her cheeks and she rolled hers in the bottom of his T-shirt.

"Can you go somewhere with me?"

"Where?"

"A dinner and then a late reception for an athletic organization. You don't have to do both."

"I can do the reception. Is it close to eight?"

He nodded, smiling.

Her insecurities settling, Vivian smiled. "I'd be glad to. I've got to go so I can get in at least six to seven hours of practice."

"You need to eat. We exercised a lot last night." He kissed her nose then her lips. "And this morning."

"Well, I'll have some protein and some fruit."

"You were trying to take all my protein."

"Jay!" she exclaimed, covering her eyes. "You're embarrassing me."

He caught her before she could get away. He planted kisses wherever he could land them.

She let herself be pulled into his arms, the day looking beautiful over his large backyard. She could get used to this. "You're a mess, Jay Smith."

"Yeah, I know. Come on, let's eat. I need to check on both my cars today."

"We can ride in my car."

He looked at her for a long minute. "Baby, your car is the size of a stamp. No offense, but I can hardly fit in there."

"You managed last night," she said, stroking his head. Though irrational, she no longer desired to leave his house or practice at all today.

"That's because I wanted to wake up with you."

"Well, you got your wish."

His kisses made her feel lazy yet powerful. Like he had some kind of power she hadn't been aware of. Jay had put on the coffee and it brewed quickly, but the sausage would take a couple minutes. He tossed in the CD she'd burned of the music for the wedding, and they began to dance. Now that it was just the two of them, they got into it, adding their own flavor and sexiness, bringing it alive.

Despite them being right there, the meat burned, and the screech from the smoke detector brought Sandy and Mike from the guesthouse.

"I will cook for you, Mr. Jay, before you burn down my nice house."

Jay and Mike shook their heads at the outspoken Hispanic woman. She took over the kitchen and sent her husband along to clean up the rooms as Jay disappeared to take a quick shower.

Vivian had offered to help, but Sandy would hear none of it. "You go outside and have fun with Mr. Jay on the swings. He built them last year and nobody swings but me."

"Who's been swinging on my swing set?" Jay asked, fresh from his shower. He was wearing jeans and a striped dress shirt. His hair was damp, but his clean-shaven face looked very handsome.

Sandy and Mike exchanged a look. "I try them out for safety," Sandy told him and shrugged.

Mike helped in the kitchen, turning the TV channel to

an all-Spanish station, while Jay and Vivian went outside to the yard.

"They're both employees?"

"No, friends of mine. Sandy has her own cleaning business, but fell on hard times back about a year ago. They take care of my place and stay in the guesthouse. I hardly come out here."

Vivian looked at the beautiful house. "You don't? It's gorgeous. Why not?"

"It's too far from the city and my job. If there's a traffic jam and news breaks, I need to be in the city."

"Why'd you buy this house then?"

"I was engaged and was living with my fiancée. Things didn't work out and the housing market had taken a turn for the worse. Sandy was living next door. She had one of the biggest cleaning businesses in the state. But when Mike got sick, their business fell apart."

"So she lives in your guesthouse?" Shocked, Vivian tried to close her mouth.

He nodded his head. "Yeah. It's nice out there. Two bathrooms, two bedrooms, a living room, a dining room and storage space. She's rebuilding her business."

"You're the best neighbor and friend ever."

Jay pulled Vivian to the swing and made her sit down. He pushed her. "I didn't do it for that reason alone. I own part of the business. It's in my best interest to see it succeed."

"That's really awesome. But how will they succeed with just the two of them?"

Vivian swung, but she could see Jay smiling down at her every time she swung back toward him. "She cleans for everyone in this subdivision. That's three hundred homes. We just hired four part-time people and bought two transport vehicles. We're expanding into upscale subdivisions. That's our brand. That's all we do. Upscale homes."

"Jay, that's great. You're a venture capitalist."

"I'm not afraid to get dirty if I have to," he proudly admitted.

"Really, Jay?"

"Yeah. Really. Every business I invest in I make sure I'm proficient in. If I have to work to make it succeed, then I work."

Vivian stopped the swing, liking him even more. Her grandmother had been a maid back in the day. The fact that he could get his hands dirty if he needed to made her feel really good.

"I'm really liking you right now."

She got up and took the stone walkway heading for the patio. Jay caught up to her and they strolled down the pathway leading to the tennis courts.

"Do you play tennis?" he asked.

"No."

"Basketball?"

"No."

"Bowling?"

"I'm a dancer." She smiled at him. "That's pretty much all I've ever done. I can throw a football but only because I have three brothers, but I'm a dancer."

He stopped. "You can't throw a football."

"I'm a great quarterback. My number is twelve and I can do that shake-your-knees dance, but nobody can tackle me. Those were always the rules."

A grin split his face. "What dance is that?"

Vivian elbowed him. "None of your business. You got a ball?"

"I'm a football player! Of course I've got a ball." He ran to a covered crate and pulled a football from the box. Tossing it, he threw it to her and she stretched out her hands and caught it.

Jay fell to the ground laughing.

Vivian ran up to him. "What's so funny?"

"You catch like a girl!"

Her eyes narrowed and he hurriedly got off the ground. "Baby, that was a good catch. Now throw me the long pass."

Vivian decided to teach him a lesson and drilled a pass to him that clicked into his hands.

His eyebrows shot up at the same time. "What the?"

He threw the ball back, this time, putting a little heat on it. Vivian backed up and caught it, tossing it back. Soon they had a game of catch going.

"Breakfast! Come and eat!"

Jay caught the high toss and shook his head at Vivian as she sashayed up the walkway and through the back door.

"Lady, this game isn't over."

"You better believe it, mister. You dropped four passes, to my three. I'm winning."

She poked him with her bottom and he grabbed it as they headed in to wash their hands and eat.

Chapter 10

Vivian refused to spend the night with Jay after the third sports reception in one week, although she'd had a good time. Parked on her driveway, Trey Songz belted out a hit from the radio that played in the background.

"You sure you don't want to come back to Ingerwood?" Jay asked, holding her hand.

Vivian leaned over and kissed his jaw, her lips softly teasing him. She'd been a hit tonight at the Sportsmen's Dinner. "Walk me to the door?"

Vivian climbed from Jay's Mercedes SUV and let him hold her hand as he walked her to her door. His Audi was still waiting on new rims that had to be special ordered.

"I'm sure. I'll see you tomorrow night at practice. I've got a surprise for everyone. We're going to dance in public because I don't want anyone to get a case of nerves when it's time to do it at the wedding."

Jay walked her to the door of her town house in the Candler Park neighborhood. The wedding was just a few days away, and they only had two practices left.

"That's a great idea. Get us primed for our debut."

He rubbed her back as they walked up the stairs to her place. Rain pelted the street, and they watched it from the porch. "Drive carefully," she advised him, her fingers tickling his palm.

"You're not going to invite me in for a few minutes?"

Her eyes were sad, but she looked more tired than anything.

He clasped her hands and tried to meet her gaze.

Vivian leaned to the side then put her head on his shoulder. "Jay, I have to sleep tonight."

He put his arm over her shoulder, pulled her onto his body until he was supporting her weight, then he massaged her back.

"You're making it impossible for me to say no."

"I don't want you to say no." He kissed her cheek, and they stayed quiet for a while.

Her keys hit the steps and Vivian rubbed between her eyes, then down her neck. "Okay. Okay, okay, okay."

She bent down, but he'd already picked up the keys. "Come on," he said. "I'll leave after you go to sleep."

Vivian shared a split-level house with a couple who lived above her in the upstairs apartment. The entire lower apartment was hers.

Jay walked inside and headed for the kitchen. He knew there were Epsom salts and a towel in the pantry. He'd put them there the last time they'd played football. He poured her a glass of wine and sat down.

Vivian headed for the bathroom. The shower turned on and he heard her getting ready to bathe.

It took the strength of ten men for him not to join her, but he didn't want to push her. Their relationship was so new. Going on three weeks for him was a record. But he liked it.

While she bathed, he pulled off his jacket, shirt and pants, laid them over the chair in the kitchen and went to the bedroom. He was watching the news from her sitting area when she came in.

Vivian entered, the silk robe kissing the top of her thighs. She saw a single glass of wine at her bedside table. Her questioning gaze landed on him. "You're not going to bed?"

"No. I soaked this towel in Epsom salts. I'm going to heat this up, put it on your back and rub it for you. Then I'll clean up, get dressed and go home."

She sat with him, nuzzled her head in his shoulder, and he kissed her.

She curled up under him. Her face was lined with exhaustion.

Her eyes were closed, so he carried her to the bed and then left to quickly heat up the towel.

When he returned to the room, Vivian had removed her robe and was flat on her stomach. Half the glass of wine was gone.

"Where should I put this?" he asked, looking at the smooth light brown skin on her back.

"My lower back."

He laid the towel on her back and stood beside the bed.

Vivian cracked her eye open and looked at him. "Get in, Jay."

He wasn't sure what to do with her. Naderia was a complete psycho compared to Vivian. He held her through the night and into the early morning, and by that time, he was sure she was the one for him.

She woke up and went through her morning routine, and then they made ravaging love before she sent Jay away with a huge smile on his face.

He couldn't wait to see her later that night for practice.

Chapter 11

The music was broadcasting as they walked into the night club and everyone was excited about dancing in public. Even Naderia. She had only recently returned to the group after paying the fine she owed for the studio floors. The club was crowded for a Thursday night, but Vivian was glad about that. They needed to be prepared for the unexpected. Noise, crowds, waiters, whatever.

Having been friends with Terico, the club owner, who was a former dancer, Vivian had sometimes come here to blow off steam. He loved when they danced together, and tonight he was in rare form.

"Vivi! My love! How are you?"

Terico was tall, light-skinned with his hair skimmed back into a swirling ponytail. He'd gained a few pounds, but he could still move on the floor. She enjoyed dancing with him, but that was as far as it went. He made no secret that he wanted more, but she made no secret that it wasn't going to happen.

"I'm good, T. These are some of my students. We've come to get a little real-life experience. I called and left a message. I hope it's okay."

"You're always welcome, baby. You know that. Can I get you something from the bar?" he asked the group.

The men ordered for everyone, and Vivian ordered bottled water.

"Go dance," she told her group. "Have fun."

The couples hit the floor, dancing, and having a good time. Vivian was going to pick the moment to see if they heard their music and how they'd react.

Women approached Elliott, but Idalia made it clear that her man was off-limits. And there were tons of women who were a constant stream for Jay, but he kept his eyes on the TV at the bar, or on her.

Naderia attracted every man who thought it was his lucky night, only to cast him aside. She was hunting big fish, and this club was in the wrong zip code for her.

Terico chose his moment when Jay was distracted to make his move. "You and him got something going?"

"No. Why you asking?"

"A man knows when another man is tapping the action."

Vivian didn't crack a smile. "I'm not action. I'm his teacher."

"I must be off my game then. My mistake. Let's dance, Vivian. It's been a while."

She shook her head, feeling Jay's gaze. "No, thanks. I'm on the clock."

If there was one thing about Terico, he was about money. "Well, baby. Scoop up that cash. Will you give me a little treat before you go?"

She relented. "Sure. Why not?" He cued the DJ and her

group's music began. They assembled and began dancing. The floor cleared as people began to pay attention to the music and choreography.

There was laughter and spontaneous applause which Vivian was thrilled to hear, especially for the men. When the dance was nearly over, the group broke formation suddenly.

"Hey! What y'all doing here?"

Beth and Naderia bear-hugged a woman, while Jay pulled Terico aside.

He pointed to the woman's back and mouthed, *the bride* to Vivian.

Suddenly Vivian's special piece of music was playing, and Terico was leading her onto the floor.

"Give us something special. Please, darling?" he said.

Swept into the music, she became caught up in the beautiful dance she'd been rehearsing for weeks. She and the movements had finally gelled.

When the music ended, Vivian felt herself stop spinning. Then she heard the applause, deafening as it ran all over her body. This was right. The very best thing that could happen to her had happened. Her dance was perfect.

Vivian began moving toward Jay when Naderia stepped in front of her and kissed him. Then with a huge smile on her face, Naderia brought the bride to Vivian. The woman had tears in her eyes.

"I don't think I've ever seen anything more beautiful in my life. I'm Destinee."

"This is one of my newest friends, Vivian," Naderia said, a big fake grin on her face.

The rest of the group gasped, but the sound was lost in the congratulations from people who milled around them.

"Oh, my god, you have to dance at my wedding," Destinee gushed. "That would be amazing."

"Oh, I'm so sorry. I can't."

"You don't even know when it is. It's a week from this Saturday in St. Croix, Virgin Islands. You would be my special gift to myself. Please consider."

Her chest full of tears, Vivian felt herself crashing emotionally. "I'm so sorry. I have an audition in New York in a couple days. I'm leaving on Wednesday. For three weeks."

Jay shook Naderia loose from Vivian and shot her a warning look. To Vivian, he asked, "When did this come up?"

"Does everyone know you?" Destinee gave Vivian a questioning look.

"Well," Vivian said, gathering her bag. "We met tonight. They're all really cute couples. I'm the odd man out here, so I'm going to say good night. It was nice meeting you all. Take care," she told them, and could barely get her foot in her leg warmer before making a break for the door. Well-wishers delayed her escape, but as graciously as she could, she finally got out of the building.

She was Naderia's friend? Hell had frozen over.

In the parking lot, she lost her bearings, forgetting where she'd parked. Walking up the aisles looking for her car, she hurried before tears exploded all over the parking lot.

She could hear Jay calling her, but she couldn't turn around. He'd see her pain and her fury. But most of all he'd see her jealousy.

Hurrying to her car, she shoved the key in the door and tried to open it. The key didn't move, but she kept wiggling it, wishing the lock would give before Jay caught up to her.

"Will you please wait? Vivian, I know you're angry."

"Out of all of you, Naderia is the only one who spoke up and claimed me as a friend? How pathetic is that?"

"Vivi, baby?"

"I'm not your baby!"

"Since when?"

"Since you decided not to claim me. You let your fake girl-friend have me first."

"She's manipulative and you know that. After she said that, didn't you see everyone's face? Here we are trying to keep up this lie for Destinee, and then Naderia goes and tells this whopper. Nobody wants to tell more lies just to keep up one lie. Plus, the dance is still supposed to be a surprise for the bride and groom, remember? And will you stop trying to break into this car? It isn't yours."

Freezing, Vivian looked inside the car and saw that it was spotless. Her car, on the other hand, was full of dance clothes, magazines and shoes.

Pissed, she scurried past him, and he caught her arm.

"You didn't claim me, Jay. I want a man who *wants* me."

"I do want you. I was just surprised. I'll go back inside right now and blow all this out the water, if it'll mean you'll stop being angry with me."

"No. I want to go home. Where's my car?"

"At the studio. You rode with me. Come on."

"What about the others?"

"They're getting a ride with Destinee."

"What does she think is going on?"

"She thinks we're planning a surprise shower for her."

"This is all too weird," Vivian said, getting into his SUV. "I can't do this in the name of false appearances. This is crazy. And she kissed you! Oh, my goodness. I can't do this."

"What? Fight for me?"

"Exactly, Jay. Women kissing you. You letting it happen. What if I let Terico kiss me on the lips?"

"Then it happens, Vivi. I would expect in your business that you would, from time to time, kiss someone on the lips. But it's the intent behind it. We all know Naderia is out of her mind. I've denied it so often. I would think that you know that she would do anything to drive a wedge between us."

"What *us,* Jay? As far as she's concerned, I'm just your dance teacher. You're paying me to teach you to dance and nothing more."

"Everyone can tell there's something between us."

"Everyone but you. I'm not a groupie or a fan of yours. I'm a real woman who exists in the real world. Men don't kiss me on the lips when I belong to someone else. Not in my world. And they damn sure don't kiss my man on the lips, either. Until you get that straight, among other things, you belong to the world and not to me."

Chapter 12

Jay finished shooting promos at 6:00 p.m. and was glad to leave work. He headed for Chow Baby on Ponce near the old City Hall East. Sitting down, he drank his black rum straight.

The man who sat beside him smelled of Usher's new cologne.

"You need to grow up. You been wearing that scent too long," Jay told his best friend, Troy.

Troy ordered from the waiter. "Patron straight." The drink arrived and he sipped the shot then threw it back. They ordered again, and their plates arrived. They began eating.

"What's your problem?" Troy asked Jay.

Troy was a big man at six feet four inches, 260 pounds, and nobody messed with him. He was an attorney moving quietly up through the district attorney's office, but he had a sixth sense when it came to his friends. "You've been acting funny and last night at the rehearsal dinner, you acted like you wanted to bounce Naderia on her head."

"I'm seeing somebody, and Naderia got in the way. We're not together, we haven't been but we're keeping up appearances for Destinee's sake. That's about to ruin me. I could've lost someone very special."

"Then don't. Destinee can't dictate your life. This wedding is about to kill me. She's emotional and upset. What should be a happy time is turning into a war, and it's all because she's pregnant."

Jay choked on his rum and Troy pounded him on the back. "Not Ms. Goody Two-shoes Destinee."

"Hey, we're very happy. We could have timed this a bit better, but she's only about a month along."

Jay laughed, staring at his friend. "Congratulations, man. And here I was so worried about offending her. No lie. I was truly scared that she'd be angry that I don't want anything to do with Naderia."

Troy threw up his hands. "Man, get her crazy butt up the aisle, and as far as I'm concerned, you don't even have to touch her walking out of the church. Your job is done."

Jay dropped his head in shock. "No dance at the reception?"

The big man's entire body shook. "Man, have we rehearsed a dance? *I* can't dance. We decided on a family dance so everyone can participate." Troy made the sign of the cross. "Man, you're free. Do your thing. Hey, bring your girl to the islands. I'd like to meet her. What's her name?"

"Vivian. She's in New York right now, but I want her with me for the wedding. I think I can get her to come, but I have my work cut out for me."

After Troy climbed into a taxi and Jay into Ashton's car, he called Vivian and prayed she'd answer. Her phone went straight to voice mail, which never used to happen. "Vivian, baby, please answer the phone."

The phone buzzed in his ear while he was leaving the message. "Hello?"

"Hi, it's me."

After three days of not talking to Vivian, her voice hit his chest heavily. Fuzzy from the rum, he sat forward and put his hand on his head. "Baby, how are you? How are the auditions?"

"Good. Okay. I'm still in the running."

She didn't sound hopeful or happy.

"Are you okay?"

"No, Jay. Everyone is younger than me. They're more limber and more exciting. I thought my dance was great and theirs are better." Her voice cracked. "I don't know what I was thinking. Oh, my…" He heard her tears, and he closed his eyes at her anguish.

"Vivian, you can't give up. You're a champion."

"Am I?" Even her sniffles broke his heart.

"Yes, baby. You're stunning. Experience is the best thing you have over them. You're going to get this, and you're going to be amazing."

"Voice call back for Franklin. Franklin?" The woman's voice in the background said she was tired, too.

He signaled for Ashton to turn the truck around. Ashton looked at him like he was crazy.

"Baby, go and be amazing. Call me tonight if you want to talk. I'll be up all night."

"Okay, bye," she said, and her phone went dead.

"I'm going to Hartsfield-Jackson airport."

"You're seriously going to New York? Are you even thinking straight?"

"Yes," he said, dialing the travel agent the company used. He specified what he needed and got a flight within ten minutes.

"What about the segment tomorrow?"

"I expect you're going to shoot it with a guest host while I'm out with *strep throat*. You'll wish me a speedy recovery."

Ashton started grinning like a fool and pounding on the steering wheel. "You're sick. That's awesome, man. I'm the lead."

"Hey," Jay snapped, getting his attention. "Don't get comfortable in my chair."

Ashton let him out at the departure gate. "Naw, man, of course not. I'm just keeping it warm. Safe travels." His exultant scream out the window as he drove away wasn't lost on Jay who dashed into the airport.

Jay checked in, bought a power cord for his phone and checked his email on his computer. No messages from Vivian. Hopefully everything was going well.

He'd been booked into a nice executive hotel, and he texted Vivian that his phone would be off for a few hours. Landing in New York, the weather was much cooler than Atlanta, but it was a little late to shop, so he hit the stores in the airport, buying only what was needed for an impromptu trip. He turned on his phone and received a message from Vivian that she was turning in early. He called her but she didn't answer.

Unwilling to have come to New York for nothing, he texted, asking for her address and she finally replied, but said that she was going to bed early and that she would call him in a day or two.

He hopped into a taxi for the ride to Vivian's walk-up.

Chapter 13

Tapping on the door drove Vivian to throw her sneaker at it. "Go away, you idiots!"

Music pounded from the studio apartment above her, and the dancers below her were having a smoke out. All she wanted to do was sleep, but she couldn't do anything but cry. "The kids" were tormenting her again tonight. Many of them had been eliminated from auditions, but they'd paid their rent through the end of the week, so they were staying and didn't care that she needed her rest. The rent was three hundred dollars for seven days, but it was the best deal in town.

The pounding intensified, and she got her bat and approached the door. Tonight she was taking off heads. Snatching the door open, the bat raised, she braced to swing.

"Baby," Jay said.

Seconds of silence hung between them. Was Jay really here...in New York?

"I was just looking at you on my phone."

He stepped toward her and gently took the bat. "Get your stuff for tomorrow. We're leaving."

Vivian went to the foldout bed she slept on and sat down. She slipped her feet into her shoes and put her coat on, rolling a scarf around her neck. Jay was really here. The truth was sinking in and her heart was beginning to race.

"Jay?"

"Yes, baby?"

"You're really here in New York, right?"

"That's right." He pointed at her dance bag she was hauling to her shoulder, but pulled it over his instead. "You don't need anything else?"

She shook her head.

Stepping into the hallway, she used the key she kept around her neck and laced her hand through his. "Are you staying far away?"

"No."

Jay looked *so good.* Vivian hadn't known how much she'd missed him. His hand was warm and his body was solid and she couldn't wait to take a bath and be next to him. He came all this way to be with her. He was her guy.

In the taxi, she rested her head on his shoulder and closed her eyes. He felt so good. She wished this feeling could last forever.

"Vivi, we're here."

Opening bleary eyes, she stared up at the hotel. She looked down at herself and then at him. "I can't go in there with you. It'll be a *Pretty Woman* moment if I ever saw one."

Jay nuzzled her cheek and kissed her. "I do not give a damn. You are my woman, and we are going into the hotel. Now get out."

Hustling her from the taxi, they walked inside hand in hand.

Check-in was far less eventful than Vivian had envisioned

as there were more exciting guests in the lobby. Jay and Vivian were escorted to their suite, and Vivian's jaw dropped at the beautiful skyline. "This place is incredible. How much is this?"

"Three ninety-five a night."

"I'm paying three hundred a week!" she exclaimed as Jay set their bags down and walked toward her.

"That place is a dump. You shouldn't be there."

"That's all I can afford with my mortgage at home and the studio. I have to be realistic."

"You've got dark circles under your eyes."

Vivian pulled her jacket closed around her body. "I'm sorry I'm not as pretty as you're used to, but it's grueling here." Tears gathered in her eyes. She was so near the breaking point, if she moved a toe she'd fall over.

He gathered her to him. "You're still beautiful to me."

"I'm not," she whispered. "If I don't get this, I'll be a huge failure." Her defenses began to crumble. Jay let her cry it out on his shoulder. When she was done, he was still holding her, rocking her, still ever-positive Jay.

"Come on now. You're tired. I'm taking a shower. Wanna come?"

She caressed his cheek. "That's the best offer I've had all week."

They showered, and Vivian washed her hair in fragrant soap and warm water. This was the first time in a week the water had been hot. She dressed in a brand-new T-shirt Jay had bought, and when she came out of the bathroom, the sheet was to his waist, and there was a spread of wine, fruit and tiny sandwiches on a tray on the bed.

Vivian ate until she was full, then she sat at the foot of the bed facing Jay, moisturizing her dry legs. His eyes lit up like Christmas-tree lights.

Jay removed the tray of food from the bed. Then he

took the lotion and squirted it into his hand. He removed her T-shirt and smoothed it over her skin. She reached for him and admired the power in his arms, the muscles and tendons, the beat of his heart in his sculpted chest, and the strength in his hips and legs. He lifted her with one arm and she moved with him, peppering him with affectionate kisses. She'd missed him, and she didn't know if she could be away from him again. Desperation flooded her and she clasped his neck, pulling him to her.

Jay collapsed on top of her and he rolled them to their sides, and looked at her. "Hey," he whispered. "I'm not going anywhere."

"Okay. I don't want you to."

"You're really close to your dream. Baby, it's coming."

She nodded.

He was at her opening and her body welcomed him. They both smiled, kissing.

"Hi," he said, kissing her.

"Hi." She kissed him back.

Their movements were slow and passionate, their lips meeting as often as their sex joined. Jay lay her on her side and curled his body around hers, entering her from behind. His body claimed hers, and she gasped with each thrust until she could hold back no longer and let her body sail free.

Jay needed her to face him, and she knew his favorite position. She turned in his arms, and straddled him. His smile was sleepy and sexy. "Oh, Vivi, I'm in love with you."

"Say that when you're not buried in me," she teased, bouncing up and down on him. She held her breasts, his hands on her waist as he aimed for Nova Scotia inside her body.

"Give it to me, baby," she begged him.

"I'm coming," he said, and sat up, grabbing her as he throbbed, growling through his climax.

Holding him, Vivian knew that she wanted to hold him

forever. She heard his even breathing and looked down. He'd fallen asleep inside her.

She kissed the top of his head and slid off him, making her way to the bathroom.

The man had crossed eight states to be there with her. He was allowed to be tired.

Cleaning them up, she hurried back to bed and as soon as she covered both of them with the sheet, he wrapped her in his arms and they went fast asleep.

Chapter 14

Jay waited in the hotel for Vivian to return. Today she'd find out if she'd gotten the part of Bess. This was a huge role for her to undertake, but one she was ready for. They'd prayed this morning, something he'd never done with anyone outside his immediate family, but she'd asked him to and it seemed right—was right.

Anxious, Jay grabbed his phone and checked the ringer, making sure it was on. It was. What was taking so long?

The phone rang and it was Ross, his boss. Answering, he shook his head. He couldn't lie about his life. This was too big a deal.

He explained everything, and Ross was surprisingly supportive, offering options Jay hadn't considered. Like relocating to New York and shooting there, or while Broadway was in season living in New York and spending the off-season in Atlanta. Jay hadn't known Broadway had a season. But first, Ross reminded him, she had to be chosen.

The room phone rang and he answered it. Vivian was downstairs.

"Ross, I've got to go. She's here."

"When you two get back in Atlanta, come out to the house and have dinner with Miriam and me."

"Thanks, Ross. We will."

Jay ran to the elevator and couldn't wait to get to the lobby.

In the lobby, Vivian was sitting near the piano player, lost in thought. He had to tap her shoulder to get her attention. "Hey, what happened?"

She stood up. "I didn't get Bess." She blinked at him. "I got Clara. I'm going to be singing the famous song 'Summertime.'"

"'Summertime and the livin' is easy,' that 'Summertime'?"

She nodded, a smile growing on her face. The piano man began to play the tune in a slow, easy way.

Jay grabbed her and danced her around the piano. "My baby is on Broadway."

They laughed and hugged to the delight of others. She drew back, looking at him. "Can we go home now?"

He looked down, surprised. "You sure you want to leave New York? When are rehearsals starting?"

"Not for three weeks and I'm very sure I want to go. Right now. I've already called, and it's going to cost me three hundred dollars that I'm happy to pay to change my ticket. How much is it for you?"

It had cost him five hundred dollars to get there and his ticket was open-ended, so he wasn't worried about it. That's what bonuses were for. "My ticket is taken care of."

He hadn't told her that he needed to be in St. Croix the next day, but Jay knew they needed to have that talk.

Vivian put her arms around his waist and squeezed. "Let's go. Besides, tomorrow is the wedding, and I wasn't going to let you miss that."

"Speaking of," he said, taking her hand and guiding her away from the piano and toward the elevator.

"What is it?"

"I want you to come to St. Croix with me."

Vivian was shaking her head no as they boarded the elevator. "I don't want to. I don't want the drama. I want to relax."

"You want to come with me," he said, gazing at her, caressing the tight bun on top of her head. Slowly his hand worked down to her neck, and he stroked her throat. "You'll miss me." Sadness lurked in her eyes, and Jay suspected Vivian didn't want to be away from him, either. "Kiss me."

She sighed softly and kissed him.

Holding her against him, they arrived at their floor. Her head rested on his chest, but they didn't get off the elevator. "What's it gonna be, baby?"

"I want to go," she said, her eyes shining.

He grinned down at her. "Come on. Our flight is in three hours."

Laughter bubbled out of her as they strode down the hall to his room.

"You're changing my whole life."

"It's all for good, baby. All for good."

Chapter 15

Walking from the wedding chapel into the balmy island sun had never felt so good. Troy and Destinee were married, and Jay was thrilled his obligations were over.

Naderia had tried to orchestrate reasons for them to be together, but he pushed her aside every time she got close to him. She'd finally promised to ruin the night for everyone. He didn't know what she had planned, and he didn't care. He rode in the car with Vivian. There was nothing that could keep him away from her.

Troy had brought Jay's tuxedo from Atlanta to St. Croix, and had forgiven him for missing the rehearsal dinner, but he knew Jay was about over the wedding drama. The last thing Troy wanted was to be without a best man.

The reception had begun and the wedding party was seated. The champagne was flowing and the party started. Vivian disappeared with Idalia and Beth, laughing and having fun. Jay breathed a sigh of relief.

He hung with his boys, and enjoyed the food, wondering where his lady was.

Then he saw Vivian again, and his heart expanded. He wasn't going to let her go.

Toasts were made by each set of parents, and then the microphone was passed to Jay.

"Troy has been my best friend for many years, and when he and Destinee started dating, she became like a best friend to me, too. I got really sick a few years ago, and my best friend did something for me few people will do for strangers. He gave me a bone marrow transplant. He gave me back my life."

There were gasps and applause, then silence.

Jay looked at the quiet district attorney, whose head was lowered. "I can never repay him for his love and kindness, so when he asked me to be his best man, I said yes. It's a small favor in comparison to the big favor he'd done for me. I'll spend the best part of my life trying to emulate the man that he is. I'm very happy for him and his lovely wife. So I ask that, with all the love in your heart, you raise your glass and send your best wishes to the happy couple."

The toast was raised and when the deafening applause died down, Jay removed his jacket signaling the guys to do the same.

Jay still had the microphone. "And there's one more thing."

Three chairs were placed in the center of the dance floor and the men took their positions. Idalia and Beth stood at the edge of the dance floor whispering and waving for Vivian to come to them.

The DJ pumped the music, and the wedding party started to dance, minus Naderia, Vivian in her place. The audience erupted, loving the dance, especially the bride and groom. With Naderia gone, the dance had flavor, personality and sensuality.

There was applause and laughter, and in the end, the bride

and groom joined in, and all four couples danced together. Nobody cared why Naderia wasn't there. She just wasn't.

The bride got on the microphone. "This evening is so special. Not only did I marry the man of my dreams, but I made a new friend. I'd like you to meet the choreographer of this wonderful dance, Ms. Vivian Franklin. Everyone has blessed my wedding, but you, Ms. Franklin, have blessed my heart with joy. Thank you all so much, and one last thing. If you haven't tried love, give it a try. There's nothing like it. Good night and God bless you all."

Jay kissed Vivian's temple as they swayed around the dance floor. "I love you."

She held him close. "You're just saying that."

"Why would I do that?" He leaned back, looking down at her.

"Because everything is going right. I'm about to go to New York."

She had a point. How would they manage travel between two distant states? Living in two cities?

"Would you rather I didn't love you? Would you rather I didn't want to stick around for the long haul? Would you rather I didn't get down on one knee and ask you to marry me?" He had barely made it down on his knee when she realized he was serious.

Vivian started jumping up and down, laughing. She nearly toppled Jay over. "I love you, too. Yes, yes!"

He stood, looking down at her beautiful smiling face. "Now we're getting somewhere."

He picked her up and they spun around, kissing.

Troy and Destinee looked on proudly as the couple forged a bond that would last a lifetime.

* * * * *

ORCHIDS AND BLISS
Felicia Mason

Chapter 1

When Baden Calloway ran away from home, she went as far west as she could. When she reached Honolulu, Hawaii—4,787 miles, six time zones and a lifetime away from Cedar Springs, North Carolina— she finally stopped running. That had been eighteen months ago. While her features carried none of the native Hawaiian, Samoan, Japanese or Pacific Islander influences of those around her, she'd managed to ditch the Southern lilt in her voice. No longer was she *malihini,* a tourist or outsider. She belonged here. She thrived here. And there was nothing to remind her of North Carolina or her Southern roots except her memories…and the cop banging on her front door.

Baden was not at all happy to see the shield of the Raleigh, North Carolina, Police Department through her peephole.

"Baden Calloway, I know you're home. May I come in?"

The Carolina drawl in his simple request set her teeth on edge.

No! she wanted to shout. *No, you cannot come in and disrupt the life I've made here. No, you can't just barge in as if nothing ever happened.*

The islands of Hawaii were Paradise on earth. The very essence of the islands—forged in the violence and heat of lava and as lush as the biblical Garden of Eden—gave her the nourishment she'd so needed to heal at a time when she thought she might never recover. As far as Baden was concerned, North Carolina, especially Cedar Springs, North Carolina, could have been a continent or more away, say North Africa or northern Antarctica; in any or either case, a place she had sworn to avoid, especially after the way she had left.

Baden belonged to Hawaii, and the island retreat she now called home was her solace and refuge. The aloha spirit lived in her and she in it. There was no room for the past.

But with his very presence, the cop on her doorstep ruined Paradise, maybe forever spoiling it and her peace of mind.

It wasn't all cops who evoked such attitude and emotion and desperation in her. It was *him,* that one on the other side of this elaborately carved teakwood door. He had been there when it had happened, and the fewer reminders she had, the better.

Baden did a quick calculation. She had enough money to disappear again. Maybe further west, to Samoa or Guam or possibly as far as Tokyo or Kyoto. She'd learned a few words and phrases of Japanese to impress clients and give her a small leg up on the competition. She could learn more, right?

The cop from her past knocked on the door again.

"Ms. Calloway? Baden, please. I just want to speak with you. I promise I won't take up much of your time."

Yeah, right, she thought, *won't take much time.*

She had yet to meet a cop who could take just a few minutes. This one in particular wanted to flay her open, expose the raw nerves that, until just a few moments ago, she thought had healed quite nicely.

Baden no longer felt—or allowed herself to feel—the scar tissue below the surface. Like the volcanoes under the sea that erupted millennia ago to eventually become what today was Hawaii, there was a seething and churning inside Baden. She'd thought it dormant. Until now. With one knock on her door, she was transported back and could feel the molten lava inside her. It threatened to erupt just like the island's volcanoes that sometimes coalesced into magnificent displays of nature's might and glory.

On the other side of the door of this cottage—on the sprawling and luxurious estate that was her temporary home away from home—stood the catalyst that would make the volcano erupt.

"Miss Calloway? Baden? Please."

Baden sighed heavily.

He promised he'd only take a few minutes of her time. But it had been just a few minutes of her time that had changed her life forever. Promises from cops had gotten her into this mess in the first place.

With her arms braced on the front door, she closed her eyes for a moment. Then with a few select muttered words, half curse, half prayer, she opened the portal to allow her past to disrupt her present.

Jesse Fremont wasn't surprised that she'd refused to see him. Had their roles been reversed, he probably would have responded in the same way.

Baden Calloway.

If just her name filled him with a longing that he knew would never be quenched, what might it have been like to actually see her again? He had, of course, known that the odds of her actually opening the door and welcoming him were about the same—if not greater—as hitting the Powerball lottery jackpot back home.

Even on the drive out here in his rental car, he had tried to form the words he'd say when he saw her—if, that is, she didn't haul off and hit him upside the head.

It's what he deserved.

If this is where she lived, Baden had obviously done quite well for herself. A plump Samoan woman in a floral muumuu who had answered the door at the main house had told him, "Miss Baden working in cottage today."

He'd followed her directions through a lush garden until he'd come to the so-called guest cottage. The lodging for guests at the spectacular up-country estate was bigger than his place back home in Cedar Springs.

He clearly was not going to see inside either the main house or the guest cottage because Baden wasn't going to talk to him.

But just as he turned to go, he heard the big door open.

Baden stood there, framed by the elegant entrance, the rich and deep red browns of the wood accenting the dark honey hue of her skin. She'd changed little since he'd last seen her. Her eyes were a light, light brown that never failed to arrest him. When he'd first met her a few years ago, he had thought their color was due to tinted contacts. Her skin remained flawless. If she wore makeup other than lipstick, it had been applied with a deft hand because he couldn't tell. A golden sundress with thin straps showed off her bare shoulders and arms, and she wore the pointy-toed high heels that women called mules.

She looked like one of the gorgeous flowers that bloomed in profusion along the walkway from the main house to the guest cottage.

"Hi, Baden," he said.

She eyed him warily, then leaned against the door, her arms folded. "What do you want, Jesse?"

What did he want?

He wanted to wrap her in his arms and never let her go. He wanted to kiss her and hug her and make love to her until she forgot how much his presence reminded her of her painful past.

But he said none of those things.

"I'm in Hawaii for a bit, and thought I'd look you up."

She swallowed, looked beyond him as if she expected a ghost or an intruder to appear from the garden. With a wry thought, he acknowledged that he probably represented both to her. And Jesse knew all too well that each of those things joined them here. Not the ghost of the *woo-woo* variety, but a ghost nonetheless.

"You're looking well, Baden."

She hadn't moved from the doorway or invited him inside.

"You said you wanted a little time to speak with me. I'm giving you five minutes."

She wasn't going to make this easy for him.

"May I come in?"

For a moment, he was sure she was going to say no; they would have this conversation standing in her front doorway. But with a sigh, she just turned and walked back in the house, leaving him to follow or not.

The interior was light and large. The foyer opened to a gallery of sorts—a front hall with a view of the ocean on the left side.

"Wow!"

Jesse couldn't suppress the exclamation. The main house must have access directly to the Pacific Ocean.

This, he thought, was serious money.

She led him into a great room furnished in all white with a large—Ultrasuede?—upholstered L-shaped sectional sofa.

She didn't sit, but instead stood behind a chair on the other side of the sofa, sending a clear message that she didn't want to be close to him.

"After all this time, I can't imagine what you want to discuss, but I've got a question. How did you know I was in Hawaii?"

How could he tell her without coming off like a stalker?

He'd been keeping tabs on Baden Calloway from the moment she'd left North Carolina. And he had used the considerable information at his disposal via the police department to know she was safe and out of harm's way. That and the fact that, since Sean's death, he had regularly checked in with Baden's aunt and uncle. They knew where Baden was, though they'd never exactly told him.

Public access sources also gave him plenty of information, even though she wasn't chatty on social media sites. Given that he was already on rocky ground with her, he decided that prudence was the road best taken in this instance.

"It was pretty easy to track you down and get the address once I knew the name of the realty company you worked with."

She pursed her lips and said, "Hmm. I will definitely have to make a point to tell the folks at the main office on the Big Island to be a little more circumspect. By the way, you have four minutes."

God, did she have a stopwatch ticking in her head?

"It's good to see you, Baden. I, well, there's no easy way to say this so I'll just come out with it."

He hated seeing the wariness creep into her eyes. She suspected he had something to do with the day her world fell apart. And he was guilty as charged on that count. If she hated him before, she'd have nothing but contempt for him after today.

"I'm in Maui on vacation," he said.

She lifted a brow. "And I'm supposed to care because why?"

"You should probably sit down," he suggested.

Baden ignored him, clearly resenting the intrusion into the life she had made for herself here in Hawaii. Jesse knew he represented her painful and debilitating past. Hawaii was her future. One that did not have him in it, especially if this cottage was what she now considered modest.

"What do you want, Jesse?"

"I'm very sorry about S—" he began.

She held up a hand and shook her head violently.

"Don't say it," she said. "I *do not* want to talk about...him or about any of that. It is done and over. Over, you hear me?"

A part of Jesse withered and died right there in her foyer.

Even after everything that had happened, after what she had done, she still loved Sean.

That was clear as could be.

No woman would have that much lingering passion about a man if she were not still emotionally tied to him.

She folded her arms across her chest, the universal "Go to hell" posture he was used to seeing while interviewing witnesses in some of the rough-and-tumble parts of Raleigh. No one ever saw anything, heard anything or knew anything. The only thing they wanted was for him to go away.

And Baden clearly conveyed that that is just what she wanted him to do: go away.

All righty then, Jesse thought. So this was not going quite the way he had anticipated it would.

But what else should he have expected? She hadn't seen him since her wedding day, and that had not been a stellar occasion for any of them.

This was not a good idea, Jesse thought. As a matter of fact, it was a monumentally horrible idea.

The envelope in his pocket felt like a hot brand on his skin. He couldn't do it. Not now.

Damn you, Sean, he thought. *Damn you for leaving me to clean up your mess.*

Jesse, who hadn't been promoted to the rank of police detective sergeant for nothing, was used to thinking fast on his feet. Now, however, he scrambled to come up with a plausible reason for showing up at her door, a door that was more than a little farther away than the twenty-five-mile drive from his place to hers back in Cedar Springs, North Carolina.

He moved closer to her, all but invading her personal space.

"I wanted to apologize," he said.

That seemed to take both of them by surprise.

She dropped her arms and regarded him.

"Well, that's not what I was expecting," she said.

"After Sean died, I thought about you," he said. "Actually, I worried about you and wondered how you were doing. What you were doing. Then, when you didn't come home for the funeral—" he looked a bit sheepish, but shrugged and continued "—more times than I can count, I headed over to your aunt and uncle's, intending to ask for your address or contact info. If I did, I knew I'd get some ribbing from Mr. Calloway even under the circumstances, but I thought Miss Henrietta might take pity on me."

Baden smiled at her aunt's name.

The smile encouraged him. And now that he had actually started, the words came out as if part of an eruption from one of the island's volcanoes he'd seen from the airplane heading into the airport.

They had been bottled up inside him for a long time. This isn't what he'd specifically come to say to her, but it needed saying.

"But I couldn't seem to do it," he said. "I kept thinking that if I could just see you or talk to you…" He shrugged, the words momentarily failing him. Then he continued, "But eighteen months ago, when you deleted me from your friends list on Facebook and didn't accept me on LinkedIn, I knew you were royally pissed and didn't want anything to do with me."

She reached a hand out and touched his arm.

"I deleted everybody when I left Carolina," she said. "I just wanted and needed to disappear from the planet."

When he glanced at her hand, she snatched it back, fluttering for a moment, before eventually clasping both of her hands in front of her. She twisted them together like a shy or uncertain schoolgirl. Jesse knew her to be neither.

That was why what she'd done to Sean confused and confounded him so much.

She had been ready to promise forever to his best friend. And then, then she'd just walked away. She had put Sean through hell, a hell that had ultimately killed him.

But that wasn't something he would *or could* ever tell her.

Baden's burden—and his own guilt over loving her and being jealous of his partner for having her—was great, and she didn't need him dumping his own mess on top of her.

She studied him for a long moment, a moment that was starting to get really uncomfortable.

"You came five thousand miles to tell me you're sorry."

She didn't sound angry or disbelieving. If Jesse weren't mistaken, she sounded more mystified than anything else.

She leaned forward and kissed him on the cheek.

The gesture stunned him.

"You've always been one of the good guys, Jesse Fremont," she said as she stepped back and again put a bit of distance between them before perching on the edge of the chair. "You said you're in Hawaii on vacation. Have you seen Maui yet?"

If surprised at the kiss, or at the abrupt change in her tone, from morose to upbeat, or even at the ultrasharp shift in conversation, Jesse didn't show it. He was a cop and knew how to roll with the punches even as he assessed the lay of the land in the middle of a volatile situation.

Besides, he reasoned, other than reminding her of the past, she had no reason to be angry with him. Did she?

"Not really," he answered her. "I checked into my hotel then decided to find you first before…"

He trailed off, catching himself before he accidentally revealed the true purpose of his visit to Hawaii.

He could hardly confess that to her. He had barely let himself think beyond what he'd do after seeing her. For the first time in his adult life, Jesse didn't have a plan.

She must have read something into his silence that he clearly had not intended because Baden smiled.

Jesse had to smile right back. "What?"

"You're in luck, Officer Fremont."

"It's sergeant now. I'm in the detective bureau."

"Oh. Well, excuse me, Detective *Sergeant* Fremont," she said lightheartedly, accenting his rank.

And then, more serious, as if the ghost of Sean were in the room with them, she added, "Congratulations, Jesse. You deserve it. Sean always said you'd go far up the ranks."

He wanted to ask more about this, wanted to ask how she knew he deserved his promotions. But he didn't want reminders of Sean to turn her back into the closed and distant woman she'd been when she'd opened the door a few minutes ago. So Jesse took the safe route for now, asking, "And why am I in luck?"

"My clients don't come in until tomorrow and I have no appointments or showings booked so I am free for the rest of the day. That means that you have your own personal tour guide."

He lifted a brow. "Tour guide?"

"You're here on vacation, right?"

If you could call six weeks of involuntary leave a vacation, sure, he was on vacation. To Baden he just nodded.

"Well, welcome to Paradise," she said. "Let me grab some flats and my bag, and I'll show you a good time."

Somehow, he doubted that the type of good time Baden referenced or was thinking of had any bearing to the kind of good time he wanted to have with her. But beggars would not be choosers, especially when offered with this gift. Jesse knew he would take the company of Baden Calloway any way he could get it.

"Be right back," she said, getting up.

True to her word, she made it quick, returning with a cell phone at her ear.

"I'm going to be out for a while, Mama Melia. I'll meet Mr. and Mrs. Li at the airport in the morning. Will you have Deato Kauhane pick up my car, please? I'll leave the keys under the seat like last time."

The cop in Jesse shuddered at that. Whatever she drove, leaving the keys in the vehicle was just an invitation for trouble. Hawaii might be known as Paradise to the thousands of tourists who flocked to the islands every year, but there was crime and a criminal element here just like everywhere else in the United States.

Let it go, he told himself. *You're a cop without authority right now, so just let it go.*

He studied her as he listened to the one-sided conversation.

There was no doubt about it. His memory and the regret of what-could-have-been had not been lacking in a single detail when it came to this woman. Baden Calloway was simply stunning.

She'd done a complete presto chango on her clothes, and he wondered if she had a cadre of assistants back there who had whisked her out of one outfit and into another. He'd seen that magic in action once when he'd been roped into the role of backstage wrangler for a benefit fashion show his sister had put on.

Instead of the sundress, she'd changed into a short flirty skirt in the same golden color and a filmy top that draped off her shoulders. That smooth dark honey-colored skin tempted him, and Jesse's body responded to the off-limits temptation.

He forced himself to ignore it. But that was a hard task.

"No, that won't be necessary, Mama Melia. Thank you for all your work," she told the person on the phone. "Yes, he found me."

Her gaze met Jesse's, and she smiled as if letting him be a party to the conversation.

She turned to reach for something on the table behind the sofa, and Jesse got a great view of those long supple legs. She'd ditched the mules for even sexier open-toed sandals that had little seashells on front, but they were hardly what he'd call flats.

Jesse's gut tightened when he noticed first the pink toenails and then a toe ring with a tiny seashell on it. Leave it to Baden to mark her own style even in Hawaii.

She motioned for him to follow, and she led him to a gourmet kitchen that had the perfectly put-together look of a set for a Food Network TV show.

"Yes, they were delicious. You're just trying to fatten me up." She laughed at whatever Melia said. "All right. I'll be sure to share. You have a relaxing rest of the day. It's show-time tomorrow. Mahalo."

She ended the call and dropped the phone in her bag. After turning off the coffeemaker, she reached for a plate on the kitchen island.

"These are the best macadamia nut clusters you will ever eat in your life," she said, extending to him the plate filled with cookies. "They're like an orgasm in the mouth."

Jesse's mouth went dry and for a moment he thought it was going to be over for him right here standing in her kitchen.

Oblivious to his torment, Baden handed him a napkin and invited him to take one of the cookies and follow her.

The next thing Jesse knew, he was moaning and it had nothing to do with the woman who turned him on.

"Oh, my God," he mumbled around chews.

She'd locked the door off the kitchen and was headed down a pathway toward a gleaming silver Jaguar XJL. But he was standing near the door chewing the last of the cookie and trying to figure out how to get back into the house and the kitchen without being brought up on B & E charges.

There were more of those cookies in there, and the fact that a law enforcement officer was willing to suffer charges of breaking and entering just to get at them spoke volumes. If his cop buddies back home ever tasted these, they'd swear off doughnuts for life.

"I want another one," he said.

Baden's laughter drifted back to him. "Come on, Jesse. Those aren't going anywhere and will be there when we get back. There are, however, other sensual delights of Hawaii awaiting you."

He shook his head.

The remnants of one sensual delight lingered in his mouth, and the other stood just a few feet away. This place truly was Paradise on earth.

With both of them buckled into the Jaguar, Baden spun out of the driveway as if she were trying to beat Jimmie Johnson's or Dale Earnhardt Jr.'s qualifying time for the Daytona 500.

"Drive fast, do you?" Jesse said drily.

Baden grinned. "This baby was made for speed."

She was telling the truth there. The car was one of the top-of-the-line models in an already top-of-the-line make.

But Jesse just said, "Hmm" and held on.

Then asked, "Did you make those cookies?"

That earned him an amused laugh from her.

"Any cookies I bake, you want to stay far, far away from," she said. "Mama Melia—that's Melia Olena Hookano on paper, but Mama Melia to anyone who knows her longer than five minutes—she made them. She makes a batch of something fattening every day. She's the housekeeper slash chef slash caretaker of the Kapule Garden Estate, at least until someone buys the place."

Despite his teasing, Baden handled the luxury car with skill. He watched her hands on the steering wheel and imagined them curved around…

Jesse cleared his throat, shifted in the passenger seat then tried to focus on what Baden was saying rather than what she was doing to him without even realizing it.

"She's very distantly related to the original Kapule family who owned the land. And she's worked for every owner for the last forty years. She *claims* she's going to move to the mainland to visit California and New Mexico after I sell the estate. Personally, I give her a week before hopping the first plane, boat or raft back to Hawaii. But everyone has to have a plan, and that is the one she's come up with."

Jesse wondered what Baden's plan was, especially now that he'd crashed into her life. Then he decided what the hell, in for an ounce, in for a pound.

"And what about your plan?"

She glanced over at him. "My plan is to show you a good time today."

Chapter 2

Baden, like many women, had mastered the art of the surreptitious glance. Something had him riled up and turned
on. She'd forgotten just how intimately cozy the confines of
a vehicle could be—with the right person sitting next to you.

So she knew, and conveniently chose to ignore, the sug-
gestive slip she'd made and how he might be responding to it.

Baden didn't want to think about Sean Mathews. But Jesse's
presence made those thoughts spring forth, unwanted and un-
bidden. Jesse and Sean went hand in hand. She'd met them the
same day at the same time so they would be forever linked in
her head—and in her heart?

Sean had been a part of her life for a long time, but that
was a lifetime ago. Because of Sean, she had found Hawaii,
and for that she would forever and always be grateful. If a
person could "get over" embarrassing herself and her family
by walking out of the church on her wedding day—before the
vows were even uttered, Baden thought she had succeeded.

She'd even dated a bit, but nothing serious. Just outings with a few safe guys, men she had no intention of falling for because, well, because she wasn't really that into them in the first place.

As for Jesse Fremont? Well, he was another story, another category unto himself.

She'd always found him incredibly sexy. The type of man that a woman instinctively knew was a protector, a provider and probably one heck of a lover. In other words, the brother was the total package, tall, dark, fine as all get out and the topic of more than his share of speculation among her girlfriends back when she was just starting to date Sean.

Though she hadn't seen Jesse since the day she was supposed to marry his partner, nothing about him had changed.

He was still the quintessential tall, dark and handsome law enforcement officer that he'd always been. If there were recruiting ads for cops, Jesse could be the poster boy. He stood just over six feet tall and had a body that wasn't earned by sitting at a desk or playing video games all day. She remembered that he did mixed martial arts as a part of his workout routine and ran several miles every morning.

The work he put in translated into high-octane eye candy.

He looked like a man who could make a woman glad she was a woman. And when he smiled… Glory!

Baden tried to keep those thoughts at bay. Hadn't just that line of thought already caused enough problems for her?

She could let Jesse's sudden appearance in her life and the apology that he'd brought from the past drag her back to that horrific period of isolation, abandonment and despair, or she could, like the islands she now called home, continue to grow and flourish from the remnants of devastation.

Her decision was an easy one.

"What's your schedule like?" she asked him.

Jesse shrugged. "When I landed at the airport, they said the islands were on aloha time. When I went to change my watch, the guy laughed and tapped his head. He said 'aloha time' was a state of mind, not a time on a clock. Once here, I was supposed to put aside all the calendars and schedules I use in the States…"

Baden glanced at him. "This *is* the States."

"I mean, what did you call it? The mainland?"

She nodded. "But I knew what you meant," she said flashing him an easy grin. "Hawaii is the closest thing Americans can get to feeling like they are in a foreign country while still on American soil right at home."

"As well as parts of Miami, and most of New Orleans," he said.

"What about Miami and New Orleans?"

Jesse glanced out the window admiring the Maui streetscape as it passed by outside. Palm trees and pedestrians marked the street with shops and houses no more than two or three stories high lining one side of the street. The ocean on the other made him smile.

"New Orleans has that 'other place' vibe to it," he said by way of explanation. "It's like you left America and went to some other country. And Miami, well, depending on where you are within that city, you might swear you were in Cuba or the Caribbean."

"I've never been to either of those places," Baden said. "So I'll have to take your word for it. I know Louisiana has a mix of cultures, French, African and Native American."

"Among others."

"Here in Hawaii, we're quite diverse. We have Native Hawaiians with a capital *N,* like Mama Melia Hookano, who are descended from the old Polynesians who settled the islands, and native Hawaiians like President Barack Obama who was born here."

She stopped at a light and waved at some people, clearly tourists with their cameras and white socks worn with sandals, waiting to cross to the beach side of the street.

"There are, of course," she continued as they waited, "a lot of Pacific Islanders. About forty percent of the population is Asian, Asian American or of some Asian descent. Whites are about twenty-five percent."

"I take it not a lot of black and brown folks live here."

Baden glanced over at him and laughed. "You'd be surprised," she said. "There are fairly sizable black and Hispanic populations across the islands. Even though several islands comprise the state, most of the density is in Honolulu."

"Okay, Miss Chamber of Commerce."

She glanced at him again and gave him a wink. "I sell real estate for a living," she said. "It's my job to know the demographics. I can break it down by ZIP Code if you'd like."

Jesse held up his hand as if in surrender. "I believe you. I believe you."

Baden grinned. "Today, I'm going to show you a little bit of Maui. If you have time, I mean."

"My time is your time," he said.

He looked it too, relaxed, confident, as if he had nothing better to do than tool around the island with her.

Once upon a time, she had entertained thoughts of fooling around with Jesse. Not as in cheating on Sean, but wondering what things may have been like had she hooked up with Jesse Fremont instead of his partner.

Jesse had a way of walking, talking and just…well, being… that made her aware of him in ways that were elemental between a man and a woman.

As she navigated the city traffic, Baden wondered if there had been more in what he had said about spending time with her…or if she just wanted there to be.

* * *

Not too long after, Jesse's Hawaiian education was about to begin.

"It's sacrilege to come to Hawaii and eat in all the chain restaurants that you can easily find on the mainland," Baden said. "So we are going to eat local today, all day."

"Hmm, that sounded fine until you added the 'all day' part. This isn't going to be one of those extreme-eating excursions where weird bugs and alligator toes are on the entrée menus, is it? If so, I need to get a couple bottles of antacid."

"Alligator toes? Really?"

But the joke was on Jesse. They started the day at one of the farmers' markets where fresh fruits and organic produce were displayed and sold like a festival in the Garden of Eden.

"There are lots of farmers' markets on Maui," she told him as she retrieved a handwoven basket from the backseat of the Jaguar. "The *locavore* movement is growing here."

"Locavore?"

"Buy local, shop local. Fresh is better for you and usually tastes better, too. The markup on imported goods is astronomical here and across all the islands. We let the tourists pay those prices."

"So I get to be a local for a day?"

"If you're nice. Otherwise, I'll dump you back at your hotel where you can probably find a banana flown in from California and pay enough to buy eight or nine of them at a fresh market."

They began with fruits and vegetables. Baden got a kick out the North Carolina boy sampling a bit of jackfruit and papaya.

"Oh, my God," Jesse groaned when he bit into a rambutan. "This is wonderful!"

"May we get half a pound to go, please?" Baden requested of the stall minder.

"It's sort of like a grape," Jesse said, reaching for another, "but it's more like…I don't know. It's sweet. It's mild. I wonder if they sell these back home."

Baden smiled as he picked up another one.

"Better make that a pound, please," she told the vendor.

"*Kane* like."

She nodded.

He placed the fruit in a clear plastic bag and used a twist tie to secure it. Baden paid the farmer, placed the bag in the straw basket that served as her shopping bag and with an "Aloha!" to the vendor, guided Jesse to the next stall.

Over the course of an hour they strolled the market and the contents of Baden's basket grew with preserves and baked goods and even a tiki doll certified "Made in Maui," because Jesse watched the artist create it while they waited.

"My niece is going to love this," he said, snapping a photo of the artist finishing up the doll. "She'll be six next month, and it'll be a great surprise for her."

The mention of a six-year-old niece had Baden wondering if Jesse had children of his own. She didn't recall Sean mentioning his partner having kids, but clearly Sean had failed to mention a lot of important things about his life.

She tried to sound casual when she asked, "Do you have kids?"

"Not a single one," he said. "I managed to avoid the baby mama drama that a lot of brothers get into. I think it was the good Lord looking out for me, 'cause I used to be a wild thing."

That was news to Baden. She'd always viewed Jesse Fremont as a stand-up sort of guy, the *all-American wife, kids and a couple dogs* type. If there was a wild one, it had been Sean. He probably had kids all over the state of North Carolina.

She stopped suddenly.

Jesse turned back to look at her. "Something wrong?"

Baden shook her head. "I was just thinking about Sean, wondering if he had kids."

"Uh," Jesse said, taking a sudden and intense interest in the ground.

Baden forced a smile and told herself to get her mind off Sean and what used to be. What *could be* was right here in front of her. And the only thing she was concerned about was right now and the immediate future. The past was where it belonged, and she'd spent enough time dwelling there to know nothing good would or could come of it.

"Oh, look," she said, grabbing Jesse's hand and tugging him along. "I would be willing to bet you have never had fresh coconut."

"That would be a bet you'd win," he said.

They joined a crowd of onlookers as a machete-wielding Tongan sliced through mounds of coconuts and an assistant served up samples.

As the shoppers applauded and asked questions of the bare-chested man with the machete, Jesse leaned over and said, "I'm starting to get why you didn't return to Carolina. If that guy was on a street corner in Raleigh or Cedar Springs with a blade looking that wicked, the 911 switchboards would be lit up. Here, it's entertainment and product merchandizing."

While she knew he referred to the feast for the senses that made up Hawaii, she couldn't help but feel as if there was more, so much more here that could or would shape her future.

Baden studied him as he asked the Tongan a few questions.

Jesse was the strong, silent type. Sometimes she got the impression that he was attracted to her, but the time was never right or the situation was not the place to make an inquiry, discreet or otherwise. And it wasn't anything he said or did; he was courteous and respectful to the extreme—too extreme, in her opinion. But every now and then at get-togethers with

Orchids and Bliss

Sean, she'd catch him watching her with the same intensity that she now regarded him.

For a brief moment, she let herself wonder, what if? What if it had been Jesse Fremont instead of Sean Mathews who had taken the initiative and asked her out that first night?

Seeing him here, in Hawaii, out of the usual context and on her turf rather than his, made her view him in a new light. He was cover-model gorgeous, but didn't seem to know or care.

At just that moment he turned toward her and smiled.

Baden's heart did a little flip, and her breath caught.

Oh, my.

After enjoying their coconut treat, she suggested one more stop at the farmers' market. "You have to have a lei."

At a flower vendor's stand, bouquets of native plants and decorative flowers spilled forth in a riot of colors and sweet fragrance. But leis were the order of the day. A group of customers, a family of five—two adults and their bored-looking kids, two of whom were furiously texting on cell phones— were choosing flower leis.

"Most people think of leis as just a string of flowers you get at the airport," Baden told Jesse. "Those are called *Kui*. But there are a lot of different types, and they're all made from various materials, not just flowers, but everything from shells to feathers. And some are made from just leaves and vines. Those are called *Kipu'u*. I have a traditional shell one at home in Honolulu. I only wear it on special occasions."

"Honolulu? I thought you lived here, on Maui."

Baden shook her head. "Nope. I'm an Oahu girl. But I'm living here temporarily, staying at the Kapule Garden Estate while it's being marketed. It's an unusual arrangement, but it makes sense for that particular property. As you probably saw, the Kapule family's former compound isn't a house for the casual buyer. I have six showings set up, and four of them are international buyers flying in to the United States just to tour the estate."

"I'm afraid to ask how much the place costs."

She laughed. "Whatever price you're thinking, add a couple million."

Jesse shook his head as if clearing it after a left hook from Mike Tyson.

At his expression she grinned. "Yeah, it's about that much," she said. Then she told him the listed price.

All he could do was shake his head again.

Jesse fingered a delicate hibiscus then paused to watch the vendor deftly create a lei.

"What kind of flower is that?" he asked.

"Plumeria," the vendor said. "I use a lot of them every day. We supply several of the hotels with leis for their guests."

The woman paused to hand a business card to Jesse.

"There are more than two thousand plant species on the islands of Hawaii," Baden said. "But only about half of them are native to the islands and several hundred are considered rare and in danger of extinction."

"How do you keep track of all this information?" he asked.

Baden and the flower vendor laughed together.

With a glance between the two women, Jesse asked, "What's so funny?"

The merchant handed Jesse a copy of the brochure that Baden had been reading.

He smirked, tipped the edge of the brochure in salute to the vendor and then had to chuckle himself.

Adorned with fragrant garlands made of plumeria and tuberose, they prepared to leave the market. Baden paused to chat with another customer. Jesse plucked a large hibiscus from the bin and pressed a finger to his mouth to warn the vendor. The woman glanced at Baden, nodded and smiled.

Jesse paid for the flower and when Baden turned, he stood before her with his gift.

"I understand all the beautiful women of the islands wear these in their hair. May I?"

When she nodded, he moved closer and tucked the flower behind her right ear.

"The blossom is pretty, but you are spectacularly enchanting."

His hand lingered near her face, and then she felt the barest of caresses as his finger traced the contours of first the hibiscus and then her jawline.

Baden's breath caught.

"Just beautiful," he said.

Their gazes met. He was so close. It would take barely a movement for them to come together.

"Jesse?"

A wisp of a smile came and went. She saw longing…and something more in his eyes.

And then the moment passed. He stepped away, seemed to gather himself emotionally and physically.

"Where to next, Miss Tour Guide?"

Baden felt bereft, as if she'd missed out on something that had spectacular and life-changing potential. But she, too, knew that they played with fire; and fire, like the lava that bubbled below the surface of the islands, could burn. She'd been burned badly once and had no inclination to again experience that emotional upheaval.

So, she too put on a game face and aimed to keep it light. "As you see—" indicating the growing crowd of people, many with cameras "—tourists have found out about our farmers' markets. I think now it's time for you to see some real Hawaii, like the natives."

He bowed and swept a hand forward like a courtier before his mistress. "Lead the way."

Jesse stashed their purchases in the trunk of her Jaguar.

"Nice ride, by the way," he said.

"It's a lease while I'm here on Maui. My Jag at home is the same year but a different model."

From someone else, it may have been a humble brag, but from Baden, it came out like just another Hawaii fact, similar to the ones she'd read him about the different types of leis.

When she got behind the wheel, she slipped on a pair of designer sunglasses, which reminded Jesse that he'd need to get a pair of shades himself since he hadn't thought to bring his own.

"You've done well for yourself here."

"I was lucky in that I had an easily marketable skill and my licensing didn't take long," she said. "The real estate market here is very different than what's going on in North Carolina.

"Most of the places I sold there were your typical middle-class houses or condo units with an occasional big listing that carried a hefty commission. Kona Realty specializes in luxury estates, so most, about 85 percent, of my listings are for multi-million dollar properties. But remember, this is Hawaii and just like some places in California and New York, it doesn't take much to be a million-dollar house. Those are pretty much just your average three-bedroom, two bath homes," she said. "And they look just like the ones you see in North Carolina. The difference between them is simply the types of trees you'll find and the location."

Baden glanced at him and grinned. "And Hawaii is the ultimate in the realty world's mantra of 'location, location, location.'"

Jesse chewed on that for a bit. After living in a place that was God's little glimpse of Paradise on earth, she would probably never want to return to eastern North Carolina. Who would? He'd been in Hawaii for little time at all and was falling in love with the place.

Or was he falling in love with the place the woman he loved loved? The question made his head hurt.

"How long are you here?" Baden asked. "In Hawaii, I mean?"

"I have a while," Jesse said. "My vacation is six weeks."

Baden gave him a sharp look.

"Six weeks? Sean would have killed for..."

She let the rest of that go unsaid, then, recovering from the apparent emotional land mine, she gave him a perky smile, like a TV news anchorwoman hyped up on coffee and Red Bull while reading about devastation and destruction across the globe.

"If you're in Hawaii for that long, you should consider leasing a condo," she said. "It'll be cheaper than a hotel, and you'll get all the comforts of a place that feels like home."

"You have any place in mind?"

She gave him a look that without a word said *Duh!*

"We can look at some if you'd like."

If it meant spending more time with Baden, Jesse was ready, willing and able to look at every vacant condo on Maui. Now all he had to do was figure out how to suggest they go swimming so he could see her in a barely there bikini. She had legs that went on forever, and judging by the strong muscles in the smooth brown thigh revealed with her short skirt, she worked out, too.

He could imagine those legs wrapped tight around him.

Jesse groaned.

The lascivious thoughts were wreaking havoc on his body. He shifted a bit in the seat of the Jaguar, hoping not to draw attention to the evidence of his arousal.

"What's wrong?" Baden asked.

"Nothing," he said, probably too gruff.

Not for the first time he wondered if the thing—was it a craving?—he had had for Baden Calloway for as long as he could recall would ever go away. But to her, he took the edge off the growl by adding, "So, where are we going?"

"To a place that cannot be found in any tour books or guides to the islands. And all the customers have sworn to never let the Food Network or the Cooking Channel or those Travel Channel roaming chefs know that Uncle Jimmy's even exists."

"Ah, here it comes," Jesse said. "You're gonna make me eat something like a lizard burger, aren't you?"

She flashed a saucy smile his way. "It would serve you right if I did. But no, we're going to a place that most tourists never heard of, and we aim to keep it that way. So you're sworn to secrecy."

"Hmm," he replied.

She said it took twenty minutes to get to their destination and instead of dwelling on their shared and troubled past, Baden assumed the role of tour guide, pointing out things along the way and giving him a running commentary on the islands' history and culture.

"Are you sure you aren't with the Chamber of Commerce or the Hawaii Tourism Association?"

She glanced over at him and smiled. "I told you, when I fell in love with Hawaii, it became a part of me."

When she finally pulled into the crushed oyster shell parking lot of a place that looked like a ramshackle fishing shack, Jesse gave her a dubious look.

"Do not judge a book by its cover," she said leading the way to the entrance.

No sign proclaimed that the place was a business, let alone a restaurant, but the lot was jammed with cars, pickup trucks and a few motorcycles and scooters. The lunch rush?

At best and most generously it could be described as a dive. At worst, well, it was probably best not to think of the worst, Jesse decided.

The interior of the place lived up to the promise from outside. The "restaurant" Baden called Uncle Jimmy's had about fifteen, maybe as many as twenty smallish tables of rough-hewn wood, many of them looking like rejects from a yard sale after a hurricane. The chairs weren't chairs at all, but benches designed for function not comfort.

Jesse wasn't a foodie but he knew this place would never win any awards for its ambience.

A line of people was at the counter, and the tables where diners were already sitting were covered with what looked like a big sheet of paper. A moment later, a woman passed by pulling a contraption that looked like a giant roll of parchment or waxed paper on a spindle. At the tabletops without a covering she pulled a length of the paper from the roll, tore it off and headed to the next table.

"What is that?" he asked Baden.

"Newsprint. The guy who owns the place buys it from the local newspaper. He says it's cheaper than washing and maintaining linens or getting place mats printed up. When you finish eating, you gather up your trash, ball it up and toss it in either the trash if there's leftover food or in the recycling bin over there."

She handed him a small laminated card, and they got in line behind six other customers waiting to put in their orders at the counter.

"The wait isn't too long for a table," Baden said. "A lot of orders are takeout. Menu," she added to explain the card. "There are only six things on it. All of them are wonderful though, so whatever you get is going to be good."

"Hmm," he said. "Six? That's not much to choose from."

"You're just a regular Doubting Thomas, aren't you?"

"No. I'm just a cop who has had his share of heartburn from bad food in greasy spoons."

She laughed. "Well, I think you're going to be pleasantly

surprised with your lunch today. My treat since you're such a wuss."

"Hey, I resemble that!"

She shook her head at Jesse. "I'm having a number three," she told him without even looking at the menu. "It's my favorite."

"Then I'll have that, too."

Baden took the menu from him and flipped it over. "What do you want to drink?"

They moved up a place in line.

Jesse snorted in amusement. "Just six food choices but there's no skimping on the libations, huh?"

More than a dozen different kinds of beers, domestic and imported, were listed, as was a full line of sodas, fizzes, waters and tropical creations. While a cold beer sounded refreshing on the warm summer day, he remembered her advice about the *locavore* movement and opted for one of the local beverages, a Kula strawberry concoction that he prayed didn't come with a little umbrella in it.

"That has a kick to it," Baden said. "It has two kinds of rum."

He spread his hands. "While in Hawaii…"

She grinned.

Just a couple minutes later, they were placing their orders. And before long, they settled at one of the tables ready to enjoy piping-hot food.

It all looked kind of foreign to Jesse, and he said as much.

"There's more to the culinary universe than Carolina-style pulled pork, coleslaw and an ice-cold Bud."

"But nothing better."

"So you say," she said in a singsong voice. "We'll just see what you're saying after a couple bites."

A few minutes later, he had to take that statement back.

"Oh, my God. What did you say this is called?"

"Laulau," Baden said. "It's pork, beef and chicken with taro. They wrap and steam them in *ti* leaves. It's like, well, I guess its closest mainland cousin would be a burrito."

"I think I'm gonna need to get another order of it."

"What? You're skipping the bugs and the alligator toes, and what was it—lizard burgers?"

He smirked and got up to place an extra order of the *laulau.*

"Save some room for *haupia,* our dessert," Baden called after him. "It's a coconut pudding that's gonna curl your toes."

His gut tightened. Jesse didn't know what was turning him on more, Baden or the way she referred to Hawaiian food.

He glanced back at her and grinned. "Promises, promises."

Heat rose to Baden's cheeks.

Jesse may have been talking about food, but the look in his eyes said he was hungry for something else entirely.

Chapter 3

Baden could not sleep that night. She padded to the kitchen of the cottage for a glass of warm milk. When she realized the very idea turned her stomach, she slipped on a silk wrapper and wandered outside to walk the grounds. She found the tropical garden soothing and definitely needed *something* to soothe her raging thoughts.

An image of being wrapped up in Jesse Fremont's strong arms came to mind.

Not that!

Although she had no doubt that, after a night of passion with Jesse, she would fall soundly, contentedly and deeply into a satiated sweet oblivion.

Along the garden pathway, Baden paused and bent to inhale the luxurious and calming scent of a hibiscus flower. Then meandered to the garden bench at the base of a *kukui* tree. Its white and yellow blooms somehow reminded her of home.

Keeping her cool under pressure served Baden well in sell-ing high-end real estate. She had negotiated complex deals by maintaining her cool. Always. She knew how to ride and best the storms, hers coming in the form of millionaires and a few billionaires who were used to flunkies and "yes men" fawning over them. But Baden was a Calloway and she, like every other Calloway, played hardball to win.

She also played poker with the best of them. She had earned superfat commissions and bonuses and every one of the Kona Realty Company's top sales awards by knowing when to push and when to retreat. She always played her hands well.

But now. This. This was something else entirely.

She got up and continued her meandering, pausing at the pool and hearing the ocean just a few steps away.

This business with Jesse, well, it wasn't business. It was personal. And for a long time now, she'd relegated *personal* to a dark corner of a closet she didn't use anymore.

She wanted Jesse.

The discipline she had honed at the negotiating table in the cutthroat real estate market served her well today. She'd kept her game face intact even though she'd been quivering on the inside.

She wanted Jesse Fremont.

After the initial shock to her system, she'd pulled herself together. Her idea to play impromptu tour guide had been a stroke of not genius but brilliance. It got her out of the con-fines of the estate and the cottage. At three thousand square feet, they hadn't really been on top of each other in the guest cottage, but Baden felt closed in, claustrophobic and on edge.

She knew what the problem was. And she knew that the elephant in the room between them would be there no mat-ter what. And so she'd run. Again.

It was infinitely simpler to get out and play, as Jesse called her, the Miss Hawaii Chamber of Commerce.

Showing him Hawaii was easy. Talking about the past, not so much.

Now though, as the lush tropical night wooed her on the lanai, she had no shield. No farmers' market or local hot spot to keep her distracted. No tourism brochures to parrot with a running commentary on island culture and customs.

With a year and a half to buffer her defenses, she found them stripped away in an afternoon. She was Baden Calloway, the runaway bride-to-be of Cedar Springs, North Carolina.

She'd embarrassed Sean, a good man whose only fault was that he had loved her.

She'd embarrassed her family, though they all stood beside and behind her during the ordeal.

But most of all, she'd embarrassed herself. While she could apologize to her family and eventually come to terms with what she'd done, there was no longer the time she thought she would have or the opportunity to apologize to Sean... to explain to him why she'd bolted. He had deserved an explanation. His death had meant that she would forever carry the guilt.

And now, now, when she had finally made some peace with herself, started a new life, learned that she could be more than her reputation back home, back home had come knocking on her front door and disrupting her life.

She hadn't run away from her wedding because of Sean.

He didn't know that. Sean hadn't known. Baden had not wanted to even acknowledge the fact to herself. But it was true.

How could she stand before God, sharing vows for a lifetime with Sean, when a part of her kept wondering if the better thing was someone else?

How pathetic was that?

* * *

Later that night at the time-share resort he'd leased for a week, Jesse stood on the balcony and watched the sun go down on the beach and wondered if he'd have the nerve to tell Baden why he'd really come to Hawaii.

Spending such a wonderful day with her made him realize that he needed to give her the message from Sean that he'd come to deliver…and that, after he did, she would probably never speak to him again.

He glanced at the envelope on the dresser top, then uttered an expletive.

There was no *probably* about it. She'd hate him for what he had to tell her and for withholding the information all this time.

Baden wasn't surprised to get a text message from Jesse first thing the next morning. He thanked her for the tour and the meal at Uncle Jimmy's, then asked if she were free that day.

As in for a date? she wanted to ask, but didn't.

It didn't matter if he was asking her out. A part of her was glad, very glad, she had appointments booked for most of the day, including shepherding the Lis on their home-buying visit to Maui.

She texted Jesse back that she wasn't available.

Then, biting her lip and wondering if what she was thinking was a really good idea, she sent another text message telling him when she *would* be free to see him.

"Let's go *holoholo*," Baden said.

Jesse had not the first clue what that meant, but it sounded like something that involved Baden not wearing many clothes, so he was all for it and told her as much two days later.

"Should I change into trunks?" he asked.

She gave him a quizzical look and then smiled. For Jesse, that smile was like the sun rising off the east side of his hotel room. "Do you even know what *holoholo* means?"

"I can't even spell it," he admitted.

She gave him the spelling and then added, "It just means hang out, do nothing in particular. You know, like a Sunday drive to nowhere."

He would hang out in hell with her if she asked. But Jesse just nodded. "Sounds cool. You can show me this island you fell in love with."

She cocked her head in that little way that he'd come to recognize and identify as her "considering things" look.

"I'll drive," she said.

Since his rental was a standard-issue sedan, slate gray, late model and looked like all the others he'd seen, he had absolutely no objection to cruising in her luxury Jag.

"About that condo you suggested earlier," Jesse began as she whipped into the island traffic and waved a thank-you when another driver let her in.

"Uh-huh."

"Can we look at a couple of them?"

She grinned. "Really?"

When he nodded, she smiled even broader. "Sweet!"

He laughed and settled in to watch her drive. He loved the way she handled the powerful car.

Relaxed and comfortable, he braced his hands behind his head, happy to just be in her company.

"Show me what your clients see," he said.

Jesse did not really have a plan for his stay in Hawaii. He'd simply come to the place where Baden was.

And he hadn't lied when he had told her that he had a hotel. It was a resort recommended by a cop buddy who rented out time-share units he owned. Jesse claimed a week and figured he would find Baden then go home. The only plan he had after that was to spend the other five weeks of his forced exile from work catching up on projects around his house, projects he'd let go undone for too long—cleaning the gutters, painting, putting in some drywall in his den, a job unfinished from the last nor'easter. That storm blew through doing damage, but not enough to warrant an insurance claim, the deductible or the hassle of the paperwork and forms his insurance company would require.

When given the choice of being Mr. Home Improvement or breathing in the scent of Baden Calloway, Jesse knew he'd let his house fall into ruin without regret or the slightest remorse.

Thank you, Dr. Kleinmann, he thought.

It was the first kind thought he'd ever had for the police department's shrink for hire.

He even spared a warm thought to the airline that would make him pay through the nose for changing the date of his return flight reservation.

When Baden mentioned something about renting a condo, he leaped at the opportunity to spend even a bit of innocuous time with her.

An hour later he realized that he hadn't exactly been specific enough on what his realistic budget was like.

The first one they looked at was the sort of place A-list Hollywood stars and professional athletes who sported Super Bowl rings and championship trophies might rent out for a Hawaiian getaway.

The great room was a three-story affair that had open and railless staircases winding up on either side of the room. A curved sofa big enough and long enough to comfortably seat the entire defensive line of the National Football League's Carolina Panthers was the centerpiece of the room. The place was clearly for someone who entertained very large groups of people very often.

"You do remember that I'm a cop, right? A cop from North

Carolina," he added as if to remind her about his decent, but still-modest salary as a public servant. "This is like a high-roller's suite on the Las Vegas strip."

Baden laughed. "You said 'show me the type of place you'd present to your clients.'"

He frowned. "Who are those people, Bill Gates and company?"

He'd been joking, but she said, "Close. I've sold to a couple of Microsoft execs. Many of my clientele are from Pacific Rim countries looking for a Hawaiian retreat."

"Well, that place back there sure fits the bill. I'm afraid to even ask how much it would cost."

She told him anyway.

Jesse stared in amazement. Just to lease the place for six months cost more than he made in a year.

"How about something a little more realistic? I just need a place to sleep for a few weeks."

Shaking her head, Baden made a *tsk-tsk* sound.

"A home, even a temporary one, should be a respite," she said, "a retreat from the hassle and hustle of everyday life. Home should be a place of serenity."

There was wistfulness in her voice that she was unable to mask. Jesse noticed it and knew that she had, as well.

"Do you miss yours?"

Baden didn't pretend to misunderstand. She briefly considered lying because the truth hurt sometimes.

"Sometimes," she told him. "I was actually thinking after I sell the Kapule Garden Estate that I might take a couple weeks and go on...go home to North Carolina." She gave a little self-deprecating laugh. "I was about to say go on vacation, but it sounds crazy to leave a place like this to go on vacation to Cedar Springs, North Carolina."

"You can always return to Paradise."

"Hmm," is all Baden said.

She felt him give her a questioning look, but she didn't elaborate. In truth, she wanted to go home to Cedar Springs. It seemed like forever since she'd seen Aunt Henrietta and Uncle Carlton. But most importantly, she felt a need to go back to North Carolina to finally put to rest the doubts she had had about why she'd never returned.

Since part of the reason for bolting was right here next to her, she may as well finish the thing and return to the scene of her crime.

At first, she knew, it was the sheer humiliation. She didn't want to face her friends, her cousins, her family or former coworkers after pulling so thoroughly a Julia Roberts in *Runaway Bride*. As the days turned into weeks and the weeks into months, it was just easier—it became easier and therefore inevitable—that she stay put and make a new life in a new place.

The islands gave birth to the new Baden, a self-assured professional woman who excelled in all things—except her lingering doubts that she was somehow flawed because she had let things get so far out of hand with Sean. He was a good man who deserved better than she had given him.

Six months ago marked the beginning of the first pangs of homesickness. That's when Aunt Henrietta had called to tell her Sean had been killed in a shoot-out in Raleigh. Online she had read all the reports and followed the case, but North Carolina was practically a world away.

She'd made a life here in Hawaii, a successful one, she had reasoned at the time. She and Sean had been over for a year by that point, and she was fully entrenched in the island life.

When an old girlfriend came to Hawaii on a business trip, they'd gotten together and it was like nothing had changed in Baden's life. She was in consistent, if not regular, contact with her aunt and uncle, so there had been no real reason to go back to Cedar Springs.

The fact that she'd flown into a tailspin when Jesse Fremont appeared on her doorstep was testament that she had unfinished business—of the sentimental variety—to tend to. They needed to talk about Sean. But she didn't want to.

Not yet at least.

Baden once confided to her cousins Phoebe and Sasha that, if she and Sean hadn't hooked up, she'd want to be with Jesse. The three women then spent the next half hour dissecting the pros and cons—they couldn't think of any of the latter—of a ménage à trois featuring each woman with Jesse Fremont and assorted celebrities and athletes.

"What are you smiling at?"

Jesse's question startled her and then made her giggle.

"I was just thinking how great it would be to hang out with my cousins again."

"Which ones? There are about a hundred of you Calloways."

"Phoebe and Sasha, also known as Miss TMZ and Miss Breaking News."

At his puzzled expression, she explained. "You probably don't know Phoebe. She lives in L.A. and Detroit."

He made a wry expression. "Now there's a clash of cultures."

"You ever heard of Jerry Noland?"

"The baller with the Detroit Pistons? Of course. He was traded to the Lakers about…" Jesse's voice faltered.

Baden cocked her head, waiting.

"Your cousin is married to him? The NBA player?"

The incredulousness in his voice made her smile.

"Yep."

"And Sasha is…"

Jesse broke in, slapping his head with his hand. "Sasha Calloway, the TV news anchor? I never even made the connection. Is everybody named Calloway in North Carolina related to you?"

She laughed. "Probably. Our roots run deep and the Calloways are generally breeders. You know," she said, "my folks and my cousin Vanessa were the only ones who had just one child. I was never lonely, though. Who had time to be lonely with tons of cousins always around and about?"

In that moment she realized she didn't know much about Jesse other than that he was a detective.

"What about you?" Baden asked. "Do you come from a big family?"

Jesse glanced out his window for a moment. "I didn't think Hawaii had so much traffic."

"It's the tourist season. Well, it's always tourist season here, but summer brings even more people. Just remember, you're on aloha time now."

He grinned. "Slower than CP Time, huh?"

"Yep."

He settled in his seat.

"My family is mostly in Charlotte," he said answering the question he'd interrupted with one of his own. "I moved east to go to school at East Carolina. I had a full-ride scholarship, so that was one kid my moms didn't have to worry about. I have a sister, older, and a brother, younger. We're stair steps with barely a year separating each of us. So we were all pretty close growing up. Even now. And everybody's still in Carolina, but we're all over the state."

"Being an only child, I think it made it a little easier for me to pick up and leave the way I did." She paused for a moment, her mind going back to the how and why of that leaving. Then, shaking her head as if shaking off the past, she continued. "I didn't have parents or siblings to dissuade me. Aunt Henrietta and Uncle Carlton put up a valiant effort though," she added with a grin.

"They're really good people."

"The best."

She pulled the Jaguar into a parking spot of a complex with lots of palm trees and a waterfall in the front courtyard. "We're here. I think you're going to like this condo."

He did, and signed the lease on the spot.

"Welcome home to Hawaii, Jesse."

Jesse didn't see Baden for two or three days. It seemed like two months after finally having her in sight again. She'd called once in full Realtor role, checking in to see how he liked the condo. Was everything to his satisfaction with the space? Did he need anything from the maintenance office or the building's concierge?

His best effort to steer the short conversation to a more personal level was thwarted by the arrival of one of her overseas clients. He stayed in a state of semiarousal just anticipating the next time he would see her, smell the scent of her, feel the softness of her skin, receive the brilliance of her smile.

"You got it bad, bro," he muttered as he settled into a chair and accepted a menu at a place he'd heard a lot about at the pool.

In the few days he'd been in Maui, he'd developed a taste for the multicultural blend of the local cuisine and especially Portuguese sweet bread and bean soup. Jesse already knew what he would probably order, if they had it here.

Baden would meet him at the restaurant for lunch after she got her clients back to the airport. He'd been looking forward to it with the same amount of anticipation that a six-year-old awaited Santa's arrival on December 25.

He saw her before she spotted him.

She looked like a tropical flower in full bloom. The lightweight, probably silk dress was one that hugged her curves and wrapped at the waist. His gaze traveled the length of her. Again, high-heeled shoes, much higher than her version of "flats." Jesse wasn't complaining. He was a leg man, and Baden was perfection personified in that department…and everywhere else.

Unfortunately, he wasn't the only person to notice.

Male heads turned as she wound her way through the tables to him.

To him.

That helped tamp down the licks of irritation—jealousy?—that made him want to do some serious bodily harm to a couple of the more aggressive leerers.

Chill out, man, he thought. *That is what got you in trouble in the first place.*

Jesse rose and she saw him. The smile that blossomed on her face and in her eyes made his heart sing.

The waiter held a chair for her, but Jesse waved him away. Baden stepped into his arms, practically vibrating. She hugged him hard and then kissed him smack on the lips.

His body responded to the nearness of her, the scent of her. But before he could parlay that exuberant kiss into something more, she was out of his arms and dropping her bag in her chair.

"I sold it, Jesse! I sold it!"

She did a little shimmy dance that had a couple men at nearby tables giving her appreciative once-overs. Glares from Jesse nipped that interest in the bud and, while he was delighted to share in her joy, he damned to hell the Japanese couple who just messed up his play with Baden. In this economy, who had that kind of money to just toss around?

Dammit! He'd just leased a condo because Baden planned to be on Maui until the garden house sold. If she up and went home to Honolulu now, he was screwed and stuck on this island while she was on another.

For her though, he put on the best happy face he could manage.

"The Kapule Garden Estate? That's terrific, Baden."

She pouted with a little moue as she slipped into her seat with his assistance.

"No, not that one. I wish," she said. "It's going to take a while on a property that size. This place is nearby though, and it has been on the market for forever. It was just waiting for the perfect buyer to come love it and I found them."

"Well, congratulations," he said.

And thank You, Jesus.

He got settled at his own place and a waiter appeared with water, menus and a plate of miniature *manapua,* the steamed and stuffed dough balls that he'd first encountered at his time-share place's nightly reception for guests. The tasty little treats were another that Jesse wished he could send home to North Carolina by the gross. Maybe Mrs. Hookano—Mama Melia—could give him a recipe.

"I missed you," he said.

The words were out before he could stop them.

Her buoyancy turned quizzical, and she reached for her water goblet. Her eyes never left his as she took a deliberate sip. Then his hand covered hers as she placed the goblet back on the table.

The moment seemed weighted and expectant with the sort of tension that had always existed between them. A tension that neither had been willing to acknowledge…because of Sean.

Then she said, "I missed you, too, Jesse."

"What do you propose we do about this mutual missing?"

Although he'd asked a question, the husky timbre of his voice left no room for doubt about what he had in mind as a suggestion.

Baden's mouth curved up for a moment and then she shook

her head, sitting back, releasing the pent-up tension that so easily flowed between them.

"Do you know what you do to me?" he asked.

She ran a hand between them. "Yes," she murmured. "I think I do."

"Ah, Baden."

Lunch was a tortured affair as each thought of a better way to spend the time. But neither of them seemed willing to actually take the next step in the relationship, a relationship which was awkward at its best—and at its worst had unfinished business by the name of Sean Mathews. She had left Sean at the altar because she knew she had feelings for Jesse.

"I have to go back to work," she said.

"I know. Tonight."

"Tonight what?"

"My place," he said.

His eyes raked her, his gaze hovering first at her mouth before dipping to the V of her dress and lingering for a moment. When his gaze finally lifted back to hers, Baden was breathing deeply.

After barely a pause, she nodded.

Jesse lifted a brow and his glass in mini-salute. "To tonight."

Chapter 4

Later that evening, a multi-vehicle accident blocked access to the street where Jesse's rental condo was located. Their rendezvous was moved to Baden's temporary residence, the guest cottage at the Kapule Garden Estate.

Secretly, Baden was glad for the distraction. It gave her some breathing room. Since lunch, she'd thought of little else but the heat generated between the two of them. The rest of the workday's business and then the traffic delay and change of venue for their tryst afforded her some room to both breathe and to think—mostly about the consequences of what she'd planned to do with Jesse.

She wanted him. There was no doubt about that—or about the fact that he clearly wanted her.

He was single. She was single.

And Sean stood between them—even from the grave creating a metaphysical divide.

Physically, however, it was the big island in the guest cottage's kitchen that separated them right now. After some awkward chitchat when he'd arrived a few minutes ago, they'd agreed that wine was in order. Instead of waiting for her to return with a bottle and some glasses, Jesse had followed her to the kitchen where she uncorked the wine.

"Looking for more cookies?"

She grinned at her own joke. Jesse smiled, but didn't engage.

My God, she thought. *Is he nervous?* That was a trait she had never associated with him.

When he shoved his hands in his pockets, she knew something was up. In the time she was with Sean, Baden had learned a little about cop body language. The vibe was suddenly wrong. And everything about Jesse right now had her suddenly not thinking about seduction, about the way his sweet enchantment would make her feel, or about the rhapsody that she would find in his arms.

She was having a primal reaction right now and everything in her told her to run.

"Baden, there's something I need to tell you."

She stopped midpour. Something in his voice told her that he was in cop-mode now. She'd heard that tone before, and it never boded well.

The wine forgotten, she came around the kitchen island to stand a few feet from where he stood.

Her insides suddenly in a knot, she braced a hand on the granite counter to steady herself.

"What is it?"

"Let's go sit in the living room and talk."

"We can talk right here, Jesse. What is it you want to say?"

He sighed, then looked toward the living room.

Baden didn't move.

"I need to tell you why I really came to Hawaii. Why I came to see you."

She eyed him warily.

"You said you were on vacation."

He grunted. "Yeah, well, that's one way to put it. I'm on a...forced vacation...from the department."

Baden's mouth dropped open even as she felt a weight lift from her. Was that all?

His eyes narrowed, and she realized she must have voiced the question aloud. She quickly added. "The way you said 'There's something I need to tell you,'" she said mimicking his deeper voice, "that had me scared and worried and thinking the worst."

"You don't think me being off the job, on an...extended vacation is the worst?"

She turned and went around the island to resume pouring wine for them. "What happened?"

"I beat up a guy."

She lifted a brow at that news. Taking a sip of wine, she held out the second glass to him. When he didn't take it, she brought it around to him and placed it on the island counter-top near him.

"What did he do to deserve getting beat up?"

"You're quick to take my side," Jesse said. "You don't even know the details."

She shrugged. "What I do know is that you're a good guy, Jesse, and a good cop. If memory serves correctly about how police internal operations work, you're on desk duty or some-thing—is it called administrative leave?—until they finish up the investigation. Then the bad guy will go to jail, and you'll be back on the streets working major crime or whatever and putting douche bags behind bars."

She took another tiny sip from her glass and regarded him.

Jesse didn't say anything for a long while. So long that the silence became uncomfortable.

"Jesse?"

"I beat the hell out of him because of Sean," Jesse said.
Sean.

There it was. The elephant in the room.

"Sean died six months ago," Baden said.

"I fucking know that," Jesse said.

He ran his hands over his face and head, then apologized. "It's not you I'm angry and frustrated with, Baden. And my timing is all wrong here, but I…" He sighed as if the weight of the world were pressing on his shoulders.

"I need to get this off my chest," he said. Jesse paced for a bit, as if he felt confined.

"You're scaring me, Jesse."

He shook his head. "I'm sorry. That wasn't my intention. Was never my intention." He took a step toward her, but Baden backed up two steps.

He paused. Sighed. "I knew I'd screw this up," he muttered.

The vulnerability she heard in that simple statement eased her. She didn't know what he was trying and failing to say, but it couldn't be as difficult as what she wanted him to know, the very thing she could never confess.

"Baden?"

From her side of the island, she clasped her hands on the granite countertop and waited. "Yes, Jesse."

"I love you."

Chapter 5

Baden stared at him uncomprehending.

Did he just say what she thought he'd said?

She shook her head as if to clear it after an afternoon at home swimming in the waters of Waikiki Beach.

"I came to Hawaii to tell you that," Jesse said. "I know it probably seems out of the blue, but I've been crazy about you since the first day we all met. But you fell for Sean, and I just had to deal with that."

Eyes wide, she stared at him.

She couldn't breathe. She couldn't think. She couldn't even grasp the meaning of the words coming out of his mouth.

"Baden, say something, please."

She shook her head.

"I…"

She shook her head again and then focused on the one thing that she could begin to comprehend even though it made about as much sense as everything else Jesse was saying.

"What did Sean have to do with the guy you beat up?"

"Huh?"

The dam broke then.

The pent-up emotions and regret and fear and anger, that she had managed to control with a steady will, broke through the emotional dam she had so carefully constructed and maintained all these months.

She thought she was ready to face this, but the truth was, on this topic—on the subject of Sean—she was a coward.

"I knew answering the door and letting you into my life, into my house was a mistake," Baden wailed. "Why don't you just go back to North Carolina and wreak some emotional havoc on the people who still live there? I don't, and I don't care about the past."

"I also came to Hawaii to deliver to you a message from Sean."

"Arghh!"

The inarticulate sound was the only thing that came out of her mouth.

If a pot had been on the kitchen island, she would have thrown it at Jesse's head in a fit of temper.

Instead she ran from the kitchen berating herself for always running away from life instead of running toward something.

Jesse followed her.

He caught up with her in the living room of the cottage where she stood near the same chair in almost the same pose as the one she'd been in that first day when he'd arrived. With one arm wrapped about her slender waist, she had the other lifted, her fist pressed to her mouth as if biting back either a full-fledged scream or tears.

She looked as if she wanted to crawl inside herself and disappear.

It hurt Jesse to see her this way, especially since he knew

that what was to come would knock her for an even bigger and probably more devastating emotional loop.

"I think you should go, Jesse."

Her voice was calm, quiet. She had reined in the storm. She'd run out of steam.

The resignation in her voice let him know the immediate storm had passed.

He came up behind her and gently guided her to the chair. Without argument she sank into the fluffy white cushions.

"If you really want me to leave, I will," he said.

Jesse wasn't necessarily a praying man, but he prayed then and there that she would let him stay.

She didn't say anything. She just sat there.

"Baden?"

She gave a slight nod. He would have missed it had he not been studying her so intently.

He let out a breath. "Okay," he said. "Okay. Thank you."

He settled on the edge of the sofa near her and braced his hands on his knees.

"I need to be honest with you and with myself," he said. "I came here, to Hawaii, specifically to find you."

"Why?"

Her look clearly conveyed the "as if I care" message as if it were in glowing neon.

"Because I made a promise to look you up if I was ever in Hawaii."

"A promise to who?"

This was the hard part.

He didn't want to dredge up hurtful memories, but there was little help for it. Everything from here on out was going to be a field strewn with land mines and live grenades.

"Sean," he said. "I made a promise to Sean."

Baden jerked as if he had hit her. Then, blinking several

times, she stood up and took a step backward, as if away from the Grim Reaper.

"Sean is dead."

Her words sounded hollow, devoid of inflection or any emotion.

From his pocket he pulled out a small envelope. Inside was a photograph that he more than suspected would just make things worse.

He held the envelope out to her.

"Sean gave this to me and made me promise to deliver it to you, in person, if anything ever happened to him."

Baden eyed the envelope as if Jesse were asking her to pet a hungry rattlesnake. "What is it?"

He leaned forward closing the distance between them and handed it to her.

For a long moment, she held his gaze and then, reluctantly, she lifted the flap on the white envelope. Inside was a photograph of a pretty brown-skinned girl of about fifteen. Her hair was braided and she wore cutoff jean shorts and what looked to be a cotton T-shirt. Something in the girl's features seemed vaguely familiar, but Baden didn't think she knew her.

Then it clicked.

It was the eyes.

The girl's eyes were Sean's eyes.

"Oh, my God," she whispered. "Who is this, Jesse? Is this his daughter? Sean had a daughter? He had a secret family? Is that why he…"

She choked on the words as thoughts tumbled through her mind and long-lost pieces of the puzzle began to appear and slip into the places where for so long there had been nothing but a void.

"I always sensed that there was something he was holding back. He was married, wasn't he?"

The words, flat and lifeless, seemed to come from somewhere deep inside her.

"Baden…"

She kept right on talking. "I knew there was something going on with him. Things weren't right, not the way they should have been, but I just chalked it up to both of us being stressed about work and all the wedding plans."

"Baden," Jesse said, taking her arm and guiding her around the chair. "You need to sit down. Please calm down, baby."

She yanked her arm free and tried, but failed, to blink back the tears.

"Don't try to tell me how I'm supposed to feel, Jesse. You don't know how I feel. You don't know what a betrayal this is."

"Baden," he said gently, "turn the picture over."

Even as he said it, he turned over the photograph in her hand. "He left a message for you."

"What?"

He pointed. "A message for you."

Baden swiped at the tears and glanced down. There was writing on the back of the snapshot but she couldn't seem to focus her eyes through the tears. She sniffled, wiped her eyes more thoroughly and looked at the handwriting on the opposite side of the photograph.

She immediately recognized it.

It was Sean's bold and confident script. She used to tease him about the A+ grades he must have gotten as a boy on his penmanship tests in school.

Sean.

Her eyes misted and she had to blink away new tears.

Letting Jesse Fremont in had been a mistake. She'd known it the moment she'd seen him standing at her front door outside her sanctuary. He was here dredging up the past…a past that was buried and doing just fine there.

Slowly, the words became more than a blur, more than scribble on the back of the photograph. There was a notation on the top, in Sean's writing but faded a bit as if it had been there for a while longer than the other words, *Me. 1993*.

Baden's gaze dropped lower, and she saw the short note written in fine-point blue Sharpie, Sean's pen of choice. She'd purchased a dozen of them for him after he had complained about the cheap ink pens issued by the police department.

She blinked back the distracting memory and focused instead on the rest of the words on the back of the image.

> *Dear Baden. I am sorry. So very, very sorry to have put you through what I did. I loved you then and now. But I wasn't honest with you. A relationship should be based on love as well as on honesty. This is the me I used to be.*
> *S—*

She cast blind eyes up at Jesse. "I don't understand."

But the shell-shocked expression on her face told him she did understand. She was having a hard time wrapping her head around the proof she held in her hands.

"How?"

This time when Jesse guided her toward the chair, she didn't resist. She sank into the plump cushion with the photo in one hand. Her mouth was open, but no words spilled forth.

Jesse had seen the look many times in his career.

Accident victims wore that expression. Tragedy survivors who have not yet realized that they were survivors seemed to be marked with that look. It was shock. They were dazed, confused and unbelieving, even as the reality slowly seeped in, forever changing their reality and view of the world.

She clutched the photo in one hand. Jesse held the other, trying to offer her what comfort he could.

"But, I…" She looked at Jesse, trying to make sense of it. "How can this be?"

When she began to weep, he was there, witness to her heartbreak.

Baden's tears were not the great big racking sobs of someone out of control. They were, instead, silent and all the more sorrowful.

He cursed Sean for leaving him to do the cleanup work, to be the messenger of this news that should have, rightfully, come from Sean. Not from him. Just not from him.

Jesse wanted to maintain his good intention. He wanted to simply hold and comfort Baden as a friend would. But he'd give lie to his own truth if he did that.

Guilt assailed him. He had told her that he loved her.

He wasn't even sure that his revelation registered with her.

And it was unfair for him to have just dumped that on her. Not when he knew what he did about the man she loved. After all, she was still emotionally Sean's woman. Right now though, Baden Calloway was the woman he'd always wanted as his own.

And she was hurting. The very least he could do was comfort her as a friend. He held her close, but Baden suddenly pulled away.

Without even a glance at the photo, she dropped it and skirted his embrace. Her fist was again at her mouth as if holding in a scream as she practically ran from the room.

She was headed to what Jesse figured would be a bedroom or other private place to grieve or cry.

Jesse had had plenty of time, years in fact, to absorb Sean's news. For Baden, it was new. And though both it and Sean were now a part of her past, she needed time to assimilate the information.

He ran a hand over his head, swore and then went to find her.

He passed two open bedroom suites. Had he not been focused on Baden, he would have paused to check out the spaces and the rest of the guesthouse. But he was worried about Baden. When he came to a set of closed double doors, he knew he'd found her.

Jesse knocked on one of the doors.

"Baden?"

He got no answer, but thought he heard water running.

Jesse sighed. He had to give her the space she needed right now.

He returned to the kitchen, picked up his glass of wine and then went to the living room to wait.

She eventually came out—more than half an hour later. She appeared in the living room standing in front of him red-eyed and with her face freshly scrubbed, looking nineteen instead of thirty-one.

"You stayed."

He simply nodded from where he sat on the white sofa, one leg propped on his knee.

"I want to know about Sean," she said.

The old photograph of the Sean she hadn't known even existed lay face down on the oversize ottoman, a not-so-subtle reminder of their unfinished conversation about an unfinished relationship.

The irony was rich; one of those little sucker-punch gifts from the universe that left you gasping for breath and reassessing everything you thought you knew about everything.

"Are you sure?" Jesse asked. "We can talk later if you'd like, if you're not up to it now."

"I've been not talking about Sean for eighteen months," she said. "So, no. Now, Jesse. I need to know now."

She sat on the chair closest to him but continued to stare at the message from her former fiancé.

Baden glanced at the picture then picked it up and read again the message her Sean had left for her. It broke her heart all over again.

She was slow in turning over the photo to look at the young woman Sean Mathews had once been.

"I see him in her," she said, touching the face of the girl in the image. "There's a sadness there that seemed to always be with Sean."

Then, suddenly, she sat up.

"What?" Jesse asked.

"Wh-what was her name?" Baden said nodding toward the picture.

"The same," Jesse said. "It was just spelled differently. *S-h a-u-n*."

Baden nodded, as if that explained everything. But it didn't. Not really.

"Why didn't he tell me? We were together for three years. Three years, Jesse. That's a long time to be with someone and not know such a fundamental part about a person's life."

"I don't know, baby. That person in the picture didn't exist for him. Maybe he thought you wouldn't love him or maybe it was something that… Hell, I don't know, Baden," he said running his hands over his head and then his face. "I've been over and through this a million times myself, and I'm no closer to having any answers. Whatever Sean wanted to say or get off his chest died with him."

"He spent a good portion of his life tormented and I didn't even know." Baden curled her feet under her on the sofa. "I thought about going home for his funeral."

"Why didn't you?"

She shrugged, then picked up one of the fringed throw pillows and hugged it to her.

"What would have been the point? Aunt Henrietta sent me all the newspaper clippings. I mourned in my own way.

And this," she said, "this note from my Sean about that other Shaun is like losing him again—for the third time."

Tears sprang to her eyes again.

Jesse winced as if he'd taken a blow. In a way he had. She'd just professed to still loving Sean.

Sean had been dead for six months, and it had been more than a full year and a half since that fateful afternoon when Baden had walked out of the Chapel of the Groves in Cedar Springs instead of marrying his partner. She'd done it with élan, though. Beautiful in a white lace gown and tear-streaked face, she stood before their friends and family and announced that the wedding was off.

He'd never forget her courage that day. She'd stood at the altar, her Aunt Henrietta and Uncle Carlton on either side of her supporting her through the ordeal. They were the parents she didn't have and loved her like one of their own daughters.

"I can't do this," she'd said. "I'm sorry. Everyone's here and there's tons of food and a beautiful cake, so please, go party," she told the two hundred stunned guests.

She then turned to leave, her uncle's arm around her shoulder as she clutched her aunt's hand. "Oh," she said, bravely facing the people who had come to wish her well. "As for the gifts, please take them with you or if you'd like, donate them to the Common Ground ministries."

That was the last moment any of them saw her again.

Jesse had found out later that she'd left the church, changed her clothes and went to the Raleigh-Durham International Airport where she spent the night until the early morning flight that would take her to her honeymoon destination: Honolulu, Hawaii.

As for the elegantly wrapped wedding gifts, he wondered if Mr. and Mrs. Calloway sent their niece a copy of the story from the weekly newspaper the *Cedar Springs Gazette* about Baden's generosity in the midst of her personal anguish.

Common Ground was a partnership among three diverse churches in Cedar Springs. Developed by the pastors as a means to spark a spiritual reawakening in the community while uniting the churches and offering aid to those in need, Common Ground operated a soup kitchen, a homeless shelter, a medical clinic and a recreation program for kids, teenagers and adults.

As a result of the non-wedding of Baden Calloway and Sean Mathews, the soup kitchen got everything from an espresso maker to top-of-the-line cookware, while Cedar Springs' homeless who spent nights in the Common Ground shelter benefited from and luxuriated on eight-hundred-thread-count Egyptian cotton sheets and toweled off after showering by using fluffy monogrammed bath linens, all courtesy of the guests who'd come to wish Sean and Baden a happily ever after.

Embarrassed at how she'd completely fallen apart on him, Baden pushed back, sniffled and wiped her eyes.

"I'm sorry," she said. "I thought I'd cried out all the tears in the bathroom."

"You have nothing to be sorry about."

She picked up the photograph that had fallen to the floor at some point. She sat there, staring at the girl.

"I never guessed," she said. "I never even suspected anything like this."

Jesse gave her the silence she needed to work through her feelings.

"Who would have even imagined anything like this, let alone suspected?" she asked. "I mean, I've heard of people finding out their partner was gay or married to a convicted felon, but this? There was nothing in or about Sean that even remotely hinted that he was born…"

Her words faded away as she worked through it all, still

fuzzy on why Sean had kept such a big part of his past secret from the woman he had supposedly loved.

Then, as her brain started fully functioning again, she realized a hard truth: Jesse's complicity in the matter.

"You knew! You knew and didn't say anything."

Jesse shook his head, denying the accusation.

"It wasn't my place or my truth to say anything," he said. "And until he gave me that photo a month before he died, I thought you knew. You were going to marry him," he said simply. "I thought you knew."

Baden shook her head.

"You were the future he wanted."

"Apparently not enough," she said.

She didn't even try to keep the bitterness out of her voice.

"The girl in that picture was his past, Baden. He loved you."

Almost reverently she placed the photo on the oversize ottoman that served as a coffee table.

"I know."

She sat there quietly, evidently for so long that Jesse got worried.

"You gonna be okay?"

She looked at him, almost surprised to even see him still there.

Baden took a deep breath and nodded.

Placing her hands on her thighs, she stared at the photo of the old Sean, and then placed it back in the envelope.

"I need some air."

She stood up, but didn't move.

When she swayed a bit, Jesse was beside her in an instant.

She stepped away from him.

"I'm not going to faint, Jesse," she said. "At least I don't think so."

He left her side and went to the kitchen. When he returned

with a glass of juice from her refrigerator, Baden was nowhere to be seen.

Then he saw the sheer panel of curtains flutter. She'd gone
outside. He went back to the kitchen, giving her a moment.

Lord knew the news he'd dumped on her would take a
while to process. He'd had years to get used to the idea of
Sean as that other person. That girl in the photograph with
the sad eyes *was* another person, one he hadn't known. How
had Sean gone so far as to have asked Baden to marry him
without telling her about his past?

Jesse found her on the lanai. She was staring at the sky.

It took him a moment to realize she was crying again.

Jesse came up behind her. He gathered her in his arms, his
chin on the top of her head and held her, just held her, offering what comfort he could.

Her silent tears ate at him.

Did she cry because she'd been lied to by Sean? Were her
tears of regret about the way they'd ended?

Before he could put voice to either question, she turned in
his arms, wrapped her own around his neck and pressed her
body and her mouth to his.

Chapter 6

He wanted to resist and knew he should.

He told himself that this was something she might regret in the morning.

He told himself that she was just trying to affirm her femininity in the wake of emotional upheaval.

He suspected it might be transference of emotion.

And he knew that grief and mourning came in all guises. In his years as a cop, first on patrol and later as a detective, he'd seen everything from total physical collapse and seemingly inappropriate-for-the-moment humor to stunned silence and abject denial. People reacted in all kinds of ways both expected and unexpected.

While he had had years to process and absorb the information about Sean's former life, Baden was just discovering critical truths about the man she been ready to pledge her life and love to.

He silently cursed Sean for leaving him with the cleanup

job, but was also thankful that his former partner afforded him the opportunity to see Baden again.

But the soft woman in his arms made it hard for him—in more ways than one—to focus on the reasons they shouldn't be doing this, especially since he'd wanted her for so long, so very, very long.

The kiss made him ache. He trembled with the want of her.

"Baden," he murmured, his mouth teasing her.

In response, she pressed closer to him.

Jesse groaned.

Then, with one last taste of Baden's sweet nectar, he pulled away.

"Jesse, don't you want me?"

He closed his eyes for a moment trying to get himself under control.

"God, Baden. I want you more than you know, almost more than I can stand."

She tried to again wrap her arms around his neck, but Jesse held firm, gently pushing her away.

"Baden, I want you. But not like this," he said. "I want us to be together because it's us. Not with Sean between us. Not with you still coming to grips about who he was and maybe getting that confused with what's going on between us now."

Her eyes narrowed and she stood taller.

"Get out."

This time, Jesse didn't question if she really meant it. Baden needed time and space. He needed a cold shower.

Without another word, he turned and left.

More than two hours and three glasses of wine later, Baden found sleep eluded her. Her thoughts continued to race with questions, questions and more questions. She regretted that she had let her emotions rather than her head, and her good sense, respond to the news about Sean.

Inside the three-thousand-square-foot guest cottage seemed as tight as a broom closet, more a claustrophobic prison cell than Hawaiian oasis. So she wandered the grounds of the Kapule Garden Estate, grateful for both its seclusion and the privacy the large property afforded.

As she walked, she wondered why, even after all the time that had passed since her wedding day and even after the months since Sean's tragic death, she felt so psychologically bound to Sean.

About a quarter after two in the morning, she figured it out: the goodbye went undone.

The unfinished business between them is what caused her guilt then...and now. That she no longer had the opportunity to explain to Sean why she'd left, and he no longer had the opportunity to tell her about that other Shaun, the girl he'd been.

But Sean had sent Jesse.

Had he known, maybe on a subconscious level, that she was interested in his partner?

Jesse had told her that Sean gave him the photo to deliver to her a month before he died. A month.

A month before he died in that shoot-out in Raleigh, Sean gave Jesse the photograph with its apology to deliver.

Had there been more to his death than what was reported by the papers and the television stations back home?

The Sean she knew was brave, true, a cop's cop. Would he have deliberately put himself in danger in the hope of getting killed in the line of duty—suicide by cop, but in a different fashion?

The very thought seemed ludicrous. But so, too, did the thought that the muscular and masculine Sean Mathews that she'd fallen in love with had spent the early part of his life as a female.

Baden rolled those thoughts and questions over and over in her head, considering what she knew then and what she now knew. What she now knew wasn't enough, though. She felt lost, confused and terribly, terribly alone.

Jesse had been right in rejecting her advance.

Great, another thing to feel guilty about, she thought.

Trying to jump Jesse's bones was a rebound move if ever one existed.

She could apologize to him for that. Right now, however, she had questions, quite a few of them in fact. And she knew who could answer those questions.

Jesse Fremont, she knew, had the answers.

When his cell phone pinged with an incoming text message, Jesse scowled.

His sister, with no accounting for the time differences, had sent three texts and two emails in the last twenty-four hours. He wasn't in the mood to deal with yet another of her well-meaning platitudes about his forced leave of absence.

In bed, but wide awake, unable to sleep since leaving Baden, he'd stretched out on top of the sheets. He glanced at the phone, though, ready to delete the message. The number caught his eye, however. It wasn't a familiar 919 or 252 area code of North Carolina or even one of many he recognized as friends scattered across the country.

There was just one telephone number in his cell phone's directory that started with 808. Hawaii.

Baden. I could really use a hug right now.

It was almost two-thirty in the morning but Jesse didn't hesitate.

Chapter 7

She sat in the dark, the only illumination came from the pool's recessed lights and the miles of fairy lighting strewn throughout the garden. She needed to tell Deato Kauhane that they could go off timer and onto motion activation now that the prospective buyers were gone.

But Baden didn't need light to see the photograph in her lap, to remember exactly what it looked like.

"It's beautiful here at night."

His voice didn't surprise or startle her.

"I was sure the cop in you would first remark about the open front door."

"It went noted," Jesse said, "but I figured you'd just done that this once."

Baden smiled.

"You got here awfully fast."

"Your text sounded like a 9–1–1. That's my specialty."

She smiled bigger, knowing he couldn't see it. "Come on around and enjoy the view."

"Did you want that hug now or later?"

"Later," she said.

"That's what I thought," Jesse said as he settled on the chaise next to hers and dropped his keys on the table between them.

"I come out here to think," she said. "And clearly I have apparently been doing too much of that tonight."

"Couldn't sleep?"

"Nope. Even the wine didn't have much of an effect."

She shifted to her side so she could see him in the intimate darkness.

"When I realized it was you at my door, I was angry and pissed and hurt and confused. Your very presence interrupted my self-imposed sentence of solitary confinement and dragged me back to that day. Back to what I'd done. What I had left behind."

"And now?"

"Now? Well, I'm just confused, and still a little hurt. Why didn't he tell me?"

"I don't know, Baden. Maybe he was afraid you wouldn't love him, wouldn't want to be with him."

She sat up, pulled her legs under her and regarded Jesse.

"Did he tell you, about her I mean?"

Baden, despite her protests to the contrary, was still having a rough time getting her head around the whole thing. That girl in the photo didn't exist for her and was like another person—Sean's sister or cousin or a distant relation. But not Sean. Not ever Sean.

"We were partners, Baden. That relationship is close. Sometimes closer than a married couple's because so much is on the line. The job…" He shook his head. "The job is why a lot of cop marriages fail in real life, not just on TV. You have to depend on that person to have your back. Your life, your partner's life depends on that."

"Jesse," she said reaching for his hands as understanding dawned. "It sounds like you're blaming yourself for what happened. Sean's death wasn't your fault."

He pulled away from her, not wanting or appreciating either her sympathy or her empathy.

"Yeah," he said. "It was. And it's more complicated than you know."

"Then help me understand."

He remained silent for a while. Then, almost reluctantly, he turned his back to her.

"We were partners, Baden. Your partner on the street has to know that you have his back unconditionally, one hundred and fifty percent. So, yeah, we talked. He told me."

She cocked her head as if divining the truth from him.

"When?" she asked. "When did he tell you?"

Jesse sighed, then swung around to face her, their knees almost touching.

"About a year after we were partnered up," he said. "We were on a case. There were a couple transvestites mixed up in it and a ruckus when they were busted for prostitution. They were both put in male holding cells. They wanted to be in the female cells. Needless to say, there were a lot of off-color comments in the squad room.

"Later, we were on the way to Fayetteville to interview a witness in another case. He told me then."

"What did he say exactly?"

He reached down for her hand, but Baden scooted away.

"Why do you want to go over all this?" he asked. "It's history."

"It's history to you, Jesse, but it's new to me. You dumped it all in my lap last night with that photo. I'm just trying to understand."

Jesse nodded. "I'm sorry, Baden. I get that."

He ran a hand over his close-cropped hair. "I get that," he repeated. Expelling a breath, he again cursed Sean for leaving him with the dirty job of being messenger and particularly under these circumstances.

"We were sitting in the car when he said, 'I need to tell you something, and I hope it won't change things between us.' He said he thought he understood what the trannies, I mean, the uh, transvestites, were complaining about. I made some smart-ass remark like 'Why, Sean, you gonna tell me you're really a girl?' He looked at me and said, 'I used to be.'"

Baden's gaze held no censure, no condemnation. She just looked curious.

"We were late getting to the witness," Jesse said. "He told me how he'd always felt like a boy, even when he was little. By the time he was twelve and had hit puberty, he said he thought he was gay because he didn't like boys the way all his friends did. At fifteen, when that picture was taken, he'd done tons of research and said he knew he'd been born in the wrong body. He started saving money then because he said he knew he was really a man trapped in a woman's body."

"That's awfully mature for a teenager."

"He was lucky. Much luckier than most kids who have gender and sexuality issues at that age."

"It doesn't sound very lucky," Baden said. "It sounds horrible and sad and very lonely. There was a gay kid in my class in middle school, a white boy named Aaron, no, Avery. Avery Bronson. His father was a preacher, one of those fire and brimstone Southern Evangelical Baptists. You know the type. Avery tried to kill himself a couple times and finally succeeded because he was bullied so much, and his father was probably telling him he was going to hell. I doubt if he'd think he was lucky."

Jesse shook his head. "That's what I thought until Sean told me he had strong family support."

"Family support? Sean didn't have any family. He only mentioned a couple aunts or some relations who were…"

She stopped as Jesse continued his head shake. "Another thing I didn't know," she surmised.

"Sean had family," Jesse said. "He called them and I quote here meaning no disrespect, but he called them 'a merry band of flakes, fags and fag hags.'"

Baden closed her eyes. "I didn't know him at all, did I? I was going to marry someone I thought I knew and loved, and it turns out I didn't know him at all."

"You knew what mattered," Jesse said.

Baden pointed to the picture in her lap. "This tells me differently."

"I think the only thing Sean died regretting was not telling you about his former life. But, Baden, keep in mind that he lived his entire adult life as the Sean you knew. He had the surgery when he was eighteen. He took a year or so to acclimate and when he enrolled in college as a freshman, he was Sean."

Baden eyed him. "You were okay with it?"

Jesse shrugged. "It took me a minute to take it all in."

When she lifted a brow, he smiled.

"All right, it was more than a minute. But in the end, it didn't matter," Jesse said. "But I've learned a lot since that night. That girl was from another life, someone I didn't know and couldn't even see in him no matter how he was born. Sean Mathews was a good friend, a good cop and a good man. And I was jealous as hell that he had you."

They fell quiet after that, each lost in his or her private thoughts and memories. The only sounds between them came from water rippling in the grotto and the calls and squawks of the tropical birds that made the garden their home.

"I'm trying to process all of this," Baden eventually said.

"Which part?"

She let out a little laugh. "All of it, Jesse. All of it. And I'm not ignoring what you said."

She needed to be sure he understood what she referred to and added, "About me. Us. It's—it's a lot to take in."

Boy, was it ever.

The man she had been trying not to think about was right here in front of her. Jesse Fremont was part of the reason she'd walked away from Sean. Now, here she was dealing with Sean again, and this time he was coming between Baden and the man she wanted.

Jesse's rebuff had hurt.

She wanted him and knew he wanted her. But he was being so frustratingly honorable.

Baden knew the timing was off. The timing was always off when it came to her and Jesse Fremont. The memory of his kiss, his hot mouth on hers still lingering, making her want to taste even more of him. But he had—her brain knew—done the right thing in pushing her aside. He probably thought she was turning to him for physical comfort while jostling any lingering feelings for Sean. But what she and Sean had was over long before their actual aborted wedding. Yes, she would always love Sean, but not *that* way.

How could she make Jesse understand that?

Baden felt torn between two worlds and versions of reality. There was the one she had actually lived and thought she knew, and the one that cast a new meaning on that history.

On top of that was Jesse.

Her feelings for him were wrapped up with her memories of Sean. But Sean was dead, and she had moved on physically. It was time to do the same emotionally, as well. Maybe that's why she'd been thinking about making a visit home to North Carolina. And then the universe or God or fate had sent North Carolina to her front door.

"It shouldn't matter," she said. "About Sean, I mean. But it's unfinished business, like not finishing a book or walking out of a movie when there's still fifteen minutes left of it."

"Sean is gone," Jesse said.

Baden nodded. "After I left him like that, I thought he might try to reconcile. You know, come out here, beg me to change my mind, try to explain that my cold feet were just a bad case of nerves, wedding-day jitters. I had this whole scenario worked out in my head about how it would all go down."

"You feel cheated."

She lifted pain-filled eyes to him. "No," she said. "I feel guilty and petty."

"Baden. There's something else."

She jumped up and backed away and put her hands over her ears like a child not willing to listen to bad news.

"Baden."

She dropped her hands. "Jesse, I don't think I can process much more of this."

He rose, came to her and took her hands in his.

"You need to know this part," he said. "There's nothing for you to feel guilty about, especially when it comes to the wedding that wasn't."

She grimaced at that, but Jesse forged on before Baden could voice an objection.

"I've been straight-up with you about my feelings for you," he said. "For a long time I walked around thinking I was just wrong for wanting my partner's woman. But something Sean told me, much, much later, made me realize that sometimes life does offer second chances and opportunities for do-overs."

He caressed her hands, running his fingers over the sensitive skin of her palm.

She swallowed, looked at his hands on hers and rallied her thoughts to focus on the words instead of the actions.

"Okay, Jesse. What did he say?"

"That he was glad you'd run. You just beat him to the moment."

Of all the things she may have expected him to say—things like Sean had changed his mind and wanted to be female again or that he was quitting the police department to become a private detective or something—this was the very last.

"Excuse me?"

"You heard right, Baden. You were minutes away from being a jilted bride instead of a runaway bride. I didn't know that he hadn't reconciled his past with you. So when he told me that, I just figured he was the one having second thoughts about getting married. In a way, he was glad you'd called it off."

Baden yanked her hands from his and turned away.

"This pisses me off more than the not telling me about her."

"Why?"

"Because," she said, "it's like we were actors in a bad romance novel or something. God, we spent thousands of dollars and months of preparation for a wedding that neither of us wanted. And not a word said about our doubts because we were afraid of hurting the other person. We were idiots."

"Don't say that, baby."

She shook her head, whether at his words or the endearment, he didn't know.

Tell her!

Everything in Jesse propelled him to tell her the rest of it, the whole truth. How and why he'd ended up suspended from his job, under police department review and in Hawaii...all because of her and because of Sean.

Six months after the shoot-out that had claimed his partner's life, Jesse was in Hawaii with the woman who had a direct nexus to both the killing and Jesse's current situation.

Tell her!

She deserved to know the whole of it, but he couldn't tell her now. She'd all but said as much. It was too much information, too much distressing and heartrending baggage to dump on someone's shoulders. He'd had victims and witnesses crack under less. He also didn't want to hurt Baden or cause her any more emotional pain. After spending a year and a half feeling guilty about the way she had left things with Sean, he saw no benefit in adding to her burden or replacing one with another equally heavy one.

There was, however, a burden *he* needed lifted. Despite the way she felt in his arms, the way she responded to him, he needed to know.

"You're still in love with him."

He didn't—couldn't—pose the question like one, but he needed to know the answer nonetheless.

Even though it was Baden who had walked away from the idea of marriage, it did not necessarily mean that her feelings for Sean had in any way diminished. As a matter of fact, if she'd been walking around harboring the guilt she said she felt, Sean's death cut off forever any opportunity to make things right between them—even if that final conversation was simply an apology.

She sat, wrapped her arms around her knees and placed her head on top. She took so long in answering that Jesse had to close his eyes to ward off the pain of loving her and never having her.

"You have to understand, Jesse," she finally said. "I spent the first three months out here throwing myself into work so I wouldn't have to think about that question, about what I did or why. I was angry with him for putting me in a position where my only viable option was to just walk away. I was angry with myself for not expressing my doubts, my concerns, my fears to the man I was going to pledge my body and my life to."

Baden pushed hair from her eyes and made a motion that could have been a shrug.

"He'll always be a part of me, Jesse. Sean will always own a little piece of my heart where good memories live. When I heard that he'd died and how, I was sad and I was angry about the senseless killing. And I wanted you guys—cops and detectives—to make sure that the people who were responsible for his death got what they all deserved and got it the hard way."

"They are," Jesse said.

As if she didn't even hear him, Baden continued. "But I wasn't devastated. Do you know what I mean? I should have been *devastated* and that I wasn't just ate at me."

Baden blinked back tears.

"What kind of person does that make me?" she asked as she continued the tortured articulation of emotions Jesse had forced her to confront.

"I cried, and I wished I had my photo albums and scrapbooks or even the engagement photo that we took— something to remind me of him other than what I'd done to him."

"You moved five thousand miles and didn't take any pictures with you?"

She shook her head. "I had one suitcase and my purse. You have to understand, I was a mess. Emotional. Scared. Embarrassed by what I'd done. I dumped my cell phone in the trash and bought a throwaway one in the airport gift shop. Not my brightest moment, I must admit. But I severed all ties. I needed to focus solely on healing me," she said. "When I finally got settled, Aunt Henrietta sent my stuff, just clothes, shoes and jewelry. I insisted she not send me anything that had to do with Sean. She told me I'd regret that. And, as usual, Henrietta knows best."

Jesse smiled at that. But Baden had not yet completed the self-flagellation she thought she so richly deserved.

"I wasn't crushed and inconsolable the way a wife would have been," she said. "The way a cop's wife should have been."

She smiled then, and it was saddest thing Jesse had ever seen. The sadness in her eyes, the depth of her regret was a stark stamp across her face.

"That's when I knew I'd finally healed," she said. "In dying, Sean released me. So in answer to your question, I'm not in love with him. Maybe I never was, although we had a mutual admiration going on. More than mutual admiration is needed to make a strong marriage, though. Did I love him? Yes. As a dear friend, as someone I wished I hadn't hurt the way I did. The street thugs who killed him took away what I thought would always be time to make things right between us. That I regret."

"Have you considered going home?"

"For a visit? Sure. For good?" She shook her head. "Hawaii has been too good to me."

"How did you choose Hawaii?" Jesse asked.

For a moment, some of the sparkle seemed to leave her eyes. Jesse groaned inwardly, too late realizing the faux pas.

Before he could retract the question, she answered.

"Sean and I were going to come here. When I—" She paused, frowned as if searching for the right word to describe what had happened. Then, with a shrug, she continued. "When the wedding didn't happen, I came anyway. Hawaii was good for me," she said.

He loved the way she said the word Hawaii, adding an exotic *V* sound for the *W* and some sort of accent on the last *I* in the state's name. He'd heard locals pronouncing it that way.

Then realized with a start that she may have been born and raised in North Carolina, but for Baden, this exotic and enchanted chain of Pacific islands was now home.

"I like to think that I was born for Hawaii," she said. "It just took me a while to make my way home."

"I'm sorry about, well, about what happened. But I was glad, too," he said.

He hadn't planned to say that. It just came out, and now the words hung in the air, like a rain cloud that promised but had yet to produce fat raindrops.

Baden relaxed a little, sitting cross-legged with her hands in her lap. "Which part are you sorry about? That he would have stood me up at our wedding if I didn't do it first? That he had a secret he couldn't tell the woman he professed to love? Or that, in the end, he took the coward's way out and got himself killed on purpose?"

Anger, instant and hot bubbled up. But the anger could not truthfully be directed at Baden. He was angry that Sean had treated this one-of-a-kind woman so badly, and he was just downright pissed that she'd come to the same conclusion he had about Sean's death.

"It was ruled…"

She cut him off. "Yeah, yeah. I know all about the internal affairs or whatever you all call it, that inquiry into the shooting. I may not be anywhere near North Carolina, but getting information is all too easy. It's called Google."

"I didn't mean to upset you."

Baden sighed. Then turning to him, she gave a small smile. "I'm sorry, Jesse. I didn't mean to snap at you. You're not responsible for what Sean did or didn't do. I just wish…"

"That he'd been straight-up with you?"

She nodded. "You know, I think some part of me knew."

"That he was transsexual?"

She shook her head, her brows furrowed as if working

through a complex scientific equation. "No, not trans, but that something was going on with him. For a minute, I thought he might be gay."

"I did, too."

A ghost of a smile parted her mouth. Jesse wanted to lean in and kiss her. Fighting the urge took more willpower than he thought he possessed.

"But that wasn't it," she said. "It really would have been so much easier if he'd just been gay."

Jesse, who had gone through these same mental machinations in the weeks and months following Sean's death, knew that she struggled to make sense of it all.

"I thought he loved me," Baden said, her eyes filling with tears. She swiped a hand at her eye as if forcing the emotional response away.

"He did," Jesse said. *And so do I.*

But those words were ones that couldn't be spoken, not now when the news of the man she'd been about to pledge her life to, was so new, so raw. And probably not ever. Even though Sean was dead and gone, buried as a hero with his name added to the Officer Down memorial, Jesse didn't have the right to go after the woman his partner had loved.

"And," Baden added, "I'm not hanging out here in Paradise because I'm afraid of or embarrassed by the past and what I did. This is home. Hawaii represents the still-growing islands of life. And they, it, this literal Paradise on earth and Eden reborn all wrapped up in one, brought me back to life. I'm here because…"

When she stopped, Jesse leaned forward.

"What?" he asked.

Baden shook her head. "It's nothing."

He wanted to press, to find out what was going on in her head. But she'd already told him so much. He was grateful for that. And grateful that she felt secure enough with him to open up.

"Hey, Jesse?"

When he glanced at her, his body responded the way a starved man looked at a porterhouse steak.

"Yeah, Baden?"

"Have you ever seen the movie *Waiting to Exhale?*"

"The one where the woman burns up all of her husband's stuff? Yeah, I saw it. Didn't like it much."

She laughed. "It wasn't just about that scene," she said. "And that's not the scene I was just thinking of. You remember when Angela Bassett met Wesley Snipes in the bar, and they spent the night together in the bed, just holding each other?"

Jesse's mouth went dry.

If she wanted him to do that, he would need to be fitted with a full body cast first.

Baden uncurled herself and rose to stand over him. Waiting for permission? Waiting to exhale?

Lord, give me strength to be the honorable man she thinks I am.

She held out a hand to him. "Will you spend the night holding me?"

He wanted to cry out that holding her was just the start of what he wanted to do with her. But he took her hand and guided her back onto the chaise where they stretched out together, Baden tucked under his arm as the lush Hawaiian night lulled them to sleep.

Chapter 8

When Jesse woke up several hours later, he was pretty sure that he'd been dreaming about holding Baden Calloway close to him. But when he opened his eyes, it wasn't to see the resort-looking bedroom suite at his rental condo.

"This is what Eden must have looked like to Adam and Eve," he said, finding himself alone for the moment.

Though he'd spent much of the night in a chaise longue instead of a bed, he felt remarkably refreshed.

With Baden.

A smile broadened across his face and he knew why he felt such a sense of contentment. He was in a beautiful place and had spent the night in the arms of a beautiful woman—not quite the way he'd for so long imagined spending the night with Baden Calloway, but the exquisite woman had been in his arms nonetheless.

He rose, stretched and turned toward the cottage.

His day improved exponentially, when he saw her walking toward him.

"Good morning," he said.

Baden had had a few awkward morning-after moments in her time. She expected this one to beat them all. But she'd awakened in such a good mood, she couldn't help but smile.

"Good morning to you," she said.

Letting Jesse sleep, she had slipped away to put together breakfast. She carried a tray with coffee, fresh-cut pineapple, strawberries, grapes and some muffins she'd filched from Mama Melia.

"Let me help you with that," Jesse offered.

He took the tray and carried it to a table set for two that he hadn't even noticed.

"You didn't have to do all this," he said as they enjoyed their breakfast.

"That's why I did it," she said, casting a smile his way.

While she was grateful and touched that he'd been a gentleman last night, there was a lingering part of their conversation that remained unfinished.

Baden knew where she stood, but wasn't at all sure that Jesse was being straight-up about how and what he felt.

He could have mailed that photo to her. But he had traveled almost five thousand miles to deliver something that the post office could have done with just one stamp.

Why?

"We need to talk," she said.

Jesse finished off a muffin then answered. "We've been doing that for a while now, Baden."

"This isn't about Sean, Jesse," she said. "This is about you and me. Why did you come here? You could have taken a vacation anywhere in the world. This planet we call Earth is a big place. If you wanted tropical, you could have gone to the Caribbean. That's way closer and far more practical from North Carolina and the East Coast than coming all the way out here."

"Baden, I came because…"

With her head cocked, she waited for his answer. She may have looked aggressive, but on the inside she felt like a fruit-filled Jell-O mold that had not yet set, wobbly and whooshy and on the verge of collapse.

Jesse closed his eyes for a moment, then met her gaze, head-on, direct and unflinching.

"I came here for a Hawaiian vacation."

He held her gaze for a moment, accenting the words with the look that must have sent many a suspect on the road to confession. It didn't work on Baden, though.

She stared him down, giving as she got and not at all falling sway to cop intimidation.

He lowered his gaze for a moment. And then met hers directly.

"I told you already, Baden. And I meant it. I came to Hawaii because I knew you were here. I think I've loved you since the first day we met. You were standing in the driveway of that house, wearing a fierce blue suit, some incredibly high-heeled shoes with ribbons at the ankles and, boy, were you pissed."

He grinned, while speaking of the day.

She remembered it, as well. "I called the police when I went to open the house for a client who was coming by and instead found a window broken and the place ransacked. RPD took its sweet time sending someone over."

"Ransacked? There was a lamp overturned and a rug askew. In dispatch's defense, Baden, they weren't going to make a fuss when all you reported was a busted window. But there you were, standing in that long driveway taking out all that mad on the two of us," Jesse said.

"I wasn't just mad," Baden said. "I was scared. That was

a million-dollar listing and, not only was it suddenly a major crime scene, I didn't have another property to show that client."

They both fell silent, remembering how that day and her initial call to the police had ended. It wasn't just a broken window at the home for sale. Jesse and Sean, with Baden right on their heels trying to get them to hurry it up, had discovered a body in the backyard pool.

"The case is still open, unsolved," Jesse said. "We never had enough evidence to make a bust."

"I know," she said. "Sean told me."

"That day, I fell hard for you," Jesse said.

She lifted an eyebrow at him displaying her skepticism. "You didn't act like it. And you didn't say anything."

"That's something I've regretted for a long time," he said quietly. "Sean asked you out first. And after he got dibs, I wasn't gonna break a *man law* and go after you, as well."

Her eyes narrowed. "Dibs? I am not an object…."

"Hold on, Gloria Steinem. I didn't mean it that way. Just that he, well, he got to you first and…"

Baden held up a hand. "You are already a foot deep, so stop with the explanation, okay?"

She wasn't about to admit it to him, but Jesse was right.

Baden knew and loved Sean, the man who was her lover, knight-errant and protector. There had been not one ounce of femininity in him. It was the testosterone that she'd been attracted to, even while the distant and quiet cool of Jesse Fremont intrigued her. But Sean had asked her out first.

He smiled and nodded.

"Getting back to your original question. This little mandatory vacation wasn't exactly my idea. But when they said six weeks, I figured it was time to see what drew you to Hawaii and why you never came back home."

"I didn't have anything to return to," Baden said, her voice barely audible. "There was no need to subject myself to whispering and finger-pointing about 'there's that poor Calloway girl who left her groom at the altar and then her hometown, all without explanation.' It was humiliating enough the first go-around. I didn't need or want the reminders. Besides," she added, "when I got here, I knew I was at home. Hawaii has healed my soul, Jesse. It's hard to explain."

He shook his head. "No, it's not hard. I feel it, too. The lushness and vitality of this place is rejuvenating. Hawaii has a good vibe."

Taking her hand in his, he raised it and pressed a kiss on the tender skin right below her wrist. "You're like a flower blooming."

She liked the image. But she liked what he was doing with his fingers even more. Ripples of want cascaded through her. She fought the urge to surrender to desire. She'd done that before and look where that had led.

"Are you afraid of breaking some sort of *man law?*"

Impertinent as it was, Jesse had to smile. "I don't give a rip about man laws," he said. "Just the ones in the North Carolina criminal codes."

Even though Jesse had said the words, he knew them to be a lie. She was then and remained now Sean's girl. He had to respect the lines that had been drawn. It was a matter of honor.

"Sean is gone," Baden said. "We're both still here."

He wanted to believe he knew what she was saying. But his heart was beating too fast and loud for him to be sure. And his body was responding to the undercurrents of desire that flowed between them.

"Baden…"

Whatever he had been about to say got cut short when she closed the distance between them and wrapped herself around him like a blanket on a cold winter night.

A moment later, there were no barriers between them. He lifted her and Baden went willingly.

"This is what she meant?" Baden asked.

"She who and what?"

"The song," Baden said. "'Killing Me Softly.' You're killing me, Jesse."

He grunted. "You think this is softly?"

She let her mouth on his warm brown skin answer the question.

He tasted like summer and honey and something that she couldn't quite identify. What Baden did know was that kissing Jesse felt like coming home, like she'd waited her entire life to be in the arms of this man.

It was a struggle, but she eventually forced herself to focus on what was actually important right now.

"You did a nice job of dancing around my question," she said. Jesse sighed.

"I didn't dodge the question, Baden. You're just not getting that I came here to find you."

"Yeah, to deliver a message from Sean."

He shook his head. "That was only part of it. I knew that that had to be dealt with before we could before I could, well, before I could approach you about a future us."

He sounded sincere. But Baden no longer trusted her ability to discern the truth. Didn't cops always withhold a part of the truth?

She could only wonder if there was more that he wasn't telling her.

"It's too much, too soon," she said. "And I refuse to be held down anymore, by guilt or by regret."

Jesse started to make a crack about lyrics of old disco tunes, but her expression told him this was not the moment to play.

Sean hadn't known how to tell Baden the truth about himself. At least he had had a legitimate excuse. While he was being honest regarding his feelings for Baden, he was withholding a vital truth—or two—from her and Jesse got the feeling that Baden sensed that. Maybe that was the cause of her reticence to acknowledge what he'd now twice told her.

Also twice he had been given the perfect segue into his extended time off from the Raleigh Police Department. Like Sean, he had taken the coward's way out of an unpleasant situation.

He was going to do it again, too.

"Do you have to work today?" he asked her.

"No, and I thought I'd surprise you with a little excursion."

"Excursion?"

"I'm putting on my Miss Hawaii Chamber of Commerce Tourism Hostess hat."

Jesse grinned.

"Where are we going?"

"To the Big Island."

The pink-and-white bikini designed to turn heads was keeping up its end of the boutique's marketing department's promise. Jesse wanted to shoot every man who looked at Baden twice. And there was a lot of Baden to see.

She filled out the bikini top in a way that let a man know he could lose himself in her bosom for hours on end. Her stomach, flat and taut, also sported a surprising gold belly ring. He wouldn't have pegged her for the type, but it looked good on her. And then those chocolate-colored legs, they just kept going on and on.

He smiled as she approached holding two froufrou drinks with umbrellas in them.

She thought it would be nice for him to see Hawaii's Big Island. But all he wanted to do was drag Baden off to a secluded spot and make sweet love to her until neither of them could see straight.

The sun was warm on his body, but it wasn't the heat of the day that had him worked up.

"I brought you a little refreshment," she said.

"I could use something to cool me down."

She eyed him, and because he was watching, he saw her surreptitious glance at his crotch. His desire for her was evident.

"*Yo-hoo!* I do declare. Is that you Baden Calloway?"

Baden placed the drinks on the small table anchored in the sand and turned to see who hailed her.

Jesse groaned. "The world is entirely too small," he muttered as he reached for a beach towel and draped it across his lap.

"What do you mean?" She put her hand up to shield the sun from her eyes and see who was calling her.

Before Jesse could answer her, she was enveloped in a hug that took her breath away.

"Baden. It is you! Howard, look who's here!"

When the woman finally let her go and she was able to take a decent breath again, Baden recognized the woman. Etta Rae Baker and her husband, Howard.

The two were in full-tourist Hawaiian gear, a long muu-muu and sandals for Miss Etta Rae, with a giant straw purse with the word *Hawaii* embroidered on it. She'd gotten her hair done for her vacation, the gray, and a liberal bit of blue-black added, was pulled back and pinned up in a twist. And Mr. Howard, who was heading to a tiki stand, wore a Hawaiian shirt, a pair of unfortunate white shorts and sandals with what looked like white tube socks.

Baden bit back a groan even as she plastered a smile on her face. Miss Etta Rae was one of the biggest gossips in Cedar

Springs. She could get news out faster than CNN, Twitter and TMZ combined.

"Well, I declare! This is such a surprise to see you. I didn't know you were in Hawaii. I'm gonna have to tell Henrietta that we ran into you. Can you believe it, right here on the beach with your, uh, friend."

"I'm so glad to see that you're not out here just wasting away after that, well, you know, the, uh…" She waved a hand in a vague motion. "That was all so terrible what happened. But I see you've settled down with a young man."

Etta Rae Baker took in Jesse, who'd stood up during the extended hug and her monologue. Curiosity faded away and a sly smile filled her round face. "Well, well, look, Howard. It's Officer Jesse."

"It's detective now, Mrs. Baker."

"Huh?" She didn't wait for an explanation. "So, how long y'all been together? You sure make a nice-looking couple."

She turned to her husband who had drifted off.

"Howard must be off getting another of those mighties."

"Mighties?" Jesse asked.

"I think she means mai tai," Baden said translating under her breath. "It's a common mispronunciation."

"Oh."

Maybe the mai tais Miss Etta Rae and her husband had been downing would make them forget running into Baden and Jesse. Baden could only hope that was the case. The last thing she needed or wanted was gossip being spread around town about her and Jesse.

"Lord, those things are good," Etta Rae was saying. "But don't you dare tell Chaplain St. Clair. Right before we left Cedar Springs, he was preaching about the seven deadlies."

"Miss Etta Rae, we're not a…"

"I heard tell that you were on some kind of extended vacation, Officer Jesse," Etta Rae said, turning her eagle eye on Jesse. "Nobody said you were out here in Hawaii." She glanced between the two and grinned. "Is this a secret honeymoon?"

"No!"

The echo blast from both Baden and Jesse startled the older woman. Then she smiled. "I'll keep your secret," she said. "I'm gonna go find Howard."

She pulled Baden in for another smothering hug. "I'm happy for you," Etta Rae whispered in her ear.

Baden knew Miss Etta Rae's words were supposed to be reassuring and uplifting, but running into the Bakers put a damper on the afternoon for her.

And the encounter brought her back to reality. She could pretend all she wanted, but there were plenty of people who hadn't forgotten what had happened between her and Sean. And then, the way Sean had died only made things worse. So much worse.

The call from cousin Vanessa came a couple hours after they'd returned from their excursion. Baden had been thinking about the repercussions of Miss Etta Rae telling everyone that she and Jesse were an item. Would it really be that terrible?

About the time she decided that it wouldn't, she got news that made everything else irrelevant.

Now, many hours and miles later, she realized she'd forgotten how comforting the Raleigh-Durham International Airport was. If Baden hadn't been so stressed about getting home and to the hospital, she would have spent time lingering, kicking back in the rocking chairs and watching people go by.

There might be time for that later, much later.

She claimed her two bags and hightailed it to ground transportation for a taxi.

En route she got a text from Phoebe who was about to board a plane from Detroit headed to Raleigh.

Where r u?

DK. Just landed. N cab 2 hosp, Baden replied.

OK. B there soon. V said it's bad.

I know. Praying hard, Baden texted.

Me too, cuz.

Of all her Calloway cousins, Baden was closest with Phoebe—the one she had the least in common with.

Gotta go. Trey is calling.

K.

She disengaged with Phoebe and greeted her other cousin, skipping the pleasantries.

"How is she, Trey?"

"Stabilized," he said.

Baden breathed her first clear breath since getting the frantic message from Mama Melia and then the phone call confirming the news. "Good," she said. "That's good to hear."

"Where are you, cousin?"

Baden glanced out the taxi window. "About five minutes away from Duke University Hospital."

"She's on the third floor in the cardiac intensive care unit. But I'll meet you in the lobby and take you up."

Chapter 9

When she didn't answer her phone, Jesse got worried. He'd sent a couple text messages and had called, but Baden was either working or ignoring him. Somehow, after their conversations and that embarrassing encounter with the Bakers, he figured she was ignoring him.

If she wouldn't answer the phone, he would just go see her in person. But there was no answer at the cottage and the silver Jaguar was gone.

Frowning, Jesse made his way to the main house.

Maybe Mama Melia Hookano would know where she was. But she had no assurances for Jesse.

"Miss Baden gone to mainland, Mr. Jesse. She no tell me when or if she return to Hawaii."

Jesse thanked Mama Melia who pressed a cellophane bag of cookies into his hand. But the cookies remained uneaten and on the front seat of his rental as Jesse contemplated the why and the I-should-have-known-better ramifications of falling for Baden Calloway.

Henrietta Calloway was sixty-seven years old and the rock of the Calloway family. A woman of strong faith and an even stronger constitution, none of her sisters, her children or the nieces she'd all but adopted, had ever seen her operating at less than 150 percent.

So it was a blow psychologically and emotionally to see her so small and frail in the hospital bed, surrounded by tubes and machines.

"She just fell asleep," Patty said as Baden came in with Trey.

Baden hugged her Aunt Patty and squeezed Aunt Vicky's hand, before making her way to the bedside where Aunt Henrietta lay. Baden placed her hand over her aunt's and stood there for a moment. Her quiet prayer was interrupted by a tap on her shoulder.

She turned to see her aunts and cousin being ushered out of the room by a nurse who looked none too pleased to see the ICU room full of people.

"Miss, you'll have to leave now."

Baden nodded. She leaned over, kissed Aunt Henrietta on the forehead and then exited in front of the nurse.

She followed her relatives to a family waiting room that the Calloways had all but commandeered. She hugged more people, then perched on the edge of one of the available chairs.

"Where's Uncle Carlton?"

"We finally convinced him to go home, get a shower and a change of clothes," Aunt Patty said. "He's been gone about an hour, so that's a good sign. This has really been hard on him."

"What happened?"

"Heart attack," Trey said. "Luckily, she was with her girl-friend, Miss Nancy. You remember her, right, Baden?"

"The nurse, yes," Baden said, vaguely recalling a tiny woman who manned the nurse's station at church.

"The Lord was looking out for Henrietta," Aunt Vicky said. Then added, "Baden, girl, let me take a look at you. It's been forever."

Catching up with her family made Baden realize just how much she had missed them all—and just how much she'd cut herself off from the support system that had defined most of her life.

She didn't think she would be able to look back with fondness at her hometown after fleeing the way she'd done. But she had forgotten that home and family were always there with open arms.

Her year and a half in Hawaii had also made her forget the slow cadence of North Carolina accents, the cacophony of Calloways, all talking at the same time.

Baden checked in with both her office at Kona Realty and with Mama Melia on the Kapule Garden Estate, letting them both know what had happened. She looked at and deleted Jesse's text messages, and ignored his calls. What, after all, was there to say to him? There was little that she could say in a text or on a voice mail that would convey her tangled emotions. Then reconsidering, she sent a quick text to him: On mainland. Family emergency. Details later.

She knew that, from Jesse's perspective, she'd again run away without explanation.

All of the family had been called in because it was touch-and-go while her aunt had been in ICU.

They all said prayers of gratitude when Henrietta's condition was upgraded. The doctors said her vitals were fine. But she was, for all intents and purposes, in a comatose state.

"She seems to respond to voices and music though," the doctor said.

That was all the Calloways needed to know.

They agreed to a schedule so someone was always with Henrietta, who had been moved from the intensive care unit to a private room. One aunt read Scripture in the mornings and another read novels by Toni Morrison, Aunt Henrietta's favorite author, in the afternoons. The senior choir from the Chapel of the Groves came and presented a mini concert to lift Henrietta's spirit, which the nurses and other patients had enjoyed, as well.

When Baden sat with her aunt in the evenings, she just talked. She poured out her heart about Sean and Hawaii and Jesse Fremont.

On the second day of Baden's vigil, she'd moved beyond her life in Hawaii and her desire for Aunt Henrietta and Uncle Carlton to come for a visit. Now, she was into personal territory, telling her aunt all the things that she'd kept bottled up inside for so long.

She'd lost her heart to yet another cop, yet another man who could hurt her by compounding the heartache that she had finally thought she'd squelched.

"I don't quite know how it happened, Aunt Henrietta. I fell for him. Hard. I just looked up one day and realized I'd fallen head over heels in love with Jesse. And it's just so…complicated," she said on a sigh. "With Sean, well, you know about all that. Jesse came all the way out to Hawaii to see me. He said he loves me, and I doubted his sincerity because I could hardly bear to go through another heartache. But my heart aches right now, Auntie. I'm so… It's just…I'm so confused. Jesse probably hates me. I ran off to come here without a word and he has no clue how I feel about him."

She fell silent for a moment, contemplating the mess of her personal life.

"I want what you and uncle Carlton have," she told her aunt. "Decades of mutual respect and love."

"Then you ought to marry this one."

Henrietta's recovery was cause for an epic Calloway family celebration. That's what Jesse walked in on in the hospital's family waiting room.

The crush of people were carrying on like it was a party when, from what he'd heard, Henrietta Calloway was close to death. He'd been angry and hurt when Baden had pulled her disappearing act. It wasn't until he got in touch with someone back home that he found out it really was a family emergency that had sent her running, not necessarily his declaration of love. Her text read like an abrupt brushoff.

He knew the moment Baden spied him at the door. His skin tingled and the air seemed to leave the room.

Jesse watched as she pushed and excused herself to get across the room to him.

"Hello, Jesse."

"Hey, Baden. My timing always seems to be off when it comes to you."

She smiled. "Your timing is just fine," she said. "Aunt Henrietta is finally awake and talking up a storm. She's also demanding to be released so she can get home and tend to her family."

"That sounds like the Henrietta Calloway I know." He paused. "Can we talk about this?" Jesse asked.

He knew Baden knew that he wasn't referring to her aunt's health but the health and longevity of their relationship.

"I'd rather not," Baden said, indicating the room full of her relatives. "But I think we have to. I'm allegedly a grown-up now despite some of my actions to the contrary. Like leaving without giving you the courtesy of an explanation."

"You were worried about Mrs. Calloway."

"That's convenient and true," she said, "but it's not an excuse for just falling off the radar. Again," she added drily.

"Is there somewhere we can go?"

"The chapel, the cafeteria?"

"Cafeteria," he said.

A few minutes later, they were seated at a table for two in a corner, cups of coffee steaming but ignored between them.

"I meant what I said back in Hawaii, Baden. I've always had a thing for you—more than a thing," he said. "I was pissed when Sean asked you out first."

"If you say he called 'dibs' again, I swear to God, Jesse…"

"No, not dibs," he said. "I don't want you slapping me upside the head or something. He just had the good sense and the good taste to know he'd found a diamond."

"In the rough?"

He shook his head. "Cut and polished to absolute perfection," Jesse said.

"How long did you know about Shaun, the girl, I mean?"

"Sean and I were partners, Baden," he said. "I told you how close a relationship that is. Each of our lives depended on the other. When he told me, yeah, I was taken aback for a bit, but it was all so far in the past it didn't matter. I did some research on transgendered people. Sean didn't fit any of the stereotypes that I'd had. That's what got me in trouble."

"In trouble? What trouble?"

"The reason I'm suspended."

Baden looked startled. "Suspended? You said you were on an extended forced vacation. I thought you meant you were being forced to take a ton of accrued vacation or comp hours."

Sighing, he shook his head. "No. I'm on a six-week suspension from the department."

"This has something to do with Sean doesn't it?"

He nodded, then rubbed his eyes.

"Go on," Baden urged.

He looked at her, a weariness in his eyes that aged him more than the work he did on the streets as a cop.

He shifted in his seat, rubbed his hands on his thighs and then clasped his hands together on top of the table.

"It was a couple weeks after the…" He paused and glanced at her.

"It's okay, Jesse. The wedding-that-wasn't is always going to be a part of our shared past."

He shook his head as if he were the one having issues in coming to grips with the past.

"It was a couple weeks after the wedding date," he said. "Sean was acting crazy. Reckless. He was taking chances that didn't need to be taken. Antagonizing suspects. Basically being an asshole. And he refused to talk about it."

"I wondered how he took my…running off."

Jesse shrugged. "Publicly he was stoic. He walked into the squad room that following Tuesday morning and said to everybody there, 'Well, if anybody had any bets going on, it's time to pay up. She dumped me. So give my number to your sisters and ex's.'"

Startled at that, Baden pressed for more information. "He made light of it?"

Jesse nodded. "In public. In private, he was a mess, just a freaking mess. I've never seen anybody go off the deep end like that. I was scared for him, Baden. Really scared. All he'd tell me was that you had more balls than he did. When I'd ask what he meant, he'd just say something like, 'Let's go kick some drug dealer butt.'"

Shaking his head, Jesse recalled that time. "Baden, he was going after perps like he had a quota to fill. Then we got called out to a club, The Palisades."

"Never heard of it."

"You wouldn't have," he said. "It was—is—a private social club for the gay, bisexual and transgendered community."

She looked stunned. "Here? In Raleigh?"

"No, Miss Sheltered from Reality. Actually it's tucked out in the county, between Raleigh and Cedar Springs. There are gay folks, you know."

She hit his arm. "I realize that. And I'm not sheltered from reality. I try to hide from it sometimes, but I've never been sheltered from it. Well, apparently except when it came to Sean."

"The Palisades is in the county, and it's been operating for about five years. Every now and then the department would get a call out about a domestic dispute or some sort of altercation, but this call out was different. A biker group came upon a couple patrons after they'd left and, let's just say, trouble ensued."

"What happened, Jesse?"

"When it was over? One guy was dead, three were in the hospital and Sean had a hit put out on him by the biker gang."

"Oh, my God."

"It was a classic cluster fuck from the get-go," he said. "Sean was like a crazy person."

"Did he kill the man?"

Jesse shook his head. "No. It was clear that the bikers picked the wrong transvestites to hassle. The two of them who were attacked could have handled the five bikers and gone on to enjoy their evening. But Sean…" Jesse shook his head. "Sean was like… I can't even describe it. The dude who was killed had his carotid artery severed by a size-thirteen, spiked high heel. Sean sent two more to the hospital where at least one of them remained for about three months."

Baden's eyes widened and she covered her mouth, horrified by the recount of the carnage.

"Why was he so violent?"

Jesse shrugged.

Baden regarded him, and then reached for and squeezed his

hand. "Jesse, we're being honest here. Please, no more secrets between us. It's the only way we can move forward as *us*."

"Us?"

She nodded.

"I know, Baden. I want there to be an us."

"Then let's get the past out of the way and put it where it belongs."

"The department cleared both of us," he said.

Baden stared at him. "The truth, Jesse."

He sighed. "The official report says two citizens were in imminent danger and that backup was stuck trying to quell the near riot from Palisades patrons trying to come to the scene."

"And the unofficial report?"

"There was no unofficial report, but I think Sean was fighting back against every slight or slur he may have suffered while he was a boy trapped in a girl's body. Seeing those two Palisades patrons being attacked and knowing that he hadn't been straight-up with you about his background, I think it was just all mixing together and came out in that moment."

Baden nodded. "I get that." Then she voiced a question she'd been wondering about ever since Jesse had given her that photograph of Shaun. "Did anyone else in the department know? About Sean, I mean."

Jesse shook his head. "No one to my knowledge except me. It wasn't something he talked about. Frankly, I don't even think it was something he thought about until…" Jesse's gaze met hers.

"Until he asked me to marry him," she finished.

"Yeah. If our backup hadn't gotten there, I think there would have been more than one fatality. And Sean refused to go to a ceremony where the Greater Raleigh LGBT group honored our so-called heroism. He got written up for not going."

"I don't understand something."

"What's that?" Jesse said taking a sip from his coffee then frowning. "It's cold now."

"This was more than a year ago. What did that have to do with your suspension?"

Jesse rubbed his eyes. "Let me get some more coffee."

He picked up the two cups and returned a few moments later, the contents again steaming. He took a sip from his, but Baden just wrapped her hands around hers.

"I mentioned a biker gang."

She nodded.

"The Sons of W.A.R., they call themselves. I mixed it up with one of them after Sean's funeral. Sent him back to the hospital."

This time it was Baden who let out the heavy and weary sigh. "An unprovoked attack."

"Oh, no," Jesse said. "There was provocation and plenty of witnesses. Thank God, not any of Sean's family, though. Between The Palisades incident, a couple cases that got pretty dicey, Sean's death and that funeral fight, well, the department's shrink decided I needed a time-out. I objected, vigorously, and when it was all over, I got six weeks to contemplate my insubordination and to think about the error of my ways."

"What happens now? With the police department, I mean?"

"I have a hearing scheduled for mid-October."

"I want to be there with you."

"That's not necessary, Baden. I made this mess."

"Jesse," she said, pushing aside the coffee cups, "I am going to be there for you."

He smiled. "All right, Baden."

She glanced at a clock on the far wall. "We should get back upstairs."

When she would have pushed her chair back to depart, Jesse stayed her.

"Baden, there's one thing you haven't told me," he said.

"What's that?"

"Why you called off your wedding to Sean."

Had her complexion been any lighter, the blush would have reddened her face. As it was, she glanced to the right, to the left, anywhere except at Jesse.

"Baden, we agreed. Total honesty."

"It's not honesty I'm avoiding here."

"What then?"

"The look you're going to give me."

"What look? Just tell me, baby."

She smiled at the endearment and then shyly looked away before taking a breath and meeting his gaze head-on.

"I couldn't marry Sean because I was in love with you."

A broad grin filled his face.

She punched him. "That look!" she said. "That's the smug and knowing look I didn't want to see."

He laughed, got up, pulled her to him and clasped his arms around her waist drawing her close, flush with his body.

"It may be smug, Baden, but that's because you just gave me the best gift ever."

He lowered his head and covered her mouth with his, sealing their forever bond.

Epilogue

"You know, Carlton, this is a lovely place for someone recently released from the hospital to make a full recuperation," Henrietta Calloway told her husband.

Indulgent but not gullible, Carlton Calloway smiled. "Nice try, dear. But we're here for a wedding, not a long-term visit."

"I'm sure Baden could find a nice condo on a beach for us to lease."

"Hey, Uncle Carl," Baden said, sidling up to her uncle. With a wink at her aunt, she said, "Do you need to be rescued?"

"As a matter of fact, I do," Carlton said. "Your auntie here was making the 'let's move to Hawaii' argument."

"It is a beautiful place to live," Baden said. "Sheer bliss."

"And perfect for a recovering cardiac patient."

Carlton shook his head. "You have milked that for five months now, Henry. And if you don't slow down, you'll find yourself right back at Duke."

"That's why I'm advocating a Hawaiian hideaway."

Baden laughed. "It's time for you to give me away," she told her uncle.

She kissed her aunt on the cheek and whispered, "I have some condo brochures you can check out. There's a three-bedroom unit I think you'll particularly love."

"I heard that," Carlton said.

The sun was setting in a fiery blaze of golden reds, deep golds and luscious oranges. An orchid-draped arbor was secured on the beachfront, as wedding guests, many of them barefoot, surrounded it. They watched as Baden, on the arm of her uncle, made her way to the arbor. The simple white dress she wore was embroidered with seed beads. Around her neck was a ceremonial lei.

An identical one graced Jesse's neck.

As she approached and Carlton handed her off to Jesse, he bent low. "I love you, Baden Calloway."

"I love you more, Jesse Fremont."

"So you two decided to do your own vows?"

Their guests giggled.

"No, Reverend," Jesse said. "It's your show now."

The bride and groom laughed along with the others. And then the vows were spoken. *To have and to hold. For richer or poorer.*

Until death do we part.

When the minister declared Jesse and Baden husband and wife a cheer went up among the assembled Calloways and Fremonts who'd flown to Hawaii for the wedding.

But Baden and Jesse didn't hear them. They were lost in love and in each other.

* * * * *

REQUEST YOUR FREE BOOKS!

2 FREE NOVELS
PLUS 2 FREE GIFTS!

KIMANI™
ROMANCE

Love's ultimate destination!

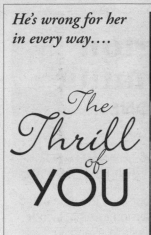
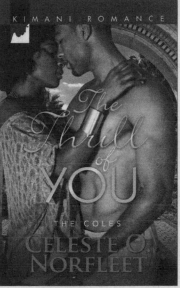